"Thank you for sha___ me, Stella."

"*My* stars?"

"Yours." His voice was low and tender. "Your stars, your special place, your memories."

Stella felt as if her heart had morphed into a supernova.

Their lips met and Stella felt a shock wave flow through her body with the energy of two suns. When they pulled away, she could barely make out his profile in the dim light, but it was there—the strong jaw, Roman nose and high forehead framed by curls as black as the sky. She traced it with her fingers like a blind woman, memorizing every feature.

She didn't understand it herself, but there was an urgency in what she felt when she was with Joiner. Like she had to act on every impulse, grab each moment before it got away.

The feeling both scared and thrilled her.

Dear Reader,

The Deep in the Heart series was the brainchild of my friend and writer extraordinaire Mae Nunn. I was blessed to have the opportunity to collaborate with her on the third and fourth books in the series and to give life to the two oldest Temple brothers, Joiner and Mac.

Lone Star Refuge is Joiner's story. Sprinkled throughout it you will find many references to stars, beginning with the heroine, who is named after my youngest daughter, Stella. I had fun with this imagery, building on Texas as the Lone Star State, but as I dug deeper into the story a couple of themes very close to my heart emerged—faith and family—and I realized that just as these are the two things that guide my life, they would also become the stars by which my characters would learn to navigate theirs.

Stella and Joiner both suffered losses in their formative years that make it challenging to trust, to commit to love with all of its joys and complications. Theirs, I hope, is a story of real people growing together to find a place of safety with each other, even as they work to create a refuge for others.

Thanks for joining me on this journey! I'd love to hear from you by email at gfaulkenberry@hotmail.com, or on Facebook, Gwendolann Adell Ford Faulkenberry.

Blessings,

Gwen

HEARTWARMING

Lone Star Refuge

—

Mae Nunn &
Gwen Ford Faulkenberry

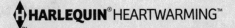

HARLEQUIN® HEARTWARMING™

Recycling programs
for this product may
not exist in your area.

ISBN-13: 978-0-373-36714-6

Lone Star Refuge

Copyright © 2015 by Mae Nunn and Gwen Ford Faulkenberry

Printed in U.S.A.

www.Harlequin.com

Mae Nunn grew up in Houston and graduated from the University of Texas with a degree in communications. When she fell for a transplanted Englishman living in Atlanta, she moved to Georgia and made an effort to behave like a Southern belle. But when she found that her husband was quite agreeable to life as a born-again Texan, Mae happily returned to her cowgirl roots and cowboy boots! In 2008 Mae retired from thirty years of corporate life to focus on her career as a full-time author.

Gwen Ford Faulkenberry lives and writes in the Ozark Mountains of Arkansas. She and her husband, Stone, have four children: Grace, Harper, Adelaide and Stella. Gwen is the author of three Christian romances, a book of prayers for couples and three devotional books. A professor of English at her local college, she holds a master's degree in liberal arts.

Other titles in the Deep in the Heart series:

Cowboy in the Kitchen
Fatherhood 101

Visit the Author Profile pages
at Harlequin.com for more titles

For Cheryl Ann Jech Smith

the real Cha Cha

CHAPTER ONE

STELLA JANE SCOUT slowly descended the stairs. She was going over the numbers again in her head, figuring on potential donors, and almost ran into her father who appeared at the bottom just as she reached it.

"Whoa there, Pretty! Raring to go to work?" He steadied himself against the door frame that led from the foot of the stairs into the dining room, which was rarely used. "I was just about to call you."

"Mornin', Pops." She kissed his cheek. "What's for breakfast?"

"Bacon and eggs. You need your protein this morning. You know, bacon and eggs stick with you."

Stella suppressed a chuckle as she followed him into the kitchen. He was always cooking up things he thought would "stick with" her, with no regard whatsoever to their fat and cholesterol content.

She sat down at the breakfast table where

they ate most meals, and laid her napkin across her lap. Buster poured coffee into the cup he'd already doctored with sugar and milk. As she sipped its rich smoothness, he set a plate in front of her with two fried eggs, three strips of bacon and a piece of whole wheat toast. Then, turning to the sound of a scratching noise on the porch, he went to the back door and let in two whirling dervishes of black-and-white.

"Mugsy! Mitzi!" Stella reached down to pet the Boston terriers that stood with their paws on her thigh. Their wiggling and wagging resulted in her napkin falling to the floor. Buster picked it up for her.

"Here you go, guys." They followed Buster to a mat that held a stainless steel bowl full of water beside the refrigerator. Buster set down two bowls with equal portions of bacon and eggs in each one and the dogs started chowing down. Next, he made his own plate and sat down at the table across from Stella, slathering his toast in butter.

"What's on your agenda today?"

"I'm going to meet with that feller who keeps pestering me about buying the north forty." Buster focused his eyes intently on his toast.

"What? I thought you discontinued that ad."

"I did, too, but apparently it still comes up

on that stinkin' internet. "Least that's where he said he got our information."

"Well, why didn't you just tell him it's not for sale?" The heat rose in her neck.

"I want to hear what he has to say. He's a polo player, so he's bound to have money, and if he wants that forty acres bad enough, well, it might help out with your new venture."

Stella snorted. "A polo player? From Texas?" She rolled her eyes. "Pops, I don't need help. Not that way, anyway. I know we're strapped and I know it's my fault—"

"Now, you just wait right there a minute. Our financial troubles are not your fault." He reached across the table for her hand. "Don't you ever say it's your fault, Pretty."

"Well, I *am* the one who persuaded you to quit the rodeo after Mom died, but I won't apologize for it. You're the only parent I've got left. We can blame it on the economy or whatever, but what it comes down to is that my riding school has drained you financially."

Buster couldn't argue with that.

"But I'm about to make that up to you. Just a little more time, a few more donors, and we'll be up and running." Stella placed her hand over his. The gnarled knuckles were rough beneath her palm. "You know I'm not in this to get rich, by any means. But I do hope we'll be solvent again. The last thing I want is for you to have to sell part of this place. It's our last connection to Moma."

Stella saw a muscle twitch in her father's jaw, even though it was covered with a shaggy salt-and-pepper beard. His bushy eyebrows furrowed into a near-scowl.

"Well, I'll keep that under consideration, but I'm not canceling the meeting. He'll be here in a few minutes."

Buster rose, taking his plate to the sink. He tucked his shirt into his jeans as he wobbled bowlegged across the kitchen and back through the dining room. He paused in the foyer to grab his workaday Panama hat off the rack. Then he turned around and winked at her.

"Stubborn ox!" Stella called, clearing the rest of the table.

Joiner Temple rolled over in the four-poster king-size bed and grabbed his phone off the rusted oil barrel Gillian, his brother Hunt's wife, had rescued from a junkyard and reimagined as a nightstand for one of the rooms in her five-star resort, Temple Territory. Hunt and Gillian had offered him the "Mason-Dixon" suite, named after his notorious grandfather. They insisted on treating him to the lap of luxury in the thirty-eight-room mansion that was the heart of the resort until he found a place of his own to rent in Kilgore.

That task had been harder than he hoped it would be, but he had a meeting today with an old rodeo guy named Buster Scout. If Joiner could get Buster to agree to sell part of his 450-acre ranch for an affordable price, it might be the best option yet for Joiner to start over.

The clock on his phone read 7:00 a.m. He'd better get a move on or he was going to be late.

Joiner jumped out of bed and showered quickly in the shale-tiled shower Gillian had designed. He pulled on jeans, a clean white T-shirt and ran a brush through his dark, wavy hair. Forgoing a shave, which would take too long, he hoped a little stubble wouldn't make a bad impression with Buster. Then he stepped into his favorite Justin boots, picked up his Stetson and, locking the door behind him, hurried down the hall and out the door.

His brother Hunt was coming up the steps of the mansion as Joiner was going down.

"Morning, bro!" Hunt flashed him the smile

that had made him famous as the Cowboy Chef. "Did you have breakfast?"

"No time. I've got to go see about that forty acres. Supposed to be there at eight o'clock."

"I can have someone feed Pistol for you."

"I've got it." Joiner reached out his fist and Hunt bumped it with his. "See you later."

Joiner crossed the lawn, passing the guest-house where Hunt and Gillian were staying while their new lodge, which would be their personal home, was under construction by the lake at the rear of the property. He headed to the lavishly remodeled barn where Pistol was boarded. Pistol looked up immediately when Joiner entered, as if he'd been waiting for him.

Man, he loved this horse. A carbon-black Argentine Thoroughbred, Pistol was the one dream Joiner had not left behind with the rest of his polo career. He filled a bucket with oats and brushed the horse till his coat shone in the soft morning light that filtered through the barn windows.

"I've got to go, but when I get back we'll go for a ride."

Pistol nuzzled him and Joiner rubbed the white star that blazed across the horse's fore-head. "Hopefully I'll have us both a place where we can finally settle down." Although, admittedly, Joiner didn't know if he'd ever be happy settling down…

THE SILVER TRUCK kicked up so much dust that Buster could see it coming more than a mile down the driveway. He finished milking Violet and Minnie, the two goats, and took the pails inside for Stella to strain. He was already gathering the eggs when the truck came to a stop under Stella's old basketball hoop. The truck wasn't that new and wasn't that shiny. A man got out and Buster sized him up as he strode toward the front door of the house. He was a good size, broad-shouldered, and what Buster's mother would have described as *too pretty to be a boy*.

"Hey there!"

Joiner started at the sound of Buster's voice from the chicken coop across the yard. He turned around.

"Mr. Scout?"

Buster ceremoniously wiped chicken poop off his hand and extended it toward Joiner. The young man hesitated only an instant before reaching out to take it. There was something like a dare in his violet eyes.

"Ha-ha! Gotcha!" Buster laughed, withdrawing his hand, and the young man laughed, too.

"You got me."

"It's nice to make your acquaintance, Mr. Temple."

It was immediately obvious to Buster that this Temple boy was very different from Stella. And it might be nice for both of them to have him around…

"CALL ME JOINER. PLEASE." He followed Buster around behind the house, where the older man set the pail of eggs down on the porch, and then pumped water from an old-fashioned spicket in order to wash his hands.

"Let's sit up here on the porch. Do you like coffee?"

"Sure, thanks." Joiner took a seat in one of the wooden rockers while Buster walked past him and into the house. He noticed that in the distance there was a ratty-looking RV parked under some trees.

Buster came back with two coffee mugs and two Boston terriers, who ran to surround his rocker. Joiner reached down to return their affection.

"I hope you like it black."

Joiner nodded, although he preferred a little cream.

"Good. I never can stand a man who doctors his coffee. My daughter takes sugar and cream—all of that girly stuff. But a man should drink black coffee." Buster plopped down in the other rocker. "It puts hair on your chest."

Joiner had all of the hair he needed but he took a sip anyhow. The coffee tasted like tar. "Thanks," he sputtered.

"This is Mugsy." Buster pointed to the bigger of the two dogs. Mugsy was twenty-five pounds of solid muscle and all black except for his three-quarter-moon white face. Brown eyes sparkled over a smashed-in nose. The mutt grinned and displayed an under bite and crooked teeth. Joiner could almost imagine him smoking a cigar.

"And this little girl right here is Mitzi." Buster's voice crooned as if he was talking to a baby. She turned over by his feet and he reached down to rub her tummy, which was none too small, even though she was more petite than Mugsy. Mitzi had more of a terrier's nose, and lots more white fur to go with the black. It was speckled with what looked like black freckles. Joiner immediately took to them both.

"So you're interested in my north forty acres. What do you want it for?"

"Well, sir, I'm searching for a place to build a

little horse-breeding operation. Nothing large-scale, but enough to get me by."

"Aren't you some kind of polo player?"

"I was. Started in college, and then I was drafted by a European team. I had some fun over there, but the truth is, I just can't afford to make polo a career." Joiner ran a hand through his hair. "I poured most of my inheritance into it before I figured that out. When people call polo 'the sport of kings' that's because only kings have enough money to play it seriously."

Buster squinted at Joiner, who hoped he was making some sense to the older man.

"How'd a Texas cowboy end up playing that sissy kind of sport, anyway, if you don't mind me asking?"

Joiner did mind. But he was used to it. Being a polo player was about as unconventional as a Texas cowboy could get. Still, the older man's prejudices were starting to get on his nerves.

"It's very competitive, and it requires a lot of skill of both the rider and the horse." He was blunt.

"Well, don't get your panties in a wad. I didn't mean nothing. I'm just trying to understand it, that's all." Buster stroked his beard. "I used to rodeo. Sunk every dime I had into it, and spent all my time on the road. I loved it, but

I have to admit I missed a lot of my daughter's growing-up years and I regret that. It may be a good thing you've got the road out of your system before you settle down and have a family."

Joiner blushed. "I have no plans for that, Mr. Scout."

"Never knew many cowboys who did."

The back door creaked open and a stunning young woman in jeans, a gingham shirt and red cowboy boots stomped through it. Some kind of silver necklace glinted on her neck when she bent to pick up the pail of eggs Buster had set on the steps. She started toward the door again, but Buster stopped her.

"Hey, Pretty, come here. I want you to meet Mr. Joiner Temple."

The girl's brown eyes looked Joiner up and down. The back of his neck prickled. Still, to be polite, he stood and offered her his hand. When she took it, her handshake was surprisingly firm.

"Nice to meet you," she said, sounding as if it really wasn't.

"You, too, Miss Scout."

"It's Stella."

"Her name means *star*," Buster explained. His chest puffed out and he gave her a little pat on the back.

Stella the Pretty Star tossed her short gold hair, turned on the heel of her boot and headed into the house, letting the screen door slam behind her.

CHAPTER TWO

"IGNORE HER," BUSTER SAID, rubbing his hands together. "You want to go for a little ride out on the range?"

"Sure, sounds great."

"You take these coffee cups in, if you don't mind, and I'll go get the pumpkin."

Joiner wondered why in the world Buster would be getting a pumpkin and how it related to their ride on the property, but he did as he was told. He was disappointed that there was no sign of Stella in the house when he set the coffee cups in the kitchen sink.

Maybe it was a good thing he didn't run into her again. She seemed to harbor some underlying hostility toward him, although he couldn't imagine why. It was as if he reminded her of the high school boyfriend who left her to dance with another girl at the prom.

He was sitting on the porch steps when Buster roared up on an orange Kubota ATV with Mugsy and Mitzi sitting beside him.

"*Pumpkin* orange," Joiner mused aloud as he took his seat beside Mugsy on the passenger's side. It was the same color as his Texas Longhorns.

"Stella named it."

Buster lurched forward and soon they were bumping at full throttle across a cattle guard and out into open pasture. There were groves of loblolly pines, pencil cedars and live oaks interspersed with vast acres of grass for grazing cattle. Joiner counted five ponds as they passed, one as big as a small lake—about twenty acres—and it was on the north-forty. It would work perfectly for Joiner's plans, and he told Buster so. The older man just nodded.

After several minutes, Buster pulled up to the edge of the spring-fed creek and cut the motor of the Kubota. The dogs jumped out to get a drink. Buster leaned back, crossing his boots on the dashboard in front of him, just to the right of the steering wheel. He gazed out across the creek. He closed his eyes and slowly breathed in and out a few times. Joiner wondered if he was praying. Then Buster turned to look at Joiner.

"Son, I'm afraid I've wasted your time. I can't sell this place. Not any part of it."

After Buster's tour and description of this

part of the property, Joiner had begun to doubt he'd be able to afford it, but he'd wanted to make an offer anyway. It was perfect for him and Pistol, whatever they decided to do. He could train and board horses, breed Pistol, teach riding; the possibilities were endless. And that was something Joiner liked—keeping his options open.

"Why not? Why did you place the ad, then?"

Buster adjusted his cowboy hat. "I can answer both of your questions with one word—*Love.*"

"Something tells me there's more to it than that." Joiner leaned closer, prompting the older man to continue.

"Son, if you think love ain't enough, you got a lot to learn."

Joiner could only imagine his brothers' responses when he recounted this story. It seemed straight out of a dime-store novel about some dying breed of cowboy-philosophers. The hooting and hollering among the Temple brothers would be abundant.

Still, in the short time he'd spent with Buster, Joiner had become somewhat impressed with the older man. No one could be more outwardly different from Joiner's own father, who'd been a doctor, even though his dad and Buster would be about the same age if Dr. Temple had still been alive. But there was a quality there that felt familiar, a certain wisdom. Joiner wondered if there were ghosts that haunted Buster, as his grandfather's tarnished reputation had haunted his father for years.

"Love?"

"I lost my wife—Stella's mama—when she was thirty-six years old. She was a rodeo queen who became a hands-on mother after we had Stella. Then one day she got on a horse like she did every other day, only this time she fell off and died. It was a freak accident. She was gone from us, just like that."

Joiner shook his head. "I'm so sorry."

"Lily was also a naturalist, loved everything homegrown. She adored this place. It belonged to her family. She rode horses all over it, had her a garden. It was her sanctuary. I was gone all the time, but I like to think because of this land she wasn't lonely." Buster sighed. The water rolling over the rocks in front of them seemed to sigh with him.

"She taught Stella at home. Not for religious reasons, like a lot of people around here. With her it was more for personal freedom and what she called 'independence of thought'." Buster smiled as he made quotation marks in the air, and then continued, "They were always into these experiments and things Stella never would have done in public school. Lily, that's my wife, she would take her to the creek here and they'd collect jars of water and come home and identify all of the little creatures under a microscope. They'd go on walks and look up wildflowers in a book to learn their names. They hung artwork all over the house, even painted constellations on the ceiling of Stella's room. They milked goats and made their own cheese."

"Wow. That's neat. And I can vouch for the fact we did *not* do that kind of stuff at Kilgore High School."

"Well, I'm not knocking the school. Stella ended up graduating from there and the teachers were good to her. She was only sixteen when her mother passed."

Joiner felt a pang, remembering how painful it had been to lose his own parents at a young age. "Is that when you retired from the rodeo?"

"Yes. I was fifty, and twenty years past a bronc rider's prime. It was time for me to hang it up, and Stella needed the stability of a home. I couldn't take her riding around Texas with me in that RV."

Joiner swallowed hard. The story was a lot

to take in. Finally, he said, "But what about my second question? What did love have to do with putting the land up for sale?"

"Stella. She has this dream and I wanted to make it come true. But I'm not exactly high on funds."

"What does she want to do?"

"She wants to open a place here where kids with problems can come be with horses. 'Equestrian therapy' she calls it." Buster made quote marks in the air again. "I don't know about the fancy name, but I am a firm believer that spending time with horses is good for you. I've had a couple horses I like better than most people."

"I can relate to that." Joiner laughed. "Right now Pistol is pretty much my guiding star. Well, he and my brothers. Since my polo funds dried up, I'm at a bit of a loss as to what to do with the rest of my life. I can't say I'll settle down in Kilgore for good, but I'd prefer to be near my brothers while I'm figuring out my next step. And one thing's for sure—whatever I do next will involve Pistol. We're a package deal."

"I like that loyalty. You know, there's an old Spanish proverb that says a man who does not love a horse cannot love a woman." Buster sat up, planting his boots back on the floorboard of the pumpkin. "I guess we better head for the house."

THEY WERE QUIET for the ride across Buster's 450-acre kingdom. Mugsy and Mitzi ran along beside them till Buster deemed they were tired out, then he slowed down for them to jump into the pumpkin. When the house came into view, Buster pointed out a barn to the far right of it. Joiner had noticed it when he was driving up—a big horse barn painted red, with a white star above the doors. He saw now that there was a riding arena behind it.

"That's Stella's setup."

Buster didn't go any closer. Instead, he veered left toward the house, and Joiner noticed the old RV again under the trees.

"Was that your rodeo mansion?" He pointed to it. Surprisingly, Buster drove up close.

"That's it. We use it as a guesthouse now. Wanna see inside?"

He turned off the motor of the pumpkin without waiting for Joiner to answer. Using a key to unlock the RV, Buster held the door open for Joiner to enter. Despite the dust, it was surprisingly well-kept inside. Kind of like a museum dedicated to the rodeo life of yesteryear.

"You know, since I can't sell the land, I'd consider renting the guesthouse if you can think of anyone who might be interested. Especially someone with a strong back for work and horses they'd like to board." Buster tugged at his whiskers. "I don't want any riffraff, though."

Joiner didn't tell the older man what he was thinking, that "riffraff" were the only ones who would be interested in the setup. Except, maybe, for him.

"What about me?" Joiner couldn't believe the words had come out of his mouth, but he didn't try to retrieve them. He liked Buster. And something, though admittedly he couldn't see what, was drawing him to the place.

"You? A pretty boy like you?"

"Mr. Scout, I need a place to live and board my horse, and you won't sell me any land." Joiner kicked a clod of dirt.

"Call me Buster."

"Okay, Buster."

"You serious?"

"I'm not afraid of hard work. If you'll let me board Pistol and breed him out of here maybe I can save up the money to get my own place when the right one becomes available." Joiner raised his eyebrows and grinned at the older man. "One that is actually for sale."

"You're a smart aleck, you know it?" Buster held out his hand for a shake. "But I don't mind a little of that—and I might be able to make a real cowboy out of you. It's a deal."

Joiner shook his hand and they hopped back into the pumpkin. Buster sped the rest of the way to the house as if he was late for a party. Joiner liked the older man's style.

"Stella!" Buster called, opening the back door. "Pretty? Stelllllaaaa!"

An image of Marlon Brando in *A Streetcar Named Desire* flashed through Joiner's mind. He followed Buster into the foyer, where Buster called her again, looking up the stairs.

"I guess she ain't in here."

"Well, sir, if you don't mind, I'll just get going. I'll start moving in tomorrow, if that's okay."

"I wanted to let you and Stella do some talking. You'll mostly be working for her, you know. Getting her business up and running."

"Oh. Well." Joiner reached out for the banister. This was a little more than he bargained for. A mixture of curiosity and acid from his lack of breakfast churned in his stomach, but he needed the arrangement to work. He was running out of money, and no other interesting options had popped up.

Joiner straightened himself up and grinned, offering his hand to Buster again. "You just tell her I am at her service."

The front door opened, and Stella walked in on them.

"Well, now you can tell her yourself!" Buster clapped his hands together.

"Tell me what?" Stella demanded.

"Joiner is going to live in the RV and be our new ranch hand."

Stella took this news as if she'd been punched in the face.

"What?"

"I decided not to sell the land, but he's going to live here and help us out on the ranch for a while."

Stella's eyes widened as the news sank in.

"You're not selling?" She smiled, but her smile was for Buster only.

"No." Buster shook his head. "But we've made an arrangement where he can board his horse here and help with chores, and he'll be help to you with the school. You won't have to pay as much for a ranch hand, and he won't have to fork over lots of money for lodging. It's a win-win."

She seemed to bristle at this idea.

Buster grabbed the front doorknob and turned it. "You two probably ought to talk a little bit among yourselves. I've got to go check my chickens." He let the screen door slam behind him.

What a crafty old goat, Joiner thought, hoping he hadn't made a big mistake in agreeing to live and work here.

Stella motioned to Joiner. "I guess we could sit on the porch?"

He followed her through the screen door and sat down in one of two rockers that flanked a small table. She took the porch swing, the farthest seat away.

"So, your dad told me about your school. I think it's a great idea."

Her head snapped to attention. "What did he tell you?"

"Just that you want to help people through therapy with horses."

"Did he mention safety?"

"Um, no. We didn't really go very far into it."

"Safety is my first concern with the school—and I saw the way you drove in here like you were in a high-speed chase."

"I'm sorry, but—"

She continued, "I don't know what you're

used to with polo, but I'd imagine it will be a lot different than what I'm doing here."

Joiner was sure it would aggravate her, but he couldn't resist. "I'm used to having fun on horses."

She snorted. "Well, I hope my clients have fun on our horses, but my first priority is that they are safe at all times." Her brown eyes bored into him. "It will have to be *your* priority too while you work here."

"Okay," Joiner said, and then added in his thoughts, *which probably won't be very long.*

CHAPTER THREE

"YOU'RE DOING WHAT?" Mac demanded as his eyeglasses clattered to the tabletop.

The four Temple brothers sat around a table on the back patio of The Wild Horse Saloon, a honky-tonk joint that also served the best steaks in Kilgore—apart from Hunt's restaurant at Temple Territory, of course. Most of the action was clustered around the stage inside where the band played. Locals, including students at Kilgore College, crowded the dance floor to do the Texas two-step and unwind after a busy work week.

Hunt's wife, Gillian, and Sarah, a young widow who'd recently wed Hunt's twin, Cullen, had taken Sarah's three daughters to Longview for a movie. The brothers saw this as an opportunity for a Meeting of the Brotherhood, as they affectionately called their impromptu men-only gatherings. They'd been calling them that as long as Joiner could remember, when he and Mac initiated the younger twins into the clubhouse that used to be in their parents' yard.

"I'm moving into an RV on that place I wanted to buy. Buster Scout's place."

Mac picked up his rectangular wire-rimmed glasses from the table and set them back on his nose, as if to see Joiner better. "The place you're not buying? You're going to squat there in an RV?"

Joiner shook his head. "The RV is a guest-house of sorts on the property. Mr. Scout is renting it to me in exchange for some help on the ranch. Plus, he has a place I can board Pistol and hopefully start breeding him so I can save some money."

"Is that what this is about? Joiner, I told you if you needed money—"

"And I appreciate that you agreed to cosign the loan with me for the land if I could buy it, but Mr. Scout decided not to sell it. And that's probably for the best right now. I can keep what little I have left in the bank and add to it, get back on my feet. Then maybe when the right place comes along down the road, I won't need a cosigner."

"Sounds like a good plan to me." Hunt's gray eyes danced as he helped the server distribute the plates. Each brother had ordered a

T-bone, but they all preferred their own degrees of doneness.

The waitress—a girl with big blond hair—studied Hunt's face for a moment as she handed him a plate. "You look just like my favorite professor!"

Hunt grinned and flung out his arm to announce that Cullen was across the table. She promptly turned all of her attention to him.

"Dr. Temple! How are you doing? I was in your American History class last semester." The girl made no effort to conceal her admiration.

"I remember you, Katie. It's nice to see you again."

When she finally exited the patio after several minutes of chatting with Cullen, Hunt cackled. Then in a falsetto voice, he said, "Oh, Dr. Cullen! Your lectures are so enthralling! I only fell asleep three times! But it's such a shame you're not as good-looking as the Cowboy Chef!"

Cullen rolled his eyes in Hunt's direction.

"I thought it was pretty funny that she compared the Cowboy Chef to Dr. Cullen, and not the other way around." Joiner cut into his steak. "That must burn."

Hunt frogged Joiner in the arm. "You just wish you were our triplet, pretty boy."

"Well, I can tell you I don't get admirers very often, even though I'm obviously the more attractive twin." Cullen forked a bite of steaming baked potato that was dripping with melted butter. "Did you find out anything on the history of Buster Scout's place while you were there?"

"Only that it belonged to his wife's family. She died a long while ago in a freak accident with a horse, and I guess it went to him and his daughter. It's a heck of a place."

"I think I remember something about that accident." Mac rubbed his chin. "It happened right after I moved back here and set up shop. I consulted with Mr. Scout over some tax issues, helped him get things with his wife's will straightened out. Nice guy. Kind of an original, as I remember."

"That's him. He could have his own reality show, he and his daughter. They're like the Texas version of characters from *Duck Dynasty*."

"And now you're joining the show."

"Well, I would hate for Hunt to be the *lone star* in our family." Joiner couldn't resist the pun.

His three brothers groaned in unison, then

Cullen asked, "What time do you want us there to help you move in the morning?"

They all looked at Joiner. He'd always been able to count on the Brotherhood, no matter what.

"Thanks, guys, but I don't have anything to move besides a few boxes and Pistol. It won't be any big deal."

"NO BIG DEAL?" Stella, remembering her earlier conversation with her father, set down her book a little too loudly and whipped off her red reading glasses. Mugsy jumped down from the couch and regarded her with suspicion.

Buster, who had kicked back in his leather recliner, didn't stir from his comfortable position. Mitzi was sprawled out across his chest lengthwise, snoring.

"I can't *believe* you think this is no big deal," she repeated.

Buster opened one eye and Stella glared into it.

He closed it quickly, like pulling down a shade.

"Pops! You should have consulted with me first before offering to let him live here. Instead you let him sweet-talk you. And I'd like to have seen his horse before you said he could board him in our stable. What if the horse is dangerous?"

"Good grief, woman. We've been through this." Buster raised his head slightly so as not to disturb Mitzi. "He didn't *sweet-talk* me. It was practically my idea. And I thought you'd be happy to have some free labor. At least I didn't sell him any land."

"I *am* happy about *that*." Stella shrugged and put her glasses back on. She smoothed her cotton pajamas and tucked her feet up under her. Then she remembered something. "But isn't there some scandal with the Temple family? I wouldn't want that to affect my school."

Buster sighed heavily. "Anybody who still cares about that scandal is nobody I'd want on my ranch, school or no school."

Stella raised her eyebrows.

Buster continued, "Pap Temple did steal oil, but the big oil companies were so greedy there was no real harm, in my opinion, in Pap taking a few million barrels. Those were different times." He snorted. "In fact, I admire his gumption for doing it, and his guts in taking his punishment after he was caught instead of filling his wells with cement like some others did to avoid prosecution."

"I didn't know all of that," Stella said quietly.

As though sensing the storm had passed, at least for the time being, Mugsy jumped back onto the couch and resumed his post at her side.

WHEN STELLA AWOKE the next morning, she was glad she had a busy day ahead. Maybe the work she had to do to get Star Stables Equestrian Therapy up and running would distract her from Joiner Temple's invasion of her property. Until he brought his horse into her barn, that is—a high-dollar thoroughbred stallion. Having that kind of horse join her operation was not at all what she had in mind. His presence would probably be as obnoxious as his owner's. No, what Stella wanted was a few other horses like Daisy, her mother's old mare, who were gentle enough to be trusted with the special-needs children Stella planned to serve.

But the agreement had been made, and there wasn't anything she could do about it now but continue with her own plans. She picked out one of her nicest shirts, a lacy cowgirl-chic top with bell sleeves that was the color of gunmetal. Pairing it with her distressed skinny jeans, she tucked the jeans into a pair of tall, vintage, gray halter boots. The brushed silver amulet she wore, a custom piece by Andrea Edmondson, perfectly complemented the color of her shirt. Her hair was easy—shoulder-length and chic—and she didn't need any makeup other than a little lip gloss. Her mahogany eyes were framed by dark lashes and brows even though her hair remained the color of a palomino.

Stella waved at her father, who was out milking the goats, as she climbed into the farm truck. She planned to grab something for breakfast at Common Grounds. A potential donor from a local family well-known for its oil money was meeting her there for coffee. She really had high hopes that she could convince him to donate to her school. Star Stables was the one thing she wanted with all of her heart—everything important to her was tied to it. It was something she could do on her own land, at home with Buster. It was a way to give back to her beloved community. And it was a way to help people—to give them better lives, and especially, to teach them how to be safe.

STELLA ROSE FROM the bistro table where she was sitting with her mocha cappuccino when the man who had to be Clint Cavender walked into Common Grounds.

"Mr. Cavender?"

He turned his gaze to her.

He was wearing Armani and some kind of lizard-skin boots. Nice.

He held out his hand. "Stella Scout? Call me Clint." Perfect teeth, dark hair, milk-chocolate-colored eyes. Stella felt as if she was talking to a movie star. She needed to get herself together.

"Please, have a seat."

"Sure, but I think I'll order first. Can I get you anything to go with your coffee?"

Stella didn't want him to buy her food. "I'll just join you."

He set down his Louis Vuitton laptop bag on one of the oak-and-iron chairs at her table and they walked together to the counter, which was just a few feet away.

"I'd like some steel-cut oats with fruit."

The guy at the counter rang her order into the cash register. "And for you, sir?"

"These are separate orders." Stella held out her debit card, but Clint Cavender shook his head.

"I'll have a ham, egg and cheese panini and a latte with two shots, please."

He paid for their order with a twenty-dollar bill, dumping all of the change into the tip jar. They waited while it was prepared.

"You didn't have to pay for my breakfast," Stella said.

"Oh, no problem."

Clint's phone vibrated and he took it out of his pocket. "Sorry. I always have to check in case it is the school."

He carried their tray back to the table, and set her oats in front of her before removing his own order. "That looks good," he commented, then set the tray on a nearby table.

Stella straightened her shoulders. "Clint, thank you for meeting with me. I know you have a very busy schedule and I appreciate you taking the time to listen to my proposal."

"It's a pleasure." His eyes were warm. "Let's hear about these plans of yours."

"Well, I am opening a facility for equestrian therapy on my family farm just outside Kilgore. We will offer hippotherapy as well as therapeutic riding for people with disabilities. My focus is geared more toward children, but I'd like to be able to offer services to all ages eventually."

Clint leaned forward, eyebrows knitted. "Wait a minute. You lost me. I thought we were talking exclusively about horses. What exactly is hippotherapy?"

"*Hippo* is the Greek word for horse." Stella laughed. "So *hippotherapy* is just a term that encompasses all kinds of therapy that uses the horse's movement. I want to offer physical, occupational and speech therapy using horses."

"So I'm assuming you'll employ professionals in these fields?"

"Yes. I have a master's degree in physical therapy myself, and I've already contracted an excellent occupational therapist assistant named Daune Holzman and a speech therapist named Jacob Hunnicutt. Of course, the amount of hours they are able to spend at the school will depend on how things work out with funding."

"It sounds very interesting." Clint took a sip of his latte. "Are there any other programs similar to this in the state of Texas?"

"Ours will be the second, and the first in East Texas. The other one is in Austin and partners with the University of Texas. I trained there and it is very cutting edge." Stella stirred her oatmeal. "These techniques have been used in Europe for about fifty years, but they are just now starting to catch on in the United States."

"It sounds like you have the vision and the expertise to really help some people."

"I believe I do."

Clint leaned back and draped an arm over the ironwork back of the chair beside his. "Stella, one reason I agreed to meet with you is that I've heard your story. You may not realize it, but you're something of a celebrity in this little town."

"Me?"

"Yes. I know you've battled hardship and overcome a lot yourself. I was away at the height of your rodeo fame but I heard about how you brought the people of Kilgore together."

"Oh, that."

"To hear my parents talk, we might as well have changed our name to 'The City of Star' instead of 'The City of Stars'."

Stella blushed. "I wouldn't go that far. I didn't really do anything. It was the people of the community who blessed my family and me over and over with their support." Her heart warmed at the memories of barbecue suppers, parades and the cards and letters that wallpapered her room at home. She also remembered the flowers that had poured in after her mother's death. Lilies. "I guess that's why I never want to move anywhere else. And in a way, this venture is a chance for me to give back to the people who have done so much for me."

Clint smiled, seeming to understand. Then he said, "The other reason I'm interested is my son, Cade. He has Asperger's syndrome. The symptoms have gotten worse since his mother left. I've done everything—spared no expense—but we've not found any therapies that have helped with his particular case."

"I'm sorry to hear that." Stella looked into his eyes and saw deep pools of pain she had not noticed before. "I'd love it if we could help him," she said softly.

"Me, too. Tell me more…"

CHAPTER FOUR

"Dios mia!" Alma made the sign of the cross as she stepped across the threshold of the RV. "Joiner, *mi cariño*, are you really so poor that you must live *here*?"

Joiner pulled the door shut behind them and plopped down on the red velvet couch, spreading out his arms and crossing a boot over his knee. "Home sweet home!"

Alma rolled her eyes. As the Temple family's housekeeper, she was the closest thing to a mother Joiner and his brothers had had since the plane accident that killed their parents when Joiner was in high school. She and her husband Felix had been their legal guardians until they came of age—and were still the glue that kept the family together.

"I thought you said it was in good shape." Alma ran a finger over the counter top and held it up for Joiner to see. The dust was thick on her soft, tawny fingertip.

"It's not that bad, is it? I mean, after you work your magic?"

"Magic? It's going to take more than magic to make this place livable. It's going to take elbow grease!"

"Well, I don't want you working too hard, Alma. Let's just get it livable. I probably won't be here very long." Joiner brought in her cleaning supplies from the truck while Alma opened all of the windows. Under her instruction, he vacuumed the red shag carpet that filled the living area and bedroom, and then scrubbed the toilet, shower and sink, as well as the linoleum in the tiny bath and kitchen.

Alma dusted the RV from top to bottom, removing all of the curtains to take home and wash, and beating the couch cushions outside with a broom. She stripped the bed of its velvet horse-print spread, remaking it with a new mattress cover, Egyptian cotton sheets, and Woolrich plaid comforter set she'd gotten from Gillian. It was a tasteful blue, red and green pattern with leather-trimmed matching pillows. She also scrubbed the small stovetop and oven and cleaned out the cabinets. Buster's shot glass collection went into a Rubbermaid tub along with various other things she collected from around the RV: an old wall calendar of famous bronc riders, several trophies, cassette tapes of country music, an enormous belt buckle.

"Whew! Let's take a break." Joiner leaned on the mop and stretched his back.

"Just a few more things first." Alma wiped her hands on her apron. "Take this tub of junk out." She handed it to him with a look of disgust. "Then, bring in those kitchen things we got at Target, and also get your bathroom stuff set up. You can put your clothes in the bedroom, too. I still have to wash all of the windows."

Joiner shook his head and grinned at her before obeying.

By noon the RV was passable by Alma's standards, which were far higher than Joiner's. It still needed power-washing on the outside, she said. But the interior gleamed. She spread out a quilt over the picnic table that sat adjacent to the RV under a tree and opened her basket.

"This table is convenient." She handed him a tortilla filled with chorizo. "If you are camping." Her brown eyes flickered with humor and something else.

Joiner grabbed an orange Fanta out of the basket and sat down to eat across from her. These were the tastes of his childhood. This woman and the sun had warmed every season of his life for as long as he could remember. "Do you still have that bracelet?"

Alma pulled up her sleeve. She wore the bracelet Joiner had made her for Mother's Day long ago—a strap of brown leather with a hammered metal piece that read, *Sky above me, Earth below me, Fire within me*. It had weathered to the caramel color of her skin. "I never take it off."

Joiner squeezed her hand from across the table. "Thank you, Alma. For everything."

"You are welcome, *mijo. De nada*."

AFTER HE DROVE Alma home, Joiner loaded up Pistol at Hunt's barn. He was glad to be finished moving himself into the RV. This way he could make sure Pistol got all the time he needed this afternoon to become acclimated to his new surroundings—and hopefully Joiner could become a little more acclimated himself.

He still wasn't fully comfortable with the idea of working under Stella. From what he could tell, she seemed pretty rigid. He wasn't used to walking around on eggshells and he didn't intend to start now. But it was what it was. At least Buster seemed to like him.

"Hey, buddy!" Buster swaggered out of the stable as Joiner was pulling up. Joiner jumped out of the truck and strode toward him. Buster shook his hand. "I thought we'd put your horse in here."

He led Joiner through the stable, pointing out an old mare with gentle eyes named Daisy who had belonged to his wife. Beside Daisy was Stella's horse, a white quarter horse named Vega. Across from Vega was the roomiest, best stall at the end of the row. There was new hay spread across the floor, oats in the feed bin and fresh water for drinking. The older man cocked his head to one side to gauge his reaction.

"Thanks, man," Joiner said. "This is a great setup."

Buster walked with him back to the horse trailer to unload Pistol. When Joiner led the shining black stallion out into the lot, he heard Buster catch his breath.

"That's a good-looking horse." Buster squinted into the sun. He pulled down his hat and then touched Pistol gently on his star. "Gosh darn, that's a fine animal."

Pistol held his head high and flared his nostrils. Then he shook his mane, pawing the ground with his front hooves.

"Do you mind if I take him for a ride around the place?" Joiner could feel the energy pulsing in Pistol's neck, and it mirrored the nervousness in his own veins. They were both in need of an outlet, an adrenaline rush. It had been a few days, and Joiner was desperate for it.

"Go for it." Buster grinned. "Just don't get lost."

While Joiner saddled Pistol, Buster walked over and held the gate that opened into the pasture. Joiner and Pistol cantered through, and then, finding their bearings, took off running hell-for-leather until they were out of sight.

CHAPTER FIVE

AFTER HER SUCCESSFUL meeting with Clint Cavender, Stella went shopping for horses. She wanted to purchase at least three to add to the two she owned, and she had some pretty good leads through her rodeo contacts. Calling on five different owners, she made offers on two mares that fit the bill perfectly. They were still young enough to work, strong-backed, but both were gentle. *Not much fire in their bellies.* Stella liked that, considering fire would be a hazard in her riding school. It was three o'clock in the afternoon when she returned home. She sent a text to Buster telling him her plans to pick up the mares that evening and asked if he'd get the stable ready. But, as she hadn't heard from him, she decided to check the stalls before she changed clothes.

"What the heck?"

The last stall across from Vega was open, and Joiner Temple stood inside it. He was brushing a horse that looked as though he belonged on the cover of *Stud* magazine, and the horse looked as if he knew it. He snorted at her as she approached.

"Hi there." The polo player grinned sheepishly. "How are you?"

"Uh, fine, thanks. But, what are you doing, exactly?"

His violet eyes flashed. "Brushing my horse. That okay with you?"

The thoroughbred seemed to glare at her but Stella held her ground. "Sure. I mean, I guess. Who told you to move your horse into this stall?"

Joiner stepped back, still holding the brush in his hand. He looked at her, then gazed off into the distance toward the goat pen. *Buster.*

Stella turned on the heel of her boot and stomped out of the stable. She found her father in the garden, tilling the ground. He shut off the tiller when he saw her.

"Hey, Pretty!"

It was usually hard for her to be mad at him for anything, but not this time.

"What is that horse doing in the best stall? Right across from Vega?"

He looked at her as if she'd grown horns. "Cooling off from a ride, I imagine."

"I'll cool him off." Stella put her hands on

her hips. "What were you thinking? I wanted to use that stall for boarding."

"In case you haven't noticed, darlin', we *are* boarding. An Argentine Thoroughbred worth lots of money."

"Why did you not consult me?"

Buster spat tobacco on the ground. "Don't be ridiculous. I'm just bein' a good host, which is more than I can say for you. Vega ain't gonna get cooties."

"I don't like it."

"You don't have to, Prissy Britches. But if you don't sit down and make some plans with your new ranch hand there may be lots more things you don't like, because I intend to make him work to earn his keep." Buster wiped the sweat from his forehead. "And if you don't need anything done for the school, I could use some help in this garden."

Stella shook her head. "Did you not get my text?"

"What text?" Buster fumbled in the pocket of his jeans, finally dragging out his phone. He squinted at the screen, then looked back up at her. "Oops."

"Don't worry about it. It will give me great pleasure to tell the polo player to get the stalls ready while I go pick up the horses."

By the time Stella made her way back into the stable, Joiner was just closing the door to his horse's stall. He turned and saw her standing at the other end, and for a moment they stared at one another, sizing each other up, as if they were about to duel.

Joiner made the first move. He walked toward her, and Stella tried not to notice the muscles that rippled under his sweaty white T-shirt. She straightened her spine.

"I'm sorry if there was a misunderstanding. I can move my horse if you want."

Was he trying to shame her? Because it was working. "No. Keep him there. I'm sorry. I'm afraid we've gotten off on the wrong foot."

"I don't want to step on anyone's toes. I just want to live in the RV, work and maybe breed out my horse."

Stella couldn't help but crack a smile. "You *want* to live in the RV?"

"Okay, so maybe I'm a little desperate." Joiner smiled back at her.

"Well, join the club. I've got to get this operation going, and it puts my dad and me in weird roles sometimes."

"I hadn't noticed any weirdness." Joiner raised an eyebrow. He was baiting her, but she decided not to bite. "Listen, Joiner. We need to sit down and talk about what I want you to do for Star Stables but right now I've got to go pick up two horses. Could you get the stable ready for them?"

"At your service, Boss Lady." He tipped his hat.

"Thanks. I'll see you in a bit."

"Any specific stalls you want to assign?"

But her back was already to him and she refused to turn to honor his question with a response.

AFTER STELLA, BUSTER and Joiner had the two new horses settled into the stable, Buster asked Joiner what he was doing for dinner.

"Alma—she's my adopted mom—left some homemade tamales with me this morning when she helped me move into the RV."

"Well, why don't you save them? I've got some T-bones we could grill. It's a nice evenin'."

Why didn't her dad just invite him to live in their house? Stella groused to herself.

"That's really kind of you, but I don't want to intrude."

"You wouldn't be intrudin' at all. And I'll let you do the dishes." Buster winked at him. "Besides, that way you and Stella can have a chance to talk and hammer out some kind of job description."

Even though her dad drove her a little crazy, and she wasn't sure how to manage things with Joiner Temple, Stella had to admit that meeting was a good idea. That was all she would admit, though, even to herself.

She told herself, therefore, that it was simply good hospitality to make homemade lemonade, beer-battered bread, twice-baked potatoes and a fresh Caesar salad to go with the steaks; and also to whip up a homemade apple pie with vanilla bean ice cream and Mexican caramel sauce for dessert. If he was impressed with her cooking, well, so be it. That was no concern of hers....

CHAPTER SIX

JOINER CLEANED UP for dinner in the RV's shower, which was about half the size of a British phone booth. Fitting his six-foot-two-inch frame in there each day to scrub off ranch grime was going to be one of the challenges of his new life. One of the many.

He bumped his head on the showerhead, which thankfully did have good water pressure, and rinsed the soap out of his hair. Then, squeezing himself out of the contraption and planting his feet on the hooked rug Alma had provided, he dried himself thoroughly and wrapped the white towel around his waist. His five o'clock shadow from yesterday was well on its way to becoming a full-fledged beard. If he didn't want to join Buster on Cowboy Dynasty, it was time for a shave.

Joiner wasn't sure what to make of Buster's dinner invitation. A part of him was ready for some downtime, some rest and a little privacy. He liked people. But he wasn't used to trusting them very quickly or easily. The benefit—or curse, depending on your point of view—of being Pap's grandson. And while Buster seemed kind in his intentions, Stella was harder to read. One moment Joiner thought she hated him. The next she was almost friendly. Oh well, maybe tonight he'd at least get some clarity on the role he was meant to play on the ranch and in her riding school.

Besides, this job was just a transition for him anyway. He could do anything—work with anyone—for a short while as long as it got him on his feet. If anything, being a good worker would help him accomplish the one long-term goal all of his brothers had—to restore honor to the family name.

"TAKE THAT RODEO stuff and put it on the porch, if you don't mind. Stella can show you what to do with it." Buster flipped a steak that Joiner judged to be at least sixteen ounces. It sizzled and popped on the gas grill.

"That smells delicious!"

The old man smiled. "You need to eat meat, boy, if you're ever going to grow up to be any size."

Joiner made a mental note of the latest Busterism so he could use it on his brothers the next time they had a barbecue.

He carried the tub of rodeo paraphernalia he and Alma had culled from the RV up to the porch and rested it on his hip while he knocked on the screen door.

Stella turned from the sink where she was squeezing lemons. She wore a vintage-inspired cotton dress with tiny pink roses against a white background. A silver pendant hung from a chain around her neck, the same one she'd worn when they'd met. Pink ballet slippers the exact color of the roses on the dress adorned her small feet. It was the first time Joiner had seen her in anything other than boots. She looked soft, feminine.

"Come on in." She wiped her hands on a towel and opened the door for him. "I hope you like lemonade."

"Yeah, it's great."

Stella glanced down at the tub in Joiner's arms. "Oh Lord." She lifted the calendar, which was yellowed around the edges, and then set it back down in the tub, skimming through the other contents. "You mean you can't use this belt buckle?"

"'Fraid not." Joiner shifted his weight. "Your dad said you could show me where to put this?"

He followed her through the kitchen and dining room into the foyer and around the stairs. There was a little door there that revealed storage space under the stairs. "Let's put it in here for right now."

As she held the door open for him, Joiner caught the scent of her. Nothing flashy or overpowering, just fresh, like rain. Clean. And maybe a hint of lemon.

"That's a pretty bracelet."

It jangled as she turned the knob of the little door to close it. Then she held the bracelet out in front of her, fingering it with her other hand. It was made of a thin leather strap, wrapped twice around her wrist, with charms that dangled from it on silver rings. Joiner noted a pink rose charm, a silver cross, a white horse, a red heart and a gold star, among others. "It's an Andrea Edmondson, ABE Designs?"

She looked a little impressed, but quickly recovered. "My favorite."

"Yeah, she's great. I like your necklace, too."

"Thanks."

"Can I see what it has on it? Is that a tree?"

She held it out to him, and he leaned in just a bit to see it.

"Oh. It says *healing*. What's that about?" Joiner pressed out of curiosity.

"A friend gave it to me when my mother died."

There was a bit of an awkward silence, and Joiner wished he'd not asked such a personal question. He followed her back to the kitchen. "Anything I can do to help with dinner?"

"You can set the table. We're going to eat outside on the porch."

Joiner rolled up the sleeves of his Wrangler shirt. He took the stack of colorful Fiesta plates she handed him, along with silverware and napkins, and went to the porch, where a red-checkered cloth covered the table. Buster met him with a platter of steaks, two enormous T-bones and one smaller one. Soon Stella came out with bread on a wooden cutting board, a bread knife and a big bowl of salad with silver tongs. Joiner followed her back into the kitchen where she directed him to take potatoes out of the oven while she poured lemonade into mason jars.

The evening sun was golden in the sky. Hues of purple and pink streaked the clouds as it began its descent, and the gentle breath of a breeze blew across the porch. The yard, trees and field beyond seemed bathed in the beauty of an emerging springtime. Buster, who sat at the head of the table, held out his hands to

Joiner and Stella, who sat on either side of him. "Let's pray."

"Lord, thank You for this day. I thank You for my family and for watching over us and taking such good care of us. Thank You for Joiner. I pray You will bless him through his time here on the ranch. We lift up those who are in need tonight, especially Cheryl, and ask that You would heal her and comfort her. We trust You will continue to guide and provide for us everything we need. In Jesus's name."

When the food had been passed around, and everyone's plate was full, Joiner asked, "Who is Cheryl, if you don't mind my asking?"

"She's my mother's best friend. She lives in Arkansas. She was just diagnosed with breast cancer."

"Oh. I'm so sorry." Joiner looked down.

"She's the one who gave me my necklace and bracelet—the necklace when my mother died, and the bracelet for high school graduation. Whenever something significant happens, she gives me a charm."

Joiner nodded, pieces of the puzzle falling into place. "How cool. She has great taste."

"She has been a second mother to Stella in many ways," Buster said. "Even though she lives about six hours from here in northwest Arkansas."

"Arkansas, huh?"

"Yeah. She's a Razorback, but we don't hold it against her." Buster wrinkled his nose when he said the word *Razorback*.

"How is she doing?" Joiner asked.

Stella sighed. "It is already stage four, and the statistics are not in her favor. But we are hopeful she will be the one in five who beats it."

"I hope so, too."

"If anyone can kick cancer's butt, it will be her!" Buster declared.

They all ate in silence for a few moments. Then Stella asked, "Joiner, you mentioned an Alma who is your adopted mother making you tamales. Is your mother not around?"

Buster motioned to her by waving his steak knife in front of his neck, but Joiner smiled at him and said, "It's okay." He continued, addressing Stella. "I was seventeen, so I think you would have been eleven, too young to remember. It was in all of the papers, but there's no reason you would have known. My parents were killed in a plane crash in the Apache Mountains."

"Oh my goodness! I'm so sorry!" Stella set down her silverware and fiddled with her napkin.

"Thanks. It was a long time ago. But something you never get over, you know."

"Yes. I understand." Her eyes held his for a long moment.

Buster cleared his throat. "Well, shall we talk about something besides disease and death? How about something interesting, like the Ice Age?"

That remark was so random it made them all laugh. They spent the rest of the evening in a lighter mood, as Buster regaled them with his heroic feats as a famous bronco rider in the rodeo.

After Stella served her apple pie to rave reviews, Buster announced he was going to bed. "I'm an old man and I'm tired. But you kids stay up awhile. Get some of these kinks worked out about our new slave laborer and his duties, okay, Pretty?"

"Okay, Pops," Stella answered, even though she had mixed feelings about being left alone with Joiner. Again. She was beginning to notice that Buster had a pattern, and wondered exactly what his motives were. Was it really about business? Or was her dad so smitten with Joiner that he hoped she would be, too?

THEY CLEARED THE TABLE together and, back inside the kitchen, Joiner filled the sink with water for the dishes.

"You don't have to do that."

"Yes I do. It was part of the arrangement I made with Buster." He submerged the mason jars and started washing.

"You're going to have to learn that my dad just blows and goes. He didn't really mean you had to do the dishes."

Joiner looked at her with wide eyes. "I'd never have guessed that. Now you're going to tell me I don't have to eat steak in order to grow to a good size!"

Stella swatted him in the side with a hand towel.

"I'm just saying you don't have to do the dishes. I can do them later."

"I'm not leaving the dishes, Boss Lady. Alma, and my own mother for that matter, raised me better than that."

Stella joined him and, working together, it didn't take long to put the kitchen back in order.

"Would you like to talk about work in here, or on the porch?" she offered.

"I'll take the porch."

Stella gathered the leftover bones from the steaks and called to Mugsy and Mitzi. She dropped the bones off the porch and into the yard, where the dogs went to town, and then sat down in one of the rockers. Joiner sat in the other one. It creaked. He stretched his long legs out in front of him and crossed his boots. It was not yet dark, but the air was purple. The color of the gloaming, or twilight.

"We're going to need a candle," Stella said, pushing herself back up out of the rocker. She returned shortly with a fat pillar candle and a box of matches. She set it on the table between them and lit it, releasing a soft, vanilla-scented glow.

"This is a beautiful place."

"Thank you. It's home. I really can't imagine being anywhere else." Stella sighed. "That's one reason why the school is so important to me. I want a job that incorporates my love of this place with a love of horses and people."

Joiner wished he felt that way about Kilgore—or anywhere, for that matter. He'd never committed a crime. So why did he always feel as if he was on the run?

"Tell me your vision for the riding school. How can I help you with it?"

Stella ran her hands through her gold hair and then folded them behind her head, leaning back in the rocker. "To be honest, my vision is still evolving. I thought I was clear on what I wanted, but it changed a little bit today."

"What happened today?"

"Well, I knew I wanted to help people, to offer physical and occupational therapy through interaction with horses in a safe environment. That's really the core of the vision I have. And of course I can teach safe riding techniques to anyone who wants to learn." Stella sighed.

"Sounds like safety's a big deal to you."

"It is. I've been all about safety ever since my mom's accident."

"Oh. I see." Joiner nodded. "Nothing wrong with that."

"But today I met with a potential donor who told me about his son, a child with Asperger's, whose symptoms have gotten worse since his parents split up. His mother abandoned him… my heart broke hearing his story. So now my vision is expanding to include spiritual therapy, too—a more holistic approach than I first imagined."

"Hmm." Joiner felt he was treading some deep water without a life jacket. It was not that he couldn't be spiritual or a deep thinker. It was just that those things usually led him to places of pain, places he'd rather avoid. That's why polo suited him so much. It was a game.

"Probably sounds crazy to you." She folded her hands in her lap.

"Not crazy. It sounds good. But I have no idea how you'll accomplish it."

"At least you're honest. I like that in a slave laborer."

Was she flirting with him? Two could play at that game. "Ha! Well, at least you make great apple pie. I like that in a Boss Lady."

Stella turned in her rocker so that she was facing him. Leaning toward the table, she ran her index finger through the candle's flame. "Did you ever do this when you were a kid?" Her eyes danced. The candle flame flickered, illuminating her face so it seemed as if the glow came from inside her.

Joiner tried it but he burned himself. "Ow!" He shook his hand in the air.

Stella giggled. "You have to do it this way, you goof." She slowly dragged her index finger through the middle of the flame again, coming out unscathed. "Give me your hand."

"I am injured!"

Stella reached out her hand. "Don't you trust me, Joiner?"

Her eyes challenged him. He placed his other hand in her palm. Extending his index finger, she enclosed his fist in both of hers, holding it firm, and then trailed his finger through the center of the flame. He felt nothing. No burning. Well, nothing in his finger.

"How was that?" She held on to his hand while she waited for an answer.

"It was excruciating!"

"What? No!" She turned his finger around, looking for a sign that it was burned.

"You just set me on fire. Now I think you're going to have to kiss it and make it better."

Stella squinted at him, but she didn't drop his hand.

"Really, Boss Lady, you better kiss my finger or I might not be able to work tomorrow."

She pecked his index finger with her lips and then tossed his hand away as though it was a hot coal.

"Ooh, that helped." Joiner held his finger in front of his eyes. "I think I'm healed. It's a miracle!"

A smile stole across Stella's face.

"No kidding. Maybe you should kiss the other one, too." He held it out like a dare.

Surprisingly, Stella took it and kissed it softly and slowly, closing her eyes. Joiner leaned forward and kissed her on the cheek. Her skin tasted like sunshine.

"Oh my." Stella's brown eyes were as wild as an untamed mustang's. She jumped back, and Joiner busted out laughing. He knew it was reckless, what just happened, but it was also wonderful. He couldn't contain his joy.

Joiner bit his lip, but another giggle escaped.

"What's so funny?" Stella demanded.

He reached up and touched her face. "I'm not laughing at you."

"Then why, may I ask, are you laughing?" She put her hands on her hips.

"I don't know." He wanted to say he felt happy, but he couldn't. "Maybe I should go."

"Go?"

She sounded disappointed. Maybe even a little panicked.

"Just to the RV. We have work to do tomorrow, unless you're going to fire me."

Her shoulders relaxed. "No." She kicked into business mode. "Okay, um, let's meet in the morning at eight. You can shadow me throughout the day and see what it's like working the horses and stuff. But of course you have to keep in mind that when the clients start coming, everything will change."

Joiner nodded. "Eight it is." He tipped his

hat to her as he headed for the steps. "Stella?" He paused on the second one. The corners of her mouth turned up when he said her name. "I think everything might have already changed."

CHAPTER SEVEN

STELLA THREW SOME yogurt and granola down her throat and was out the door at sunrise the next morning. It was rare that she beat Buster to the kitchen, but she hadn't slept too well the night before. Thoughts of Joiner buzzed around in her head like hummingbirds in a bed of zinnias. She had to get outside.

Vega seemed a little agitated, too. She was already up and eyeing her new stable partner from across the way. She tossed her snowy white mane when Stella greeted her.

Joiner's horse, however, snorted when Stella came near. She didn't open the door to his stall, but took the moment alone to size him up. Every inch of him evoked power. An Argentine Thoroughbred stallion. She had to admit he was pretty incredible. "You're a beautiful boy."

A door creaked. "Thanks. But who are you calling a boy?"

Stella turned to see Joiner standing at the opposite end of the stable where she'd stood just yesterday, ready to duel him.

"Do you have X-ray ears or something?"

He walked toward her. "I don't think that's a thing."

He'd tucked a white T-shirt into distressed Levi's that she couldn't call loose, and wore a flannel shirt the color of twilight open like a jacket. Brown belt, brown work boots. Wavy hair as dark as his horse peeked out from under his cowboy hat, and Stella willed herself not to remember how soft his hair had been against her cheek last night.

"What are you doing up so early? You don't have to clock in till eight."

"I figured I'd try to impress my boss."

There were lots of ways Stella could have replied to that. Instead, she said, "Well, I'm not on the clock yet, either. Vega and I are going for a ride."

"Care if Pistol and I join you?"

"Suit yourself."

They saddled the horses and walked them slowly through the gate. Once out in the pasture, Stella and Vega took the lead, riding swiftly but surely. Joiner had to contain Pistol to keep from passing them. He followed for a while, and then pulled up beside her.

"Where are we going?"

"The north forty. There's a lake…"

"We'll see you there."

Pistol shot forward, kicking up plugs of grass and dirt behind him, reminding Stella of just the type of dangerous horse—and rider—she was dealing with.

Vega kept the pace Stella had set earlier, as if in silent understanding with her rider. They arrived at the shore of the lake to find Joiner sitting on a rock, and Pistol getting a drink from the clear, cool water.

Stella dismounted. She led Vega to drink several steps away from Pistol. When Pistol had drunk his fill, Joiner tied him to a tree. Stella let Vega go but the horse stayed close by her master.

"Want to sit?" Joiner motioned to the rock and Stella sat down on it with him.

The sight was so peaceful and so filled with memories, Stella's irritation melted away. They lounged side by side, looking out over the lake as the sun spilled its warmth across it. Ducks dived for their breakfast, creating golden ripples, and a heron peered at them from down the bank. Water bugs zigzagged in a pattern at the edge, right in front of the rock. A fish flopped, then another.

"My mom and I used to come here a lot when I was a little girl. It was our favorite place." Stella fingered her silver necklace and then brought it to her lips, touching it to them as though it was some religious relic. "There are all kinds of lily pads down at the other end—I named it Lake Lily."

"Your dad told me that she homeschooled you. She must have been really great."

"She *was* a great mom. Taught me so many things. I just wish…"

Joiner stared at her intently. In his eyes Stella thought she saw tenderness, as well as compassion mixed with a certain curiosity. When he spoke his voice was kind. "What do you wish?"

"I wish she'd been more careful."

They sat in heavy silence for a few moments, then Stella tried to explain what she still didn't really understand herself, even after eight years. "I'm not angry with her, not anymore. And I don't mean she was reckless. It's just that, well, the free spirit that made her so amazing also made her sometimes—"

"Not safe?"

"Yeah. Or not careful enough to keep herself safe."

"And that's why you want to teach people riding lessons. To keep them safe."

Stella nodded. "That's also why I want to emphasize safety in my therapy sessions. So my disabled clients won't come to any harm on my watch. I want Star Stables to be a place of healing."

"Well…" Joiner sighed. "My expertise is more of the ride fast, play hard variety. But I do know how to muck out stables."

"That's a plus." Stella laughed, grateful for his effort at a lighter mood, even though his comment about riding fast and playing hard bothered her.

"Do you have any kind of schedule in mind for me?"

She thought out loud. "We're opening the doors in a week. I already have several clients signed up, but I need to finalize the schedule with my occupational therapist assistant and speech therapist. Funding is a huge issue there but after the donation I got yesterday I can budget enough to contract them each for a few months."

"That sounds good."

"Yes. It was really a relief getting that money."

"So what do you want my role to be?"

"This week, let's work together with the

horses, especially the new ones. I'll show you some basic hippotherapy techniques."

"Okay."

"And there will be a lot of grunt work. Your mucking skills will probably be in high demand."

Joiner rose from the rock and offered her a hand up. "I guess we better get to it, huh, boss?"

"We're burning daylight." As they climbed onto their horses, Stella wondered if maybe her father hadn't been completely crazy to hire Joiner after all.

BACK AT THE STABLES, they tended to their own horses and then worked with Daisy and the two others Stella had just purchased. One of them was a paint named Picasso, and the other a red quarter horse with a black mane and tail named Dakota. Stella was happy with how calmly they behaved, and was impressed by Joiner's expertise in handling them. He was obviously a natural with horses. He picked up quickly on everything she showed him about hippotherapy, even if he seemed a little bit bored.

Around noon a car came up the driveway. Stella recognized it from the previous morning as Clint Cavender's black Mercedes S600 Guard. He stepped out in shiny black leather boots with a matching belt, starched jeans and a black silk shirt that Stella guessed was probably Prada. A black cowboy hat completed the look that screamed *rich*. But his smile was as down-to-earth as he was.

"Clint Cavender?" Joiner shocked her by speaking his name. She was further surprised when he jumped over the fence of the pen and strode in Clint's direction, who was just as eagerly jogging toward him.

"Joiner Temple! Is that really you? I can't believe my eyes."

Joiner wiped his hands on his jeans and offered his hand to Clint, who took it and pulled Joiner into a bear hug.

"Hey, man, don't get your fancy clothes dirty!"

"Shoot. I don't give a dang about that."

Stella, who had walked across the pen toward them, leaned on the fence. "You two know each other?"

Clint took his hat off to address her. "Hi there."

"Know each other?" Joiner said. "You mean you've never heard of the dynamic duo of Kilgore High School?"

"Can't say that I have."

"Oh, well, I forgot we were a little bit before your time." Joiner clapped Clint on the shoulder. "This guy right here was the quarterback when Kilgore won the state championship, and I was his receiver. We were what you might call football gods."

Clint blushed.

Stella made a bowing motion. "Oh, forgive me."

"I believe we were outshone by a little rodeo star who showed up a few years later." Clint elbowed Joiner. "Her name is the one on the Welcome to Kilgore sign."

"We were robbed."

It was Stella's turn to blush.

"It's great to see you, man," Clint said to Joiner. "What brings you back to God's country? I thought you were traveling the globe on a polo pony."

Joiner kicked an invisible football. "I was, but polo's too expensive for a regular cowboy. It would be okay for one like you, though."

"Too bad I'm no good on a horse."

"You never were." Joiner grinned. "You were pretty good with numbers, though, as I remember. Did you finish up at Harvard?"

Stella was learning a lot by listening to them.

"Yes, thank God. I got enough of living in Yankeeland to last me a lifetime."

"What are you up to now? You live here?"

"I do. I built a house, and I'm running the family business for my dad, and raising my son, Cade." Clint pulled out his wallet to show Joiner Cade's picture.

"He's the one I told you about," Stella interjected, giving Joiner a look she hoped he'd understand. "I'm excited about having him at the school."

Joiner nodded in understanding. "Oh yeah." Then he turned back to Clint. "Well, cool! Maybe I'll get to hang out with him some. I'm this lady's new ranch hand."

They visited awhile longer by the fence and then Clint said, "Well, Stella, I was just in the neighborhood and thought I'd stop by to see your operation. But I don't want to keep you guys any longer from what you were doing."

"It's fine. I'm glad you came."

"Me, too," said Joiner. "It's awesome to see you, Cavender." He turned to Stella. "Hey, Boss Lady, I could finish up while you show him around if you want."

"Thanks. We do need to keep our donors happy."

She'd meant it as a joke, but for some reason

Joiner's smile faded. He glanced between the two of them, then jumped back over the fence and into the pen without another word.

CHAPTER EIGHT

TAP...TAP...TAP.

Joiner looked up from the book he was reading on the couch. He hoped the person at the door was one of his brothers, or at least Buster, as he was in his boxers and nothing else.

"Joiner? It's me, Stella."

"Oh! Uh, just a second!" He ducked underneath the windows and sprinted into the bedroom in a crouch, pulling on a gray T-shirt and jeans before he went back to the door. He caught his breath when he opened it, but not from the hurry.

Stella stood before him in an exotic lace-trimmed georgette dress, light blue with a colorful landscape print. The hem flirted a little above the knees in the front before it tapered down to midcalf length in the back. Leather Andromeda boots had been hand-finished with studded stars that looked as if they'd been scattered across a tan sky.

"Hello, Boss Lady."

"Hey. Sorry to bother you."

"You're not bothering me." Joiner opened the door wider. "Want to come in?"

"Sure." Stella stepped inside the RV and Joiner closed the door behind her. "I've got some dinner here for you. You want it in the fridge?"

Joiner suddenly noticed the covered dish in her hand.

"Buster—I mean my dad—is afraid you're going to starve to death or something. He wanted me to bring you this." She set it on the counter.

"It's probably because he's seen how hard you work me." Joiner peeked under the aluminum foil to find pot roast and potatoes. "Yum. Really, this is very nice. Tell him I said thank you."

"It's something he does. Feeds people."

"That's a great quality. In fact, I don't know where I'd find a better deal. Home-cooked meals, deluxe accommodations..." Joiner motioned around the room.

Stella laughed. "Well, one out of two isn't bad."

"You insulting my house? Don't do that before I take you on a tour."

Joiner led her on a three-minute guided tour of the stripped, scrubbed and redecorated RV.

"This is not bad. I like what you've done with it. Or should I say what Alma has done?"

"Alma. With a little input from my brother Hunt's wife, Gillian."

"I see you kept the red couch, though."

"Couldn't get rid of that." Joiner leaned against the counter which was the boundary of the kitchen, just inches from where Stella stood in the living area. He peeled the foil back from the plate of pot roast and took a bite.

Stella picked up the book from the couch where Joiner had left it. *"The Fault in Our Stars?"*

"Yeah. I just started it, but it looks like it's going to be really good. One of my nieces recommended it."

Stella set it back down. "John Green. Cool."

"So, what's going on tonight? You got a hot date or something?" Joiner tried to play it down, but he felt a pang of jealousy at the thought, remembering how Clint Cavender had just been *in the neighborhood.*

Stella blushed and looked down at her boots. "What? No!" Then she looked him in the eye. "I'm actually going to church."

Joiner choked on a piece of potato. "Church on Saturday night. You Catholic?"

"No. And I'm not going to a church service. The Presbyterian Church here in town is having a guest speaker tonight who happens to be one of my favorite authors, Adrienne Rutella. I'm going to hear her speak."

"Well, gosh dang." That was the last thing Joiner would have ever guessed, but this gal was full of surprises. "Sounds interesting."

"Do you really think so?"

"I'm not in the habit of saying things I don't mean."

Stella stared at him as if she was deciding whether or not to believe him. Nodding, she said, "Why don't you go with me, then?" There was a dare in her espresso-colored eyes.

"Are you asking me out, Boss Lady?"

"What if I am?"

He rubbed a hand across his stubbly face, contemplating. "I'd say you're a pretty bold woman."

"Well, I'm not."

"Not what?"

"Not asking you out."

Joiner feigned sadness. "Darn it!"

"You can go if you want to—I mean, it's fine. I mean, I'd like you to go. But I'm not asking." Stella twisted her hands together. "And I'm not a bold woman. Not at all. You just make me do things I wouldn't normally do."

Joiner liked the sound of that. "Such as?"

"Such as kiss a stranger's finger, for one thing."

"Stranger? Thanks a lot!"

"Well, you were practically a stranger, then."

"You tried to set me on fire."

Stella's face turned crimson. "That's what I'm talking about. You have this weird effect on me."

"Go on." Joiner laughed, enjoying her embarrassment.

"Go on? Well, this. I just came to give you food. My dad made me. And now…"

"Now?"

"Now you think I'm asking you out." Her voice was just above a whisper.

"He had to make you? Really?"

Stella rolled her eyes.

"Would you normally drink a glass of wine after dinner?" He reached in the refrigerator for a bottle of Banfi Brunello di Montalcino and poured two glasses.

Stella shook her head. Her golden hair shimmered like sunshine on a lake.

"Well, why don't you sit down on that beau-

tiful red couch, and do another crazy thing."
He handed her one of the glasses. Then he sat
down beside her, clinking his glass against
hers, and took a drink before digging back into
the pot roast.

She sipped her wine, then put it down.

After Joiner finished a few more bites, he
asked, "What time is this speaking engage-
ment?"

"In about an hour. But I want to get there
early to get a good seat."

"It does sound like the place to be on a Saturday night in Kilgore. I bet it will be packed."

Stella punched him in the leg, but he saw the
hint of a smile on her lips.

Joiner got up from the couch and in two
strides he was in the kitchen. He set down his
still-full glass in the sink, re-covered the plate
Stella brought him with foil and placed it in the
refrigerator. Facing her, he bowed. "Madam,
if you will allow me to accompany you, I'd be
honored, even if I must go to church on a Saturday night."

HE OPENED THE passenger door to his Chevy
Silverado and settled Stella into the dark
gray leather seat. Then he got in beside her
and drove to the First Presbyterian Church of

Kilgore, which was an old church that served an old population. Joiner didn't know anyone his age who went there.

"How's this bunch bringing somebody as young and famous as Adrienne Rutella to Kilgore?"

"I read about it online. A parishioner left them a trust fund for things like this—for education."

"But she's not Presbyterian, least I don't think so."

"No, you're right. That's part of the trust, too. It's to foster interdenominational relationships. Max Lucado is coming next."

"Pretty cool."

"Yeah. It is." Stella raised an eyebrow. "If you don't mind my asking, how do you know about Adrienne Rutella?"

"What do you take me for? Some redneck Texas hick?"

"If the boot fits…"

"She was one of my teachers at UT."

"Oh, how awesome."

Joiner pulled into a parking space in front of the church. "Yeah. It was. She won't remember me, but I'll never forget her classes."

"You're really lucky." Stella suddenly seemed far away.

Joiner walked around to open her door, and offered her his hand. "What is she speaking about?"

Stella took his hand to climb out of the truck, then released it. "I believe the upcoming season."

"Spring?"

"Lent."

AFTER THE TALK by Adrienne Rutella, they bought one of her books of short stories. She signed it for them and they chitchatted awhile. It turned out she did remember Joiner from their class at UT, which was kind of fun. Stella seemed impressed, anyway. When they left the church, Joiner made the split-second decision not to head toward Stella's home. Oddly, thinking about Lent had given him another idea.

"You want to go dancing, Stella?"

She looked at him as if he was crazy. But not necessarily a bad kind of crazy. "Really?"

He just grinned and gunned the engine.

"Sure. Okay."

He headed across town to The Wild Horse Saloon. The truck clock said nine thirty, and the parking lot was already overflowing. A neon sign told them Hellcat Susie was the featured band. Joiner found a spot to park the truck and escorted Stella toward the entrance. Music blared as they opened the door, and a few women in boots and colorful cowgirl hats spilled out.

Stella stayed close to Joiner. She didn't say a word. He guided her to a wood table in the corner where a candle flickered in a red votive holder.

"You hungry?"

"Not really."

He couldn't hear her very well so he leaned forward. She yelled it again.

"They have some mean desserts," he yelled back.

When the server came, a college-aged girl in tight blingy jeans and thick makeup, Joiner ordered himself a soda and a piece of pecan pie with two forks. Stella said she'd take a soda, too.

They watched the people on the dance floor for a few moments. Then Joiner moved from across the table to sit beside Stella. "I want to be able to hear you," he said without having to yell this time.

Stella smiled but looked as though she might bolt for the door. She played with her necklace.

"Have you ever been here before?"

"Of course. Who hasn't?"

"So why do you have a deer-in-the-headlights expression on your face?" He thought her big eyes were as beautiful as a doe's but didn't know whether she'd take that as a compliment, so he kept his mouth shut.

"Well, it was more of a thing I did in college."

"Oh. Yeah."

The server brought the pie and drinks, and Joiner thanked her.

"Look at those ladies. They seem like they're having a good time." He drew her attention to a couple of women who Joiner pegged as midsixties, maybe older, who were dancing together. Both wore outdated Western dresses, heavily fringed, and sequined boots. With no regard for who was watching, they moved their bodies and laughed out loud. Every once in a while they'd smile and wave in the direction of a table where two old men sat, playing a game of checkers.

"They must have been friends forever," Stella observed.

Joiner handed her a fork. "You've got to try this pie, it's warm. And be sure you get a bite of ice cream."

"Yum." She savored it, then took another bite.

Joiner grinned and put his arm around her.

"You need to get out more, Boss Lady. Loosen up. Learn to have a little fun."

"I know how to have fun." She poked his hand gently with her fork.

"Okay, why don't you show me, then. Ready to cut a rug?"

Her fork clattered to the plate. "As a matter of fact, I am." She threw back her soda as though it was a shot of whiskey and pushed back her chair.

Hellcat Susie launched into their rendition of "Footloose" and then followed with "Hillbilly Bone" and "Baby Likes to Rock It." Joiner nodded his admiration and tried to keep up as Stella stomped her boots and twirled her dress in reckless abandon. She dragged him into a line dance with the older ladies, their husbands and a group of college kids, and when Alan Jackson's "Good Time" finally gave way to a slow song, Joiner was panting.

He pulled Stella close and they laughed, catching their breath. Then, to Joiner's surprise, Stella laid her head on his chest. He held her, rocking slowly back and forth. Her fingers threaded their way through the curls at the nape of his neck. In his hands her waist seemed tiny and fragile, almost as if she might break. As a new song started, he ran one hand up her spine, gently patting the song's rhythm on her back. The lead singer belted out, "It was no accident, me finding you. Someone had a hand in it, long before we knew."

Tracy Byrd's "Keeper of the Stars." Could this woman be his star to keep? He certainly wasn't looking for someone, but here she was in his arms. He knew he held something precious, something valuable. Joiner kissed her on top of her head, his lips brushing her silken hair.

"I can hear your heart beating," she whispered, gazing up at him with her doe's eyes.

He touched her cheek. "Pretty star."

She laid her head back on his chest and they stayed like that, suspended in time, until the song ended. Slowly, they came apart.

"Want to get out of here?"

She nodded, and there was mischief in her eyes.

CHAPTER NINE

BACK AT THE RANCH, Stella had Joiner stop the truck at the barn. He was obviously clueless as to what she was thinking, and she liked the feeling of keeping him guessing. Of being in control. It was her turn to surprise him, to throw him off guard for once, as he so often had that effect on her.

"What are you doing?"

"Patience, grasshopper. You'll see." The streetlamp outside provided enough light for them to find their way into the barn, and Stella led Joiner into her office, where she switched on the light. She fished a key out of her top desk drawer.

He picked up a photo and studied it, but she didn't comment. It seemed obvious enough that the photo was of her and her mom. "Stay here a minute. I need to grab something."

Stella left the office and walked down the corridor to a closet containing supplies. She was back in a flash with a couple of gray horse blankets, soft to the touch, but kind of heavy. Joiner took them from her. Stella couldn't help but notice how his biceps balled up under his plaid cotton shirt. With those violet eyes, coal-black hair and that body, he reminded her of Superman. Superman and some kind of cowboy Adonis.

Joiner gave her a quizzical look. "You're not putting me on a horse in the dark, are you?"

"You scared, cowboy?"

"Nope, but I'm also not Paul Revere."

"Oh, come on. The only riding we're doing is on a pumpkin." She winked at him.

"Well, that sounds safe."

"Since when are you so concerned about safety?"

Stella led him around the back of the barn where the ATV was housed.

"Ah, yes. The pumpkin."

She took the blankets from him and dumped them into the backseat. Then she climbed behind the steering wheel and Joiner stepped into the passenger side. The Gator motor was quiet as she turned toward the pasture.

"Can you get the gate?"

"You're the boss." He jumped out and opened the gate in the glow of the Gator's headlights.

When Stella pulled through, he closed it behind her and got in.

"Where are you taking me, and what are you planning to do with me?"

"To an undisclosed location."

"That answers one of my questions, sort of."

"You'll see what I'm planning. And you'll like it—I think."

Joiner sat back and relaxed. He stretched his long legs out in front of him as much as he could in the Gator, which admittedly wasn't much, and laid his arm casually across the back of the seat. The touch of his hand on her shoulder was electrifying. Stella had to concentrate to remember where she was going, even though she'd been there a million times.

Finally, they pulled into a pine thicket. Joiner straightened in his seat, and Stella carefully maneuvered the Gator through the dense woods.

"I didn't know this ranch had a heart of darkness," Joiner commented. "Your father didn't take me here."

Stella glanced sideways at him and grinned. "Maybe you should come closer to me so you won't be so afraid."

"That's as good an excuse as any," Joiner said. "I'll take it." He scooted over till he was right beside her, their bodies touching, and Stella could feel his warmth. He smelled of leather. "I need an excuse, too. Since we're practically strangers."

Stella nudged him in the ribs. The muscles of his abdomen were rock-solid.

They traveled farther, winding their way through what seemed like an unending network of loblolly pines. The shadows were palpable. Then the Gator crawled out into an opening about half the size of a football field. Stella drove to the center and cut the motor but left on the headlights.

"Would you mind grabbing those blankets?"

Joiner did as he was told, and he and Stella spread the blankets on the ground a few feet away. Then she went back to the Gator and switched off the lights, leaving them in complete darkness. Joiner was standing nearby, waiting for her, and she stumbled into him on her way back. They fell into a pile on the blankets.

He laughed—a deep, sexy sound. Stella had fallen on top of him and he held her there, face-to-face.

"This is all part of your plan, isn't it? To bring me out in the middle of nowhere and ravish me in the dark."

Stella laughed.

"And you say you're not bold." Joiner nudged her nose with his. "What's bold if you're not? You're a blonde assassin!"

Stella did not give in to her urge to kiss him. Instead, she wrestled away and lay down on her back beside him.

"Look up."

Joiner wriggled his broad shoulders to get more comfortable and then he was still. Stella listened to him breathing.

"What am I looking at?"

"Stars."

He glanced over at her, and then back to the sky. "No kidding."

"Well, stars and planets." She lifted her hand to draw an imaginary line from west to east. "There's Jupiter, Mars and then Saturn."

"No way! Cool!"

"See those two stars just east of Jupiter? That's Gemini. The twins. Their names are Castor and Pollux."

Stella pointed toward them.

Joiner squinted until he said, "I see 'em. There. Yeah."

"Of course, Ursa Major is directly overhead. It's also called the Great Bear. And notice how it points to Polaris?"

Joiner nodded. "Polaris?"

"The pole star."

"That's really something. Look how it stands out like a diamond in this pitch-black spot. How do you know all of this stuff?"

"My mom and I used to come here when Buster was away at the rodeo. She taught me all of the constellations."

Joiner rose up on one elbow. "Your mom brought you out here in the middle of the night?"

"Yeah, she did," Stella said softly. Her thoughts drifted to her mother and those moments they'd shared, how they used to lie in this very place underneath the stars and talk for hours.

Joiner's voice broke her reverie. "Were you ever afraid?"

"No. Not back then," Stella said. "She wasn't, so I wasn't either. I guess I took my cues from her."

"Man, she must have been an amazing woman."

"Best mom ever." Stella bit her lip. "I guess that's why every inch of this ranch is so important to me. It represents her, and our connection."

"Still, I can't imagine a mother and a little

girl out here alone. What if some wild animal came up?"

"She always brought her shotgun with us." Stella smiled at the memory.

"No way!" Joiner exclaimed. "She was packin'?"

Stella laughed. "Uh-huh."

He lay back down and sighed. "I think I'm in love with this lady."

They lay there in silence for a few moments before Stella spoke again. Pointing to the northeastern sky, she said, "Look there. The Summer Triangle is just rising."

"Where?"

"Here." She took his hand and pointed toward it so he could see. "That's Altair and Deneb, and this one's Vega."

"Like your horse."

Stella nodded. "It's an Arabic constellation. Her name means *the swooping eagle*. Vega's the fifth brightest star in the sky."

"How cool is that?"

"Vega will become more and more prominent as we get closer to summer." She brought her hand back down, still holding on to his.

Joiner turned on his side and faced her. "Thank you for sharing your stars with me."

"*My* stars?"

"Yours." His voice was low and tender. "Your stars, your special place, your memories." He pulled her hand toward him and kissed each one of her fingertips.

Stella suddenly felt as if her heart had morphed into a supernova. What was it about this man that drove her so crazy? She reached up and yanked his face toward hers, tangling her fingers in his hair and kissing him hard on the mouth. Joiner responded with another kiss just as explosive, just as hungry. As their lips collided, Stella felt a shock wave flow through her body with the energy of two suns. It was a long time before they came up for air.

When they did pull away, Stella lay back, but Joiner stayed on his side. She could barely make out his profile in the dimness, but it was there—the strong jaw, Roman nose, and high forehead framed by curls as black as the sky. She traced it with her fingers like a blind woman, memorizing every feature.

She didn't understand it herself, but there was an urgency in what she felt when she was with Joiner. As if she had to seize the day, act on every impulse…grab each moment before it got away. Like when she used to ride barrels, the feeling both scared and thrilled her.

His eyes sparkled as he looked down at her face. "My turn," he whispered. With fingers roughened from reining a horse, he brushed back her hair and began to trace the outline of her face, starting from her widow's peak and going down her jawline, then up the other side. With his thumb he rubbed each cheekbone as if it was a piece of fine china, and then he touched his pointer finger on the end of her nose. "Close your eyes."

Stella obeyed, and Joiner began to kiss her softly. His lips were like velvet. One kiss on the forehead, one on each eyelid, one on each cheekbone, one on her nose. Then her chin.

He moved in closer. Stella breathed in the scent of leather as his waist brushed against her hip. His head was at her shoulder. Then she felt his cool breath on her neck.

Low, just at the collar of her dress, his lips caressed her skin. He followed the lacy trim in its rounded shape from shoulder to shoulder and back again.

He began moving upward. Stella's skin prickled till she thought she was going to catch on fire. She grabbed a handful of his hair and tried to pull him forward as she raised her head to kiss him.

"Patience, grasshopper."

The words formed on his lips in the dip of her neck and she felt him smile crookedly. He kissed all around her necklace. Then he was at her jaw, nibbling her ears and finally—*finally*—his lips found hers again.

She rose up to meet him, wrapping her hands around his neck. As they kissed she explored his back, tracing each taut muscle, every sinew and the strong, hard, edges of his shoulder blades. Every fiber of his body seemed to radiate heat at her touch.

When they finally stopped kissing, Joiner took her by the waist and carefully eased her onto her side with her back to him, fitting her against his body. He massaged her shoulders as they lay there like a pair of spoons.

"Joiner?"

All was quiet. Stella's heart pounded in her chest.

"I'm not like my mom was."

"What do you mean?"

"I'm really not bold."

Joiner laughed. "You keep saying that, but…"

"Joiner, listen. Please."

"Okay. I'm listening. But let me be the first to say that I rather enjoy your boldness." He kissed her on the top of her head.

"I'm not like my mom was, though, and I don't think I want to be."

"Why not?"

"Because that's what killed her."

CHAPTER TEN

BUSTER HADN'T BEEN this excited since his last rodeo. He jumped out of bed before his alarm sounded, pulled on his best overalls, and headed to the kitchen. Mugsy and Mitzi had stirred from their respective sleeping arrangements when they heard him get up, as they always did, so he let them out the back door in a whirl of black and white before getting down to business. He'd invited Joiner for breakfast, but his biggest reason for cooking was that he wanted to make sure Stella had a good start on the opening day of Star Stables.

Donning a red commercial-type apron, Buster made the coffee and then preheated the oven to four hundred fifty degrees. He liked to rev the oven up and then cut it down to a hundred when he popped his biscuits in. Biscuits and gravy was Stella's favorite breakfast and Buster's favorite to make, besides pancakes.

Taking out his favorite stainless steel bowl, he poured in the right amount of self-rising flour. No need to measure. Then he added a pinch of salt and about a tablespoon of sugar and stirred them together. Next he took out the Crisco and, using a big spoon, dropped a few dollops of the butter-flavored shortening onto the flour mixture. He cut this in with a pastry blender till it was what he called "mealy."

Making a well in the middle of the bowl, Buster then poured in buttermilk, again not measuring. He'd done it so many times he knew just by sight. He stirred the mixture till it was doughy, then dumped it out onto a floured board. After mashing it down to about an inch thickness, being careful not to handle it too much, he cut out the biscuits with a walnut biscuit cutter Stella and her mother had brought back from War Eagle a long time ago. Placing the biscuits about an inch apart on a baking stone, Buster set them in the oven. Then he turned his attention to the gravy.

As Buster made sausage patties out of Jimmy Dean sage, thin like Stella preferred them, he heard a knock at the back door.

"Come in," he said, and Joiner emerged with Mugsy and Mitzi at his heels.

"Good morning!"

"Good morning, yourself!" Buster answered.

"Can I do anything to help you?"

"You can set the table," Buster instructed. Then, motioning with his shoulder because his hands were full, he pointed at the cabinet where the plates were housed.

WHILE JOINER SET the table, Buster got the gravy going.

Stella came down looking pretty as a picture in her Wranglers and boots, and she kissed him on the cheek to say good-morning. Buster noticed a hand squeeze between her and Joiner, who seemed happy as a little pup to see her, and who could blame him? Buster imagined every cowboy would like to be in Joiner's boots right now, living on his place and working side by side with Stella. Yep, Joiner was a lucky man.

Stella got the butter and jelly out of the refrigerator and made herself a cup of coffee. "Want me to cut up some fruit?"

"That would be nice. I've got strawberries, blueberries, grapes and peaches—all of your favorites. And there are pecans and walnuts to mix in."

"Has he always spoiled you like this?" Joiner teased her.

"'Fraid so."

"Well, when I was here," Buster corrected. He wished he'd been around more when she was younger. He had missed so much. But he was here now, he reminded himself. Like riding broncs, the most important thing was to finish strong. Buster breathed a prayer to God, thanking Him for allowing him to be here on this day that was so important to Stella.

"Are ya nervous?" he asked as they sat down to eat.

"Yes." Stella nodded. "I'd be lying if I said I wasn't. But I am also very ready to get started." She spread butter on a flaky biscuit and took a bite.

"I know what you mean. It's like bein' in the chute when you're about to come out of there on a buckin' bronco." Buster grinned. But when Joiner closed his eyes as if he was waiting for something to crash, he stopped grinning.

Stella almost choked. "Pops, what am I going to do with you? Bucking broncos? Really?"

Buster chuckled. "Well, it is. I can remember being so nervous, my adrenaline pumping, like if I had to wait in that chute another second I might explode."

Stella shook her head at him. "Despite the danger involved in your analogy, I must admit it's probably a similar feeling."

Buster winked at Joiner and forked a bite of biscuits and gravy. "If you're interested, boy, I might be able to get you on a bronco."

"Sure!"

"No one here is getting on a bronco. Pops, are you crazy—"

"This is delicious," Joiner said, changing the subject.

Stella sighed but went along with it. "Yes, it is, Pops. These biscuits are perfection."

"You always said nobody else's measure up."

"It's you who always says that," Stella pointed her fork in Buster's direction, scolding him. "But of course, you're right."

He smiled. "And what exactly is your role today, cowboy?" Buster asked Joiner.

"Whatever Stella says it is."

"That's a darn good answer."

Stella said, "I hope you remember what I've told you to do, because right now I don't know that I'll keep it all straight."

Joiner sat up straight as a soldier. He even saluted. "Basically, I'm going to do whatever it takes to make the clients feel safe and secure at all times, and when my help is not needed with clients, I'll be taking care of the horses."

"Sounds reasonable," said Buster. "And you know I'll do anything that's required, Pretty." He patted Stella's arm.

"I'm counting on you both."

AFTER BREAKFAST, BUSTER offered to clean up so
Stella and Joiner could go on over to the barn
to set up. They had a staff meeting at seven
thirty and clients would start arriving at eight
o'clock. He finished the kitchen as quickly as
he could, and then his chores, so he could be
there to watch Stella's dream unfold.

Buster wobbled over to the stable area as
soon as the goats were milked. The first client was there, a boy about six years old. This
was the one Stella had talked about; the one
whose dad was a big supporter. Buster was a
little leery of the Cavenders. He thought they
were basically good people, but he was a little suspicious of anybody who had money out
the wazoo. Still, when he saw Clint Cavender
leaning up against the pipe fence that housed
the arena, he lifted his hand in greeting. The
young man's face was strung tight as a new
barbed-wire fence.

"How's it going there?" Buster leaned on the
fence next to Clint.

"Not bad so far, I think."

"That your boy?" Buster nodded in the direction of the little boy who was on Stella's gen-
tlest horse, just sitting, surrounded by Stella,
Joiner and the occupational therapist, Daune.

"It is." Clint exhaled. "Sorry, sir." He stuck

out his hand to shake Buster's gnarled one. "I guess I'm a little nervous."

Buster's heart softened. "No need to worry, son. Stella will take good care of your boy."

"Oh, I believe that." Clint bobbed his hand up and down. "This is just…so…new."

"It is, but it's logical, ain't it? Horses been helping people a long time."

The tension in Clint's face eased a little. "I suppose you're right. I hadn't thought of it that way."

As they talked, Stella began to lead the boy's horse in a slow motion around the arena. It took forever, it seemed, for the entourage to come near where Buster and Clint were standing. Buster could see that Joiner had a firm grip on the boy on one side, and Daune held him on the other.

Buster wondered what they hoped to accomplish with this kind of ride. It seemed so simple, so slow. But when they finally drew near, the look on the little boy's face said it all.

There were no points of tension anywhere. His mouth was open in a wide grin and his eyes were shining. Buster looked from him to his father. Tears were streaming down Clint's cheeks.

THAT FIRST CLIENT, that first moment, was the highlight of the day for Buster. He had listened for months while Stella explained her ideas, supported her vision both in money and work, and encouraged her all the way. But not until he saw that boy on the horse, with his expression of pure joy, did he understand what Stella had known all along. This was a life-changing thing they were doing. And it only made him prouder than he already was of his daughter. He hoped it would make her prouder of herself.

CHAPTER ELEVEN

JOINER DRAGGED INTO the RV feeling tired but satisfied. It had been a great day for Star Stables: a full schedule, new clients clamoring for a spot, all of the horses in good shape, and Boss Lady was happy, which made Joiner happy. He warmed at the thought of Stella.

Leaving his boots at the door, he hung his hat on the hook Buster had left, and stripped off his socks. Tossing his iPhone onto the kitchen counter, he walked across the RV, shedding his sweaty shirt and jeans. They were scuffed with dirt and horse manure, and he had to stuff them into the laundry hamper Alma had left in his room. He hadn't had time to think about laundry, and the hamper was overflowing.

The shower was fantastic. He felt like a new man—a clean one—when he finished. After he dried off he headed straight into his bedroom to dress, rather than lounging around with no shirt in a towel or boxers. He'd learned his lesson about that the hard way.

As all of his jeans were dirty, he put on some sweats and an old UT Polo T-shirt. Then he walked barefoot into the kitchen to find some grub. The leftovers from Hunt's last catering event, which Gillian had brought by for him, would do nicely.

He was taking his first bite when his phone started buzzing on the counter. He slid it over to look at it.

A group text from the Brotherhood read:

McCarthy Temple: Need tax stuff ASAP.

Hunt Temple: Dropped ours off last week. You were out so left it with hot new assistant at front desk.

Cullen Temple: Working on it.

McCarthy Temple: Just found yours, Hunt. Good thing, too, since it takes the longest. And you're a married man. Joiner?
    Anyone heard from the prodigal son?

Hunt Temple: Gillian saw him yesterday.

Cullen Temple: He was texting with Carrie last night. They're both reading a book about stars.

McCarthy Temple: Is it The Fault in Our Stars?

Cullen Temple: Idk. Maybe. That sounds familiar.

Hunt Temple: Mac knows the title of a recent novel? No way!

Joiner decided to enter the conversation. He typed in his message.

Joiner Temple: You boys having a meeting of the minds? I better jump in and boost the IQ level before my phone blows up.

McCarthy Temple: The prodigal returns!

Hunt Temple: Hey, man!

Cullen Temple: Howdy!

Joiner Temple: How's it goin', Temple bros?

McCarthy Temple: I need your tax stuff. Yesterday.

Joiner Temple: Oops! Is it April already?

McCarthy Temple: I don't provide free tax services in April.

Hunt Temple: Is your brain still in Europe?

Joiner Temple: I'll get it to you, Mac.

Cullen Temple: Gotta go. Grading essays. Love you guys. Will get taxes to you soon, Mac.

Hunt Temple: Fish to fry. Ditto on the love.

McCarthy Temple: Ok, and ditto.

Joiner Temple: Mac, my taxes are easy. Basically no income or possessions.

McCarthy Temple: Just a Horse and His Boy.

Joiner Temple: I love it when you talk literary.

McCarthy Temple: Any way you can bring it by tonight?

Joiner Temple: Your washing machine work?

McCarthy Temple: Yes. Dryer, too.

Joiner Temple: See you in a few.
  And ditto, bros.

JOINER SLIPPED ON clean socks and running shoes. Then he grabbed the lockbox from the shelf in his closet, pulled the drawstring bag full of clothes out of the clothes hamper and headed to his truck.

Buster waved at him from the goat pen where he was milking. "Hey, Santy Claus!"

Joiner chuckled. He was carrying a sack on his back, but Buster was the one who looked like Santa Claus. A Santa Claus with bowed legs. "Hey there!"

"You had any dinner yet?"

"Yes, I have, thanks. I'm on my way to my brother's house to do some laundry."

"You're welcome to use my laundry room anytime you want." Buster patted Violet on the back.

"Thank you very much. See ya." Joiner walked on, but remembered something and turned back toward the older man. "Hey! You hear anything more about that bronc busting you told me about?"

"No, but I've got my ears open. I've never seen a man so eager to get his butt whooped by a horse." Buster chuckled. "Unless maybe it was me."

Joiner whispered, albeit loudly, so Buster could still hear him. "You game, even though your daughter will probably skin us?"

Buster's eyes darted in the direction of the stable. "I can't say I'm not concerned about her reaction, but maybe she'll understand because of the money. It's all for her."

"I hope so. I've got to try it anyway or go nuts. All of this caution around the school has me pretty wound up."

"I hear ya, man. I hear ya."

Mac was on the porch with a cup of hot tea when Joiner drove up to his lake house.

"Man, don't let our twin brothers see you drinking that. They think tea's for girls."

"They also think polo is for sissies. That's why you and I have to stick together." Mac clapped Joiner on the back.

"We really didn't raise those twins to respect their elders."

"No. We definitely failed in that regard." Mac opened the front door. "Come on in. Looks like you better start a load of laundry."

Joiner hauled in his bag. He handed the

lockbox with his tax information over to Mac, and then went into the laundry room where he started a load of darks.

"I'm assuming you brought the key to this?" Mac said when Joiner joined him at the kitchen table.

"Oops."

Mac shook his head and rolled his eyes.

"Just kidding, bro." Joiner took the key out of his pocket and opened the box. "All that's in here of value is Pistol's papers." He took out the papers for *Pistol Gun Pete.*

"That name is so hilarious," Mac said.

"It's a good name for a stud like him."

Mac grinned. "So you are going into the horse breeding business?"

"Yes, once I had the arrangement with Buster, I decided to go for it. I've had several people approach me. I'm hopeful that it's going to be a productive—or reproductive—season."

"Ha-ha."

Joiner drummed his fingers on the table. "The arrangement I made with Buster is pretty cool. We're going to bring the mares to the ranch and turn them out to pasture with Pistol for breeding. Like everything with Buster, it's kind of old-school, but in this case I agree with him because I think it's best for the horses. More natural."

"How do you schedule that? Pistol have a dance card?"

"Well, a mare has what's called an estrous cycle that lasts about three weeks. During the first week she's receptive to a stallion, and she ovulates during the last part of that week."

"TMI, bro, TMI."

Joiner raised his eyebrows. "You asked." He continued, "And mares are more fertile in the spring and summer because there's more daylight. Some mares have a cycle in the fall, but not as many."

"So Pistol has to make hay while there's still daylight."

"Or make money. Yeah."

"How much money are we talking about, if you don't mind me asking?" Mac took off his glasses and folded them in his hands.

"I'm going to breed Pistol for $10,000 a pop."

"Whoa, you think you can get that?"

"Dude, this is why I've held on to that horse for dear life. Well, besides the fact that he's my favorite. But he's a beast. I've already got twenty mares lined up for the season."

"Man, I'm in the wrong business!"

"Well, because of you I said that the owners have to bring the mares to the ranch by April 15."

"Tax day!"

"Yep. We will put those twenty out to pasture—and I could allow up to ten more. The section is about the size of a square mile."

"Pistol's gonna be busy," Mac observed.

"The mares have to be together about two weeks to get used to each other, to sort of form a herd. Then we turn Pistol in there with them and the dance begins."

"How long will you keep all of these mares?"

"Till the end of August."

"Will that affect the school any?"

"Well, I have to admit, Stella may be uncomfortable breeding the horses this way."

"Why?" Mac asked.

"It can be messy. It's not totally controlled like insemination or other methods. This way is most natural, but it can be a little rough as they go through all of the stages of courtship."

Mac nodded cautiously. "Sounds like people."

"What I mean is that they dance around, and bite, and sometimes it's kind of wild. There can be injuries."

"I see."

"But it's not like her clients will be in the pasture with them."

"Still, it might not be particularly attractive for clients and onlookers to witness, and some might be worried about their children."

"The pasture is far away from where the kids will be riding. I'm hoping for the best."

"Well, otherwise it sounds like a sweet deal."

"There's a lot involved, but yeah. If it goes according to plan, I'll pocket a good chunk of change." Joiner ran a hand through his hair. "Hopefully get myself in a position to buy my own land, maybe expand the breeding operation, and even start a foundation for wild mustangs in Pap's name."

"Since when has this been your dream?"

Joiner was matter-of-fact. "Since I figured out I wasn't going to make it as a professional polo player. You know, Mac, since then I've really been searching for a new dream. A purpose. Maybe this is it."

"I hope it works out for you, dude." Mac squeezed Joiner's shoulder. "I really do." He gathered the tax documents together and put them back in the box.

"Hey, try to work me up a miracle this year,

okay, Mac? A tax refund would help out in a big way."

"Sure, Joiner. I'm on it." Mac laughed.

Mac made Joiner a cappuccino in his fancy machine and they moved to the deck to watch the sun set over the water. While Joiner's laundry was washing and drying, they sat in cedar Adirondack chairs and caught up with one another.

"So who's the hottie in your office?"

Mac cleared his throat.

"Are you blushing?" Joiner leaned over to inspect his brother's face. "You are! Your face is as red as Texas clay! Spill the beans!"

"There are none to spill."

"That's a bunch of malarkey." Joiner punched him gently in the ribs.

"Really, there are none. I hired a beautiful woman to be my assistant but she would never be interested in me, and I have no time for a relationship anyway."

"But you think she's beautiful."

"I have eyes."

"That's not all, is it?" Joiner pressed. "You like her."

"Well, she is an interesting person. You'd like her, too. She has spent a lot of time overseas."

"And?"

"And she has a degree in literature, like you. Just couldn't find a job in her field."

Joiner set down his cappuccino and slapped both of his knees. "So that's how you knew about *The Fault in Our Stars*!"

Mac nodded. "She's crazy about it. Has been reading it during her lunch break." He took off his glasses and rubbed his forehead, a smile escaping his lips. "One day I went in there to get some yogurt out of the fridge and she was sobbing. Literally sobbing. She said, 'Oh my goodness! You have to read this book!'"

"So you read it?"

"What else could I do?"

"Did you enjoy it?"

"Yes, I mean, as much as you can enjoy something full of tragedy."

"But it's funny, too."

"Yes. And wise, and, well—"

"I know. I'm taking Carrie to see the movie next week. The local theater is bringing it back for a limited release."

"You're taking Cullen's Carrie? Well, aren't you uncle of the year."

"I try."

"Well, you'll like it. It's great." Mac sat back in his chair. "Really excel—"

"Oh. My. Gosh."

Mac closed his eyes, and Joiner whooped and hollered.

"You took her to see the movie! The hot assistant!"

"So what if I did?"

"I'm proud of you, man. Steppin' out there!" Joiner pushed Mac's knee and Mac playfully pushed him back.

Still, he seemed eager to change the subject. "So, other than getting rich breeding Pistol, how's it going for you out at the Scout ranch?"

"Good. Really good."

"What is it you're doing? I mean, what exactly is Stella's new operation?"

"I didn't really understand it myself until today, after we opened the doors." Joiner leaned back in Mac's Adirondack chair. "It's Stella's dream. It's a riding school, really, where anyone can learn to ride horses. But the focus is equine therapy for people—children especially—with disabilities."

"Sounds pretty cutting-edge."

"It is."

"Well, then, what do you do?"

"I'm the ranch hand, so I do a lot of the grunt work. But they—Buster and Stella—respect my riding and training skills. I think I'll be spending a lot of time with the horses."

"What about the clients?" Mac inquired.

"It's interesting. I was skeptical of her whole 'holistic' approach, but after the first day I'm kind of a fan." Joiner smiled. "Stella is a physical therapist, and there's an occupational therapist assistant and a speech therapist who work there. They evaluate what the clients need and then we try to work on it using the horses." Joiner got excited talking about it. "You remember Clint Cavender?"

"Sure. Football. Oil dynasty."

"That's the one. Well, he has a son with all kinds of communication and sensory problems. But when we got that kid on a horse today, there was this transformation. He seemed so free."

"That sounds kind of like you, actually."

"Minus the problems."

"Yeah, not those kind. But remember when you first got on a horse after Mom and Dad died? You became a different person."

On his way home, Joiner thought about what Mac had said, about how he'd become a different person when he started riding after his parents' deaths. Mac was right.

An idea came to him, something that might

be good for Cade Cavender. He couldn't wait to try it out.

The next morning Joiner was out at the stables bright and early. When he knocked on the door, he found Stella already in her office going over the schedule and making a plan for the day.

Ever since the night they'd spent under the stars—three nights ago now—there had been a closeness between them, a deeper understanding. They'd been really busy the day before, on opening day, but it seemed to Joiner that they'd moved and breathed as a team. He knew she wouldn't be happy about the breeding or about the bronc riding, and she was still insistent that he pay more attention to safety, but for now he was determined to enjoy their newfound camaraderie.

"Hey, Boss Lady."

"Hey, yourself." She looked up from the schedule and smiled at him. Big brown eyes sparkled underneath long, curling lashes, and her straw Atwood matched the color of her hair. She wore work jeans, a gauzy white shirt and blue Ropers, which were propped up on the desk.

Joiner sat down in the chair across from her. "Ready for day two?"

"Yeah," she said. "I'm excited. Yesterday went well, and today should, too, I hope."

"Yesterday was cool."

She nodded at him as if they shared a secret.

"I mean, I understand your vision for this place so much better now. After just one day—it sort of came together for me."

She reached across the desk for his hand and squeezed it. "I honestly don't think we'd have made it happen without you."

He could have kissed her then and there, but Joiner heard the sound of a vehicle pulling up, followed closely by another. Pretty soon Jacob Hunnicutt and Daune Holzman appeared at the door of the office. "Hey, guys!"

Joiner liked both of them, but Daune in particular. He was impressed with her grit. Laid off from a manufacturing plant in town where she'd worked for twenty-five years, she'd gone to the community college in Kilgore and earned her degree in OTA. She had a passion for helping people, and she was seasoned, real. Stella trusted her a lot, and that was saying something.

As clients arrived, Jacob took one for speech therapy, and Stella another for physical therapy. Daune and Joiner were assigned to Cade Cavender when he arrived.

"Hey there, Cade!"

Daune's friendly greeting went unanswered by the boy. Clint tipped his hat to her and shook Joiner's hand.

The kid was a carbon copy of his dad—olive skin, warm brown eyes and dark hair. But Clint's brown eyes said *Welcome*. They invited you in. Always had—that was his personality. But Cade's expression was closed. He looked through you, past you, and into some void. Except when he got on a horse.

"You know, Cade," Joiner began. "You did so great yesterday on Daisy. And I got to thinking, if you keep working hard with her, I might let you try riding Pistol." Before starting therapy, Cade had come by with his dad one day while Joiner was bathing Pistol, and he had introduced them. He knew the boy was fascinated by his beautiful horse.

Cade's eyes registered interest. At least it was a start. Joiner hoped it would motivate him to overcome his problems. There was so much potential in the boy.

They got Cade up on Daisy, and Daune worked with him on improving his sensory issues. They remained stationary until Cade was comfortable with the reins, the feel of Daisy's mane and the concept of keeping his feet in the stirrups and his rear end in the saddle. Then they started walking.

Every movement of the horse challenged Cade's balance as well as his sensory system. Daune was extremely patient, and so was Daisy, as Cade worked on his responses to the horse's movements. They walked round and round the arena, and with each circuit Cade gained confidence. His responses became more natural. Then, they actually trotted. As Joiner jogged alongside him, there mostly for support, Cade seemed genuinely happy. He tried to do everything perfectly—and he did.

When an hour was up, Clint came forward from where he was watching on the other side of the fence. Cade dismounted Daisy with Daune's help, and Clint patted him on the back. "Good job, son!"

Cade stood still with one hand on Daisy's neck.

"Didn't he do well?" Daune smiled at Clint.

"He sure did. Thanks for working with him, Mrs. Daune." Then, to Joiner, he said, "I'm really impressed with what I'm seeing here, and I'm glad you're a part of it."

"Thanks, man."

"It's great to have a place like this to bring him, especially right here at home."

"Well," Daune said, crouching down to Cade's level and looking him right in the eyes, "You come back tomorrow. We'll be counting on you, okay?"

"Pistol," Cade said. "Ride Pistol."

Daune glanced at Joiner who turned to Clint.

"What, buddy?" Clint got down on one knee to look Cade in the eye, as well. "What did you say?"

"I want to ride Pistol." There was something like excitement on the little boy's face. "Mr. Joiner said."

Daune grimaced in Clint's direction. "I'm not so sure that's a great idea today, buddy. You are doing really great with Daisy. Mr. Joiner meant that sometime, down the road—"

The life seemed to drain from Cade like air from a balloon. His little shoulders slumped.

"It won't be long till you are ready, buddy." Joiner felt that giving Cade the chance to ride Pistol—the chance at that wild sense of freedom—might just be the kid's salvation, as it had been his. He didn't want to wait too long.

Clint stood and looked at Joiner. "I wonder if we could possibly have a little ride together on Pistol today?"

A smile broke out over Joiner's face. "We could definitely do that." He turned to Cade.

"You want to take your daddy on a little ride? Show him how it's done?"

The boy smiled and nodded.

WHEN JOINER CAME BACK with Pistol, the arena was empty except for Clint and Cade.

"Where'd Mrs. Daune go?" he asked Cade.

But Cade didn't answer. His mouth had fallen open and his eyes were as wide as platters. Joiner took his hand and placed it on Pistol's huge, pulsing neck. They stood there for several moments, stroking the horse and letting Cade get to know him.

Clint spoke up. "She's just putting up Daisy, I think."

"Can you still ride, Clint?"

"Much as I ever could." Clint chuckled. "But you'll be holding on to us, right?"

"Right."

Clint climbed into the saddle and Joiner helped Cade up in front of him. Cade was grinning from ear to ear. Joiner handed him the reins, keeping a hold on Pistol's bridle.

"Okay, buddy. Let's take it slow."

They made one circle in the arena. Joiner was proud of his horse and the little boy. As they loped around a second time, Cade actually said, "Go faster!"

Clint nodded, and Joiner allowed Pistol to trot.

Jogging along beside them, Joiner felt such warmth rise up in his heart that he thought it might burst.

Up to this point, horses—and, most of all, Pistol—had been a thrill for him because of the freedom he felt when he was riding, the reckless abandon, the rush. The faster he galloped away on a horse, the better he felt.

But here, in these moments with Clint and Cade, Joiner had never felt more alive. The look on Cade's face said it all. And Joiner and Pistol were making that happen—giving him that gift. *This is a real rush.*

Just then Mugsy and Mitzi came from out of nowhere, running as fast as cheetahs and barking at the top of their lungs. A calico cat sprinted under the pipe fence in front of them and headed straight across the arena toward the barn. The two dogs scooted under the fence and followed in hot pursuit, entirely ignoring the horse and the three people who were in their wake.

At the sudden commotion, Pistol reared on his hind legs. He jerked the bridle from Joiner's hand and galloped the length of the arena, making a sharp turn at the end that would impress any barrel racer. As he spun, he dumped Clint and Cade into the dirt, and Cade screamed. Joiner reached them just as Stella appeared in the barn doorway.

CHAPTER TWELVE

"Oh my goodness!" Stella ran toward the crumpled mess on the arena floor, with Daune Holzman close behind her.

Clint Cavender, her biggest donor to date, was bent in an awkward position around his son, who was in the fetal position, shaking his head from side to side and screaming. Clint's dark chocolate Stetson lay ten feet away, crushed. Blood streamed from a big dirty smudge on the child's knee.

When he saw her approaching, Clint lifted his hand to stop her. Joiner was quietly leading Pistol away. *Pistol!*

"I'll go get the first aid kit," whispered Daune.

"Okay."

Stella waited, frozen to her spot, and watched Clint attempt to soothe Cade. He ran his hand down the child's back, slowly, then started over at the top again. "It's okay, Cade. Daddy's here. Daddy's here."

Her heart beat a hollow sound in her ears, like a keg drum.

After what seemed like forever, Cade's screams turned to whimpers, and finally he was quiet. Daune and Joiner were back by then, and they hovered near Stella, unsure of what to do.

Clint rose painfully, lifting Cade from the ground. Until then Stella hadn't noticed that Clint's jeans were ripped. His whole backside was covered with dirt. With Cade in his arms he limped toward them, and Joiner met him, supporting Clint on one side. Other than an occasional sniff from Cade, the arena was as silent as a mausoleum. They all walked together to the barn.

"Can you bring him in here, Clint?" Daune motioned to one of the therapy rooms. "We can check him out."

"Or I can take you straight to the emergency room if you'd rather," Stella offered.

"I think he's okay. We're just shaken up."

The boy stayed curled in a ball, rocking himself in Clint's arms. His hands formed a death grip around Clint's neck. When Daune tried to clean his knee he made a sound like a wild animal.

"I doubt he'll need stitches," Daune said. "Thank goodness."

"What about you, Cavender?" Joiner placed a chair behind Clint and helped him ease into it. "You're limping pretty bad."

"It's my ankle."

Daune and Stella worked together to remove the Sienna full quill ostrich Lucchese boot from Clint's foot. Clint gritted his teeth while they wriggled it off, revealing an angry purple sprain that seemed to swell before their eyes.

"You should ice that," Daune advised. "And stay off it for at least a few days, maybe more." She took an Ace bandage out of the first aid kit and wrapped his ankle carefully, in her thorough, deliberate way.

Rising from the chair, Clint said, "Thank you, Mrs. Daune. Now, I need to get this boy home. I'm just going to call my assistant." Cade had fallen asleep in his arms. "This is kind of embarrassing, but can somebody help me get my phone out of my back pocket?" He leaned forward in the chair, and Stella reached into his pocket. She twisted free an iPhone with a newly cracked screen.

"Why don't you let me drive you?" Stella offered.

"Oh no, that won't be necessary." Clint

smiled at her with tired eyes. He reached out for his phone. "I'm sure it still works."

"Please, let us give you a ride," Joiner interjected. "Stella can drive your car and I'll follow and bring her back in my truck. It's the least I can do."

Joiner was practically pleading. It was obvious he felt horrible for what had happened.

Which he certainly should. Just wait until I get him alone.

WHEN CLINT AND Cade were safe in their home—which, by the way, was the most luxurious place Stella had ever seen—and both were in the care of his assistant, Stella and Joiner walked out to Joiner's truck. She was waiting until they were out of earshot to unleash her fury.

As Joiner tried to open her door, she wrested the handle from him and opened it herself, climbing into the truck and slamming the door behind her. He moved cautiously around to the other side and opened the driver's door. He gave her a sideways glance when he got in the truck and that was all it took for her to bust.

"What were you thinking, putting the child on that animal?"

He started the truck. "I was trying to help him."

"Help him?" Stella raised her hand to her head, which was throbbing. "That's a good one. Are you kidding me?"

Joiner drove a few miles without answering, knuckles white on the steering wheel. His silence was even more enraging than his response to her first question.

"Look. I hate that Clint and Cade got hurt, and I'm sorry it happened at your school. But as long as they're okay, I don't think it's as big of a deal as you're making it out to be."

"Oh really. And you should know because you have so much experience to draw from."

He paused before answering, as though weighing his words. "That's true."

"I was being sarcastic, Joiner." She rolled her eyes. "What experience does a polo player have with things like this? Good grief! I should have never given you so much responsibility." She spit the words out.

Joiner bit his lip but said nothing. He sped up the truck, which was already going too fast for her liking, and looked straight ahead. *Well, fine. Two can play at this game.*

When they pulled into the driveway, Joiner parked beside the stable. He got out and walked around to open her door, clearly not having taken the hint back at the Cavenders. She almost hit him with the door when she opened it. "You're done for the day," she told him.

He squinted at her, eyes smoldering underneath the brim of his hat. They were the same color as a bruise.

Then he turned to get back into his truck. "You're the boss."

Stella didn't watch in which direction he went. She stomped to her office, still as angry as a rodeo bull, and slammed the door behind her, locking it.

A look at the schedule told her Daune and Jacob were both serving clients, and thankfully, there was no one else on Stella's calendar for the rest of the day.

As she let out her breath, the shaking started. It began in her hands, and then moved up her arms, causing tremors in her whole body. Her cheeks burned white hot. They felt as though they were flaming from within.

Her legs had turned to lead and she sat down in her chair just before she fell. She took off her hat and tossed it across the room. Icy sweat broke out all over her, drenching her clothes.

Even her hair was wet. Her ears rang and her head pounded. She lay her head down on her desk as the sobs came.

Stella didn't know how long the anxiety

attack lasted. It could have been minutes or hours. The next conscious thought she registered was someone banging on her office door.

"Stella! You in there? Open this door!"

She dragged herself up and over to the door, unlocking it.

"What in the Sam Houston?" Buster grabbed her by both shoulders. "Are you okay?"

"I am now."

"Tell me what happened." Buster put his arm around her. "But let's go home first."

They walked across the yard to the house and went inside through the front door. Once in the living room, Stella sat down on the couch and put her head in her hands. Buster sat beside her. "What's the matter, Pretty? I'm here."

A single tear escaped from each of Stella's eyes and she wiped them on her sleeve. Those were practically the same words Clint had said to comfort Cade, words she'd heard before. Buster pulled a bandana out of his overalls' pocket and handed it to her. She blew her nose.

"We had an accident at the school. That stupid Joiner put Clint Cavender's son on his giant thoroughbred polo horse and it bucked him off. He and his father both! I walked in to find them on the ground in the arena, bleeding. The little boy was screaming!"

"Was anyone seriously hurt?"

"Clint has a sprained ankle and Cade had a cut on his knee. But they'll be okay."

"Oh. That's good."

"I should fire Joiner. I thought he was really good, and he is a hard worker, but..."

Buster made a face. "Fire him? Joiner? What in heck are you talking about?"

Stella looked up at her daddy. "He's reckless, Pops. He proved that today. Oh, did he ever prove it! I can't have that around Star Stables. I won't!"

"Whoa, whoa, whoa. Just a minute here." Buster scratched his beard. "What exactly is going on?"

Stella sighed heavily. "Daune said Cade and his dad made a big deal over Pistol on the first day. The little boy thought the horse was really awesome. So apparently, Joiner made some kind of offer to the little boy that if he did well with Daisy, he could try riding Pistol. So he puts him on Pistol today—the second day we're even open! Without consulting me first!"

"*Did* the little boy do well with Daisy?"

"Duane said he did great, and that he begged to get on Pistol. But that's beside the point!"

"You said his father was there, too..."

"He was on the horse with him."

"So Clint thought it was a good idea? Something that would be okay for Cade to try?"

"I guess. But Clint obviously had no idea what was going to happen."

"That's the thing. Most of us rarely *do* know what will happen. We just do the best we can."

Stella shook her head. "I can't believe you."

"What?"

"You're siding with Joiner Temple over me!"

"I didn't realize this was a competition."

"It's not! Star Stables is my vision—mine and yours—a way to honor Moma's memory. And the first and most important thing to me is safety!"

Buster patted her knee. "Pretty, you'll have to work this thing out with Joiner, what happened today. You're right that the school is yours. And he works for you, even though he and I have an arrangement. But I don't think that's all that's going on here."

"What do you mean?"

"I mean, you had one of your anxiety attacks, didn't you? Back at the barn."

"I did. It was brutal."

"What happened today with the Cavenders was bad, but what made it unbearable for you is that it was a trigger for something else—your grief over losing your mother. A desire to make sure no accident like hers happens again. Not here. Not in our arena."

Another tear escaped down Stella's cheek. This time Buster wiped it for her.

"I'd make sure it didn't happen anywhere, ever again, to anyone else, if I could."

"But you can't, kiddo." Buster looked her hard in the eyes. "You can't. And maybe it's time you quit trying."

CHAPTER THIRTEEN

JOINER DROVE OUT of town, not really knowing where he was going. The good thing about
East Texas was that there were plenty of long,
straight, country highways, and not so many
cops that a man couldn't drive fast now and
then when he needed to think. Joiner turned
up the stereo loud so George Strait could keep
him company.

He passed a lot of cows. Also some horses.
Oil wells dotted the landscape, which was
mostly flat and green. His phone buzzed but
Joiner didn't answer it, didn't even look at it.
Whoever was calling could wait. For their sake
as well as his own, Joiner couldn't talk right
now.

The question uppermost in his mind was not
whether it had been right to put Cade up on Pistol. Maybe it had been right and maybe it had
been wrong. Either way, he was sorry the boy
had gotten hurt. Clint, too. But it was a freak
accident. Sure, Daisy wasn't as big and power-

ful as Pistol, but the same kind of thing could have happened when Cade was riding her. It could happen any time a horse got spooked.

What bothered Joiner was how Stella had reacted. He'd only been trying to help one of her clients. But she hadn't even listened to his side, she'd just flipped a switch. The same woman who'd freaked out on him was the same amazing lady who just three nights ago had laid beside him on a blanket and kissed him.

He'd felt things that night he'd never felt with anyone else. Even aside from the physical attraction between them, it had been the most perfect night of his life. *And now she'll want nothing to do with me.*

He had to make things right.

Up ahead, to his surprise, Joiner saw a sign for Longview. Had he really driven that far? He exited, and pulled into the Love's station, where he gassed up his truck. While he was inside paying for the gas, he strolled through the tacky tourist trinkets offered at every Love's station in Texas. He noticed a miniature horse that resembled Pistol as much as a plastic toy could. He bought it. He also picked up a king-size box of plain M&M's, a pack of Big League Chew gum and a bag of Funyuns. Then he headed back to Kilgore.

When he got to Chateau Cavender, as the locals in Kilgore called it, Clint's assistant opened the front door. She walked him through a vast living room with ceilings two stories high, and into a sunroom on the back of the house. It faced the pool. Clint sat in a cinnamon-colored leather wingback chair with his ankle up on a matching ottoman. He was reading *The Wall Street Journal*, and Cade was in front of him on the floor, playing video games.

"Hey, man!" A genuine smile flooded Clint's face when he saw Joiner. He folded the paper and straightened in his chair, setting the newspaper down beside it.

Cade looked up at Joiner for about a nanosecond before getting back to his game.

Clint motioned to Joiner. "Have a seat."

"This place is amazing, dude."

"Thanks. My wife wanted it. Kind of embarrassing, but whatever." He sighed. "It's Cade's and my bachelor pad now."

Joiner took off his boots before stepping onto the calfskin rug. He walked around Cade and sat on the couch which was opposite Clint's chair and ottoman. "How's the ankle?"

"Terrible. May keep me out of work for several days." Clint winked. "At least one can hope."

Joiner chuckled. "Really. I'm so sorry you were hurt, Clint. I should have played it safer."

"Well, that's not really your style, is it, Temple?"

"I guess not."

"I've always liked that about you." Clint went on to recount several heroic moves Joiner had made when they'd played football together. "Nothing ventured, nothing gained. And you gained us plenty of yardage."

"I was hoping to help Cade gain confidence today. But that was an epic fail."

Clint sighed. "I knew what you were doing, and I agreed with you. Bad call on both of our parts. I feel as lousy about it as you do."

"How is he?" Joiner nodded toward Cade, speaking softly.

Clint shrugged. "In some ways I know that kid better than I know myself, but in others, he is such a mystery. He hasn't talked since we got home. And he's done a lot of his repetitive behaviors, like swaying, tapping." Clint looked up at Joiner. "I hope—and believe—he'll be fine, though. Just a little bump in the road."

Joiner eased down off the couch and sat beside Cade. Cade glanced nervously at Joiner, but kept playing his game.

"Hey, buddy," Joiner started.

Cade ignored him.

Joiner took the bag of Funyuns out of his sack and opened them. He popped one in his mouth, then offered the bag to Clint. Clint took one. "Yum," Joiner said. "These are really good, aren't they, Cavender?"

"Yeah. They're delicious."

"So crunchy."

No verbal response from Cade, but he licked his lips.

Joiner took out the M&M's and rattled the box. "You like M&M's, Clint?"

"I do."

"I thought I saw something about that on your chart at the school. Here, take some."

Clint said, "That must have been Cade's chart. They're actually his favorite."

"Really?" Joiner feigned surprise. "No way!" He held out the bag to Cade. "Want some?"

Cade blinked his eyes several times.

Joiner reached into the bag again. He pulled out the little horse. Cade's eyes widened.

Joiner turned the horse over in his palm a few times. Then he spoke softly. "Cade, Pistol wanted me to tell you he's sorry." Joiner slowly galloped the toy horse on the floor toward Cade. "And I am sorry, too. I put you in a dangerous situation and you got hurt. Will you forgive us?"

Cade looked at the horse, and then he looked at Joiner. He took the little horse in his hand, rearing it on its hind legs. Then he proceeded to play with it, galloping it back toward Joiner. When Joiner smiled, Cade smiled back.

They played together for a few more minutes and then Joiner rose to go. He patted Cade's shoulder. "Well, you boys take it easy. I better get back to the ranch."

Clint said he needed to get up and move a little bit himself, so he hobbled toward the door with his guest. "Hey, Temple, I've got a question to ask you."

"Okay, shoot."

"It's about Stella Scout."

Joiner's stomach tightened. He wasn't sure he could answer any questions about Stella right now.

"Is she…dating anyone? That you know of?"

Joiner felt the heat rising in his neck. *Oh no. Why did I come here?* He swallowed hard.

"I realize she's quite a bit younger than us." Clint shifted his weight. "I don't know. She just seems pretty sweet."

Joiner laughed weakly.

"And of course there's the matter of her being gorgeous." Clint laughed.

"Yeah. There's that."

"Well, have you heard her talk about anyone? Or seen any guy over there hanging out with her?" Clint urged him. "Come on, man. Aren't you any good as a spy?"

"I don't think so, Cavender." Joiner rubbed his eyes.

"You don't think there is anyone?"

"I don't think I'm a good spy." He gave Clint a truthful stare. "I have to be honest with you, man. We've had a couple of dates."

Clint's eyes widened. "Oh. Oh my gosh. Well, I feel stupid. That's great for you. Really, man. That's great." He smiled.

"I have no idea where it's going. We really just started getting to know each other. And she may hate me now, after what happened to you and Cade."

Clint laughed. "Why? Well, surely she'll get over that. That's no big deal at all."

"It was to her."

Clint put out his hand to shake Joiner's. "Well, good luck, man."

"Thanks. I'm going to need it."

IT WAS LATE AFTERNOON when Joiner arrived at the ranch. He and Buster had plans over the weekend to fix the fence around the section of pasture they had designated for breeding, but if Stella wasn't going to want him around the school the rest of the week, he figured he might as well get started now. He decided to take Pistol for a ride that would serve the dual purpose of stress release and preparation. First they'd ride like the wind wherever it took them, and then they'd blow around the perimeter and see what he needed for the fence.

The horse was restless in his stall. Joiner kicked himself for not turning Pistol out when he'd brought Stella home. He'd been preoccupied with everything that had happened, and had simply not thought of it. Joiner of all people understood why Pistol wouldn't want to be pinned in all day.

He saddled up as quick as he could and led Pistol through the gate. Then he mounted and took off, giving Pistol all of the freedom he himself craved.

They rode hard. Pistol took a few jumps that were exhilarating, and even swam across a small pond with Joiner on his back. Joiner had to hold up his boots, but he didn't mind. It was actually kind of fun. The water was cold on his skin as Pistol jerked them through the water. The horse's panting was loud. When he got to the other side Pistol shook and shivered, but snorted with pride. He tossed his mane, and Joiner shook his black hair, yelling, "Whoo!"

It was the first time since that morning when he'd jogged beside Cade on Pistol—before the fall—that Joiner had felt alive.

CHAPTER FOURTEEN

STELLA LOOKED AT her phone for what had to be the hundredth time. There was still no reply from Joiner. She'd texted him hours ago. Why was he punishing her this way?

She set the phone on her nightstand and changed into her pajamas, which amounted to sweats and one of Buster's old rodeo T-shirts. Mugsy snored, curled up into a ball on her faux-fur beanbag. The window was open and a nice rain-scented breeze stirred her lace curtains. She still slept in the room she'd had since she was a little girl, although its decor had evolved along with her tastes, at least up to a certain point.

Her bed had been a white canopy bed when she'd picked it out as a six-year-old at the local furniture store. Texas bluebonnets were painted on the headboard and matching dresser, desk and nightstand, and her bedding had been pale yellow eyelet.

As a teen, she'd talked her mother into painting the furniture orange—the color of a sunset, which was her favorite color. They'd also painted the walls four different colors Stella had chosen: purple, sky blue, metallic gold and black. The black was actually a chalkboard. She and her friends had spent endless hours drawing on it, writing the names of their crushes and erasing them, doodling quotes from their favorite books.

After Lily died, Stella's tastes continued to change, but she'd never wanted to redo her room. It was one of those things that kept her connected to the past, when she still had her mother. Even if much of her life had become black-and-white when she'd lost her, Stella could still climb into her bed and dream in color.

She switched on her bedside lamp. Crawling under the pile of vintage quilts—she had replaced the owl-themed duvet cover, too—she picked up the journal she'd taken with her to Adrienne Rutella's talk. She opened to her notes.

Lent is not a season that starts and ends. Think of it as a continual spring. Lent is a lifestyle. And then: *Lent is not so much about death as it is a summons to live anew.*

After that Stella had written, *What do I need*

to give up for Lent? Not as penance. What keeps me from leading a full, happy life?

Stella raised her silver pendant to her lips. The talk that night had challenged her. She'd never thought of Lent in that way. As a Baptist, she'd never thought about Lent much at all, to be honest. But her Catholic friends always treated it as a time to give up something they liked, as a sacrifice they could offer to God during those weeks. She smiled when she remembered that one of them had given up French fries. And another chocolate. They were always so happy when Lent was over. But Adrienne Rutella was suggesting something different.

Stella closed the journal and set it back down by her bed. She wasn't sure what fullness in life even was. Ever since her mom died, her focus had been more on survival than anything else. She'd tried to order everything around her in such a way as to survive, and keep others safe. Buster said she couldn't do it. And she knew she couldn't change the whole world. But maybe if she was more careful, if she worked harder…maybe she could at least make it happen at Star Stables.

The rain pattered against her window and she got up to close it. When she turned back toward her bed, her phone was buzzing. She almost tripped over Mugsy, upsetting him to the point that he bit her toe as she tumbled onto the bed.

Joiner Temple: Me, too.

What in the heck did that mean? Should she take it literally? Her text had said *I'm sorry.* So was he saying he was sorry too? For being reckless, putting a child in danger and risking the reputation of her school? Or did he mean he was sorry she'd acted so crazy and mean to him and ruined the great thing they'd seemed to have going on?

Either one would be legitimate, she had to admit. Stella felt sick. She had to know. So she typed in What are you sorry for? And waited for his reply. The words popped up fast.

Joiner Temple: What are you sorry for?

Oh my goodness! This man is exasperating. But it was actually a valid question. What exactly was she sorry for?

She texted, I'm sorry for how I acted. I treated you badly. Please forgive me.

Joiner Temple: Okay.

After that, there was a long period of silence. *What does he mean by "okay?"* Stella wanted more, but she wasn't getting it. She wrote, Now you answer my question.

Joiner Temple: As previously stated, I am sorry for what happened today.

As previously stated? Really? She wrote, Well, hopefully a lesson learned for all of us. Just have to be more careful.

Joiner Temple: Safety first at Star Stables.

Stella giggled. She typed, That's my motto. She also thought, *And it needs to be yours!* but decided not to push it.

Joiner Temple: Open your window wide.

Stella typed, It's raining!

Joiner Temple: Open it anyway.

She didn't know why, but she did what he said. When she opened it, a calf rope sailed through. Her phone buzzed on her nightstand.

Joiner Temple: Tie it to your bed.

Stella couldn't believe what was happening. Tie a rope to her bed? She typed, Done.

Joiner Temple: Now sit on your bed.

Stella sat down on the mattress, looking at her window. All she could see was the rope, which now trailed from her bed and fell out over the windowsill into the dark. It was raining harder than she'd realized. Mugsy growled and started to bark, but she grabbed him and shushed him. She didn't want him to wake Buster.

Suddenly, Joiner appeared at her window, and climbed in headfirst. He toppled onto her floor, laughing. Mugsy jumped down from the bed and started licking his face.

"Um, did that just really happen?" Stella got up from her bed, pulling one of the quilts off with her. She wrapped it around Joiner, who was soaking wet. Then she went to the window and shut it. As he dried himself with her quilt, Joiner's face reminded her of the night they'd first kissed on the porch. He laughed and his violet eyes danced. With raindrops in his lashes, he was practically sparkling with pure delight.

"Hi," he said.

"Hi, yourself. You know, you could have used the door. I would have opened it and everything."

"Doors are boring. It is far too romantic an occasion for doors."

"Romantic occasion? What has been the slightest bit romantic about this day?" Stella eyed him suspiciously. "The first time you learn that I'm a lunatic? Our first fight? Really?"

"Stella, Stella, Stella. Those were not romantic occasions. Nor was when you learned I am the world's worst hippotherapist. These are learning experiences, but they are not romantic in the least." He tucked a stray wisp of hair behind her ear.

"Well, what is romantic then? Besides that, I mean."

Joiner smiled wickedly. "Making up."

CHAPTER FIFTEEN

THE NEXT FEW WEEKS went more smoothly for the riding school, and for Joiner and Stella. Joiner tried to be more careful, and there were no more accidents. New clients arrived every day. In a mutual agreement with Stella, Joiner worked more with the clients who just came to learn to ride, and less with the kids who needed therapy. He was thrilled, however, to see that Cade returned and seemed happy enough to be back on Daisy for his therapy with Daune.

Joiner was also extra busy with the breeding operation. He had seven more calls from owners who wanted to breed their mares to Pistol, and he accepted five of them, bringing the herd of mares to a total of twenty-five. He and Buster worked together for several hours on the weekends fencing the pasture area, and Joiner put in quite a few more on his own after Star Stables closed for the day. He also had piles of paperwork to process, as all of the mares had to pass an examination by a veterinarian to make sure they were healthy, and would not bring any diseases into the herd—or pass them on to Pistol.

By mid-April things were in good shape for the breeding to commence. The excitement on the ranch was palpable as the mares started to arrive. Quarter horses, palominos, Arabians, Appaloosas, paints. These ladies were some of the prettiest horses he'd ever seen. Joiner loved them, loved watching the herd take shape. He had also vetted the owners and liked most of them real well. He had the sense they felt about their horses the way he felt about Pistol: conscientious of their values, but also nurturing and respectful of their souls.

Joiner tried to schedule all of the deliveries after school hours, and for the most part, he was successful. The few that had come through while the school was open had been handled carefully, however, and no problems had been caused. The clients liked watching the mares arrive. It was fun for everyone. Well, everyone, it seemed, except for Stella.

Joiner thought she'd be glad he was breeding the more natural way, instead of using artificial insemination. But Stella worried about the uncontrolled nature of the open-pasture method. She was afraid clients would be put off if they

saw the horses breeding, and worse, that they'd
be scared if they witnessed the biting and other
behavior that could occur. She worried about
mares being injured, and possible liabilities,
even though Joiner assured her that wouldn't
happen. She worried, she worried, she worried. Even though he tried to understand her
perspective, if he was honest, it was more than
a little aggravating.

At least Buster saw things more like Joiner
did. Wherever he was on the ranch, and whatever else he was doing, Buster usually made
his way over to the corral when a new mare arrived. He loved chatting with the owners and
seeing all of the horses. He was an amazing
help.

Buster and Joiner had bonded while they'd
built the fence. The older man seemed to like
just hanging out, telling stories, having another
guy to share the hard work of ranching. As
Joiner's father had been a doctor and not really much of a cowboy type, there had been
lots of things he couldn't relate to while Joiner
was growing up, like Joiner's love for horses.
And of course Joiner's passion for riding and
then polo had come after his father was gone.
It was nice to have someone to look up to and
learn from.

"Joiner. Psst, Joiner." Buster motioned for Joiner to follow him after the last mare had been handled and her owner was gone.

Buster wobbled back into the barn with Joiner following him, avoiding Stella's office, though Joiner didn't know why at first.

"I've got a proposition for you."

Joiner's interest was piqued. He hoped the older man wasn't going to try to change the terms of their agreement now that it was clear breeding Pistol was going to be extremely profitable. But surely he wouldn't do that. He seemed like a man of his word.

Buster ducked into an unused therapy room and Joiner followed. Buster closed the door behind him. "Lookie here what I got." He pulled two tickets from his overalls' pocket and held them out for Joiner to see. They were for the Nacogdoches Rodeo.

"There's going to be some big names there. Jesse Lovelace is the stock contractor and he's the best." Buster was so excited he could hardly keep his voice to a whisper.

"He brings in horses that produce winning rides. Everybody knows that, so some of the big names will swing up from the rodeo in Houston to ride in Nacogdoches. I used to do the same thing." Buster ducked his head, lowering his voice again. "Anyway, me and Jesse are old pals. He's a retired bareback rider, too. He's the one sent me these tickets."

"What about Stella?" Joiner asked.

"Shh!" Buster put his finger to his lips. "You want to get me in trouble?"

"You mean she's not going?"

"What rock you been under? Stella hates the rodeo."

"I know she doesn't want to participate— and doesn't want you to—but do you mean she won't even go to a rodeo as a spectator?"

"That's right, Sherlock. And I ain't been in years. But I thought if you wanted to go we might sneak down to this one while she's at Cheryl's house this weekend."

Joiner laughed. "Buster, we're grown men. If we want to go to a rodeo, we don't have to sneak."

"I know that, you idget." Buster rolled his eyes. "I thought you was some kind of English major. You never heard of a figure of speech?"

"Well, what did you mean, then?"

"Do you want to go to the rodeo or not? It's my treat. You're 'bout to get rich. We're celebratin'."

Joiner put his hands in his pockets. "I'd love to."

"You would?" The older man's face broke

into a huge smile. His eyes almost disappeared in all of the crinkles.

"Yeah. That would be awesome."

"Good." He clapped his hands together. "Now *you* can tell Stella." Buster turned on his heel and left Joiner standing alone holding the tickets, mouth open.

Might as well get it over with. He put the tickets in his shirt pocket and walked down the hallway to her office. "Boss Lady? You got a minute?" he said as he knocked on the door.

"Come in."

Stella was sitting at her desk wearing glasses, which was a rare sight.

"What's happening?" He sat down in a chair.

"Oh, nothing. Just going over some facts and figures." She rubbed one of her temples.

"They making your head hurt?"

"They are, actually. That's why I put these on. I thought they might help."

"Want a shoulder rub?"

"I'd love one."

He walked around behind her and she leaned into him. He placed his hands on her narrow, yet muscular shoulders. "Gosh, girl, you're tight." He put his thumbs right between her shoulder blades and pulled back, stretching her muscles to work out the tension.

"I know. I know…" Her voice became slurred. "Oooh. That feels so good."

Joiner found a knot the size of a golf ball. He pressed as hard as he dared, then tried to work it out in a downward motion.

"That's…so…perfect."

Can a girl get drunk on a massage?

"How…did…you…learn…how…to…do…this?"

He started on a knot beneath the other shoulder blade. "I get them in the same place."

"Oh. Well, I definitely owe you a massage, then."

"I'll be happy to take you up on that sometime."

She leaned her head back and smiled at him upside-down. Then she lifted her hand to pat his where it rested on her shoulder. "That feels so much better. Thanks."

"What's troubling your pretty head?"

"Take a look at these numbers."

Stella rose, and invited him to sit in her chair. Then she sat down on his lap.

"See this column? Receipts." She pointed to a column that had some numbers, but also a lot of blank lines. Then she pointed to the other, which had no blanks. "Expenses."

Joiner studied the paperwork for several

moments, keeping one arm around her waist. When he set it down, he said, "I see two things. We could use some more big donations, but people are also going to have to start paying for their services."

"That's my biggest problem right now." Stella sighed. "I've got the Cavenders' big grant and the one from Mike Gibbons at the bank. I think the one from the Rodeo Association may also come through. What's not working is the day-to-day income."

"What's the deal? Why aren't people paying? Do we need to set up a billing system or something?" Joiner didn't understand. "Maybe Mac can help."

Stella shook her head. "The ones who can pay, do."

"And the ones who can't?"

"I'm not turning them away, Joiner."

"Oh. I see."

She twisted away from the desk to face him, still sitting sideways on his lap. "I'll figure something out, though."

"Sounds to me like you've got a little Robin Hood thing going."

"Maybe I do." She grinned up at him and touched his face. It was after five, and as usual, he had a five o'clock shadow.

"Now, did you just come in here to seduce me with your good looks or was there something you needed to talk about?"

Joiner took a deep breath and inhaled rain with a hint of lemon. The seduction thing sounded good. He'd rather kiss her than say what he'd come here to say.

"I just wanted to tell you that I'm babysitting your dad while you're at your friend Cheryl's this weekend."

"Oh. That's nice. You know how I hate leaving him." She turned to fully face him, straddling him with her long legs. They were bent so that her knees touched the back of the chair, and for a moment she towered above him. Then she lowered herself back onto his lap.

"What are you guys going to do?"

"We're going to hang out, probably grill some steaks, maybe work on some fence."

"Uh-huh. That sounds good. You could bring your brothers out, too, to see the ranch."

"I hadn't thought of that."

She leaned forward and kissed him. "Don't you have too much fun without me, though."

"Not much chance of that."

He wrapped his arms around her and she rose slightly, clutching his head to her chest as he gripped her waist. Joiner could hear the steady beat of her heart and felt the imprint of her necklace against his cheek. They held each other for several moments in that position. Then he looked up into her eyes. He wanted her lips.

She shifted her weight, sinking into him again until they were face-to-face. She kissed him lightly the first time, and then the kisses grew in intensity. Joiner felt as if the room was whirling, but it was a ride he didn't want to get off.

When she pulled away, her ivory skin was scratched. He rubbed it gently. "Sorry," he said.

"Sorry for what?"

"You look like you've been in a fight with a cactus."

She grinned. "Who won?"

"I'm afraid it was the cactus."

"Well, the cactus may have to shave."

"I shave every morning."

"Ooh. You're just so manly it grows back out."

"Pretty much." He beat his chest like a gorilla.

"I like it."

"Even if it scratches you?"

"It's a small price to pay." She kissed him again.

"Well, so is shaving twice for you, if that's what it takes."

She kissed him again.

"Hey," he said when they came up for air. "I need to tell you something."

"You like me?"

"Yes. I do. Very much."

She kissed him. "You want to go steady?"

"If we're in high school, definitely. And you can wear my class ring."

"Ha-ha." She kissed him again. "What is it, really?"

"Your dad and I are going to the rodeo."

She pulled back several inches, her playful mood vanishing.

"He got two tickets from an old friend and invited me today. I asked if you were going too but he said you wouldn't want to. We're going one—maybe two—of the nights you're staying with Cheryl."

"I see."

Joiner could tell she was making an effort not to blow her top. For some reason, he found this hilarious. He started laughing.

"May I ask what you find so funny?"

"You." Joiner snorted. "You, Stella Scout, are funny."

"What about me is funny?"

"You're mad! Because two grown men are going to a rodeo!"

She pushed off his lap and sat down on her desk, still facing him. She kicked his chair with her boots. Her hands gripped the edge of her desk as if it was the edge of a cliff.

"Why would you want to go to a rodeo?"

Joiner rubbed his chin. "Let's see. Maybe... because it's fun?"

"I don't think it is."

"Well, I don't believe that, since you were once a national barrel racing champion, but whatever. It's okay with me if it's not fun to you anymore. Rodeos are still fun to a lot of people."

"What interest do you have in rodeos? I thought you were a polo player."

Joiner cocked his head to one side. "I guess you'd call it a mild interest in rodeos, but a bigger interest in Buster."

"What's that supposed to mean?"

"There's no hidden meaning. I like your dad. He's been good to me. He loves the rodeo— misses it. Going with him to something he's so excited about will be fun."

"If you're trying to make me feel bad it's not going to work." Stella crossed her arms.

"I'm not trying to make anyone feel bad.

You're the one who asked me to defend why I want to go to the rodeo. We're just going to watch."

Stella suppressed a smile.

"Go on," Joiner coaxed.

"Go on with what?"

"Go on and smile."

She raised one eyebrow.

Joiner nodded. "Come on. I know you can do it."

She snorted and then finally, she smiled. He had broken her.

He scooted his seat up to the desk and pulled her gently back down onto his lap.

"You're a pain in the butt, you know?"

"Yeah," she said, "well, so are you."

He twirled a piece of her hair around his finger. "Can we still go steady?"

"Absolutely."

CHAPTER SIXTEEN

STELLA DROVE UP Texas State Highway 135 North till she got to US 271 North. That took her fairly deep into Oklahoma, but she had to take three more roads before she crossed the border into Arkansas. After passing through a quaint little town called Siloam Springs, she turned on Arkansas Highway 59 North, which took her straight into Gentry. Population 3,298.

Her mother's best friend lived on Rust Street in a historic flagstone house that Stella had always associated with gingerbread. Maybe that was because, for as long as she could remember, she and her mother had visited Cheryl at Christmas, and every time they drove up, Cheryl would turn on her Charlie Brown Christmas lights that Uncle Steve had strung along all of the eaves, much to Stella's delight.

Cha Cha's house was one of the supreme delights of Stella's childhood. Lily had no siblings, and Cha Cha had no kids. So she was the closest thing Stella would ever have to an aunt, and Stella was her surrogate daughter. Stella had named her Cha Cha on one of her early visits.

Stella was a year old, and they were playing a game of peekaboo. Lily and Stella were in the screened-in porch just off the living room, and Cheryl was on the other side of the door. Lily asked Stella, "Where's Cheryl?" And Cheryl would open the door, peek in and say, "Peeka-boo!" and then close the door and disappear, only for a few seconds. Then they would repeat.

They played the game several times until Cheryl decided to go to the kitchen to get a drink, so she didn't open the door again. According to her mother's account, Stella had urged her mother to open the door, and she toddled after Cheryl, crying, "Cha! Cha!" Cheryl picked her up and kissed her, and the nickname Cha Cha was born.

When Lily passed away, Cha Cha was the only one other than Buster who'd grieved as Stella had grieved. She was the only one who'd recognized who Lily was, what they had truly lost. The friendship between the two women had been more than just a friendship. It had been a sisterhood. And with Lily gone, Cheryl stuck to Stella like glue.

Because Cheryl and her husband, Steve, ran

their own business, she'd been able to leave
Gentry and come and stay with Stella after her
mom died. She'd lived with them for a month,
and Uncle Steve had driven down on weekends. One of the things Stella remembered most
about that time was how Cheryl had cooked for
her and Buster. She'd filled the kitchen with
wonderful smells, and the house with life and
laughter. Stella was hoping now that in some
small measure she could return the favor.

"Stella Luna!" Cha Cha called, using the
childhood nickname that still made Stella
smile.

Cha Cha rose slowly from the swing on her
front porch where she'd apparently been waiting. Stella left her luggage beside her car in
the driveway and ran up the steps to meet her.
They hugged for a long time.

"How do you like my hairdo?" Cheryl took
off the Razorback ball cap she was wearing to
reveal the ravages of chemo. Where there had
been a thick, lustrous mane of red hair, there
was now nothing. "You can feel my head," she
offered. "It's smooth as silk."

They sat together in the swing and Stella felt
herself slipping into the easy peace that had always been her norm at Cha Cha's. In so many
ways Cha Cha was the opposite of Stella—at

least the post-Lily Stella. Cha Cha's motto was "If you can laugh at it, you can live with it." So she did a lot of laughing at her cancer.

She told Stella about the embarrassing bodily functions brought on by her condition. Tears rolled down Stella's cheeks and her sides hurt from laughing. "Well, Cha Cha, I'm glad I came here to cheer you up!"

"Me, too, baby. Me, too." She patted Stella's knee.

"I do hope you feel like eating."

Cha Cha pursed her lips. "Do you know that I have actually *gained* weight since being diagnosed with cancer?"

"Really?" Stella said. "That's weird. You don't look it, though."

"Well, that's nice of you to say, but it's true. You'd think I'd at least get the perk of losing these twenty extra pounds I've been carrying around, but so far, nope. Although I am nauseous a lot."

"Well, I brought lots of goodies to cook. And my plan is to fill your freezer with things that will be easy for you and Steve to take out and heat up when you are hungry."

"That sounds wonderful."

"I just need to bring a few things into the house."

When she had finished unpacking her car, and transferred all of the ingredients she'd brought with her from the bags and ice chest to Cheryl's kitchen, they sat together in the living room adjacent to the screened-in porch. Cheryl was bundled up in a fuzzy afghan even though it wasn't cold, and she leaned back in a leather recliner. Stella sat on the couch beside her.

"So what's new with you? Is Buster behaving himself?"

Stella shook her head. "Not really. Does he ever?"

"No."

They both laughed.

"In fact, while we speak, he is off to the rodeo with our new ranch hand, probably corrupting him."

"Is this the cute ranch hand you texted me a picture of?"

Stella blushed. "That would be the one."

Cheryl picked up her phone, which was lying on the table beside her recliner.

"He can't be this handsome in person."

Stella took the phone from her and studied the picture. "He is. Maybe more."

"Those eyes! I've never seen that color before. You always read about it in novels. So-

and-So had violet eyes. I never thought they were real. But his really are."

"I know," Stella said dreamily.

"Stella Jane Scout, I have never seen you act this way."

"What way?"

"Like you're in love." Cheryl smiled at her.

"Well, I wouldn't go that far. But I do like him."

Cheryl's blue eyes shone with curiosity. "Tell me about him."

"Well," Stella started. "He's smart, funny, kind and...adventurous."

"Adventurous. I like the sound of that."

"I know you do."

"It's not a word I'd typically associate with you, though."

"Thanks a lot."

Cheryl grinned at her, pulling the covers up to her chin. "Just keeping it real, Stella. Just keeping it real."

"That's another word I'd associate with him, come to think of it. *Real*."

"What do you mean?"

"Well, he just is who he is. I mean, he's kind of blunt in the way he says things. He doesn't beat around the bush."

"Ooh. That's a really good quality."

"It is. It drives me crazy sometimes, but in the end I appreciate it. You kind of know where you stand."

"Give me some examples. How has he let you know where you stand with him?"

"Well, one time I freaked out about something."

"Imagine that! What was it?"

"Oh, it's a long story but it had to do with the safety of one of my clients."

"Okay."

"Anyway, I talked pretty rudely to him… okay, really rudely."

"Uh-oh. How did that turn out?"

"I apologized and he accepted, but he didn't act as if it was no big deal. He made it clear that it *was* a big deal."

"But did he forgive you?"

"Yes. Totally. That ended up being one of the most romantic nights of my life."

"Do tell!" Cha Cha leaned forward.

"Well, he climbed up a calf rope and came through the window into my room."

"Do I want to hear what happened next? Or will it be too much for my tender ears?"

Stella's face flooded with red. "It was very sweet. And fairly chaste."

"*Fairly* chaste? How is something *fairly* chaste? Is that like being *fairly* married?"

"Oh geez. All we did was kiss. That's what it means."

Cheryl shrugged. "Whatever."

"Really!"

"Okay, okay! I believe you!"

"Another time was when he told me he and Buster were going to the rodeo this weekend."

"Rodeos are fun!" Cheryl interjected.

"No, not fun! I hate rodeos, remember?"

"Oh yeah. Safety first." Cheryl saluted like a soldier.

"That's right. I'd be happy if no one I care about ever stepped foot back in a rodeo arena. And now he and Buster are going while I'm away."

"So please tell me you did not act crazy."

"I didn't. I kept myself reined in." Stella looked down. "Well, I mean maybe I did fuss a little bit."

"Oh no, you didn't."

"I did. But he pretty much told me to get over it."

"He did? Good for him! What exactly did he say?"

"Cha Cha, you evil woman!"

"What can I say? We're all in a conspiracy to help you get over it."

"He basically said that if two grown men want to go to the rodeo, they're going to go."

"I like this guy."

"I do, too, even though he exasperates the soup out of me."

"Well, he's right that if they want to go to the rodeo it's their own decision."

"I get that, it's just, well, I just hope it doesn't lead to other things for Buster, or for Joiner, for that matter."

"What do you mean?" Cha Cha asked.

"Joiner reminds me a little bit of Pops as a younger man. He's very tender and kind, but he has a reckless side. I hope Pops can help him temper that, but sometimes I'm afraid it could be the other way around."

"You mean that he could corrupt Buster?" Cha Cha choked on a giggle.

"I know that sounds ridiculous."

"Yes, it does. Besides, sweet girl, you have to learn to let go sometimes, to remember you're not in control. They'll be okay. And it seems to me that he's trying to tell you that in a not-so-subtle way."

"I know, right? I mean, he's sort of able to

say that kind of stuff to me in a gentle way. He's gentle, but firm."

"And what do you do for him?"

"I have no idea. I've asked myself the same question." Stella fingered her necklace. "I mean, I think I make him happy, because he laughs a lot when we're together."

"Is he laughing *at* you, or *with* you?"

"Probably some of both."

Cheryl sighed. "Well, it's good to have fun with somebody. It's an important part of any friendship or other relationship." She looked at Stella with so much love in her eyes. "Your mother and I had the most fun of any two people I know."

Stella smiled. That was true; she remembered.

"You're a beautiful woman inside and out. Any man would be lucky to be with you."

"Thanks."

Cha Cha was too tired and weak from chemo to go out and do their usual shopping, or even to get a pedicure, which they sometimes did, too. So for three days straight all they did was lie around and talk when Stella wasn't cooking and stocking the freezer. Still, when their three days were up, it felt as though the weekend had flown by. That's how it always was when she went to Cha Cha's house. The thought made Stella ache. Like her time with her mother, it had just slipped through her fingers like sand. There was never enough time.

CHAPTER SEVENTEEN

STELLA LEFT AT noon on Friday to go to her friend's house in Arkansas. They usually closed things down at the school together, but this time she was depending on Joiner to do it all himself. So after the school closed at three thirty, Joiner made a special effort to put things up the way she liked them and tend to all of the horses' needs.

He and Buster were leaving for the rodeo at five thirty. The rodeo in Nacogdoches officially started at seven forty-five, but they wanted to eat at a joint Hunt recommended beforehand, and Nacogdoches was an hour away. At five o'clock, Buster was banging on the door of the RV. Joiner walked up behind him.

"Shoot! You scared me!"

"Man, don't you look snazzy?" Joiner had never seen Buster dressed in anything but overalls, usually paired with a sleeveless T-shirt.

But tonight Buster grinned from underneath a black Stetson trimmed in peacock feathers.

A studded turquoise shirt stretched across his belly, which was contained somewhat by a belt buckle the size of a dinner platter. It glittered silver and gold, with a bronco rider cast in gold as the centerpiece. Bowed-out legs in tight Wranglers tapered into a shiny pair of black Justins. "Thanks. I look better than you, that's for sure."

"Apparently just one of us had to work today." Joiner clapped him on the shoulder and ushered him inside the RV. "Want to have a seat while I get cleaned up?"

"I reckon I do."

Joiner grabbed a cold water bottle out of the fridge and offered it to Buster, who waved it away. "Never touch the stuff. You got any sweet tea in there?"

"Are we in East Texas?" Joiner poured him a glass over ice.

While Buster sipped his tea on the couch, Joiner showered as quickly as he could. Then he put on Wranglers and paired them with a dark purple poplin shirt by Ariat, with contrast stitching on the front and back yokes. His thirteen-year-old niece Carrie had helped him pick it out when they went to see *The Fault in Our Stars*. "Contemporary Cowboy Style," she had called it.

Leaving out the curved hem, per Carrie's instructions, meant there was no need for a belt. So he slipped on his black Justins—which were matte leather, not shiny—and grabbed his plain black hat.

"I'm glad Stella's not here," said Buster, sizing Joiner up when he reappeared in the living area.

"Why in the world not?" Joiner rather disagreed.

"'Cause you'd a had to primp a lot longer than that, and I'm hungry."

JOINER DROVE. They pulled into the parking lot of Butcher Boy's at six fifteen. It was packed.

"I guess it's a good thing you drive like a bat out of hell," Buster said, "or we'd miss the rodeo."

"We can go somewhere else if you want."

"No, those chefs like your brother always say to ask the locals where the best food is. Judging from this parking lot, I'd say Hunt directed us right."

Joiner squeezed his truck into a spot that wasn't really a parking place. "All right. Let's do this."

When they entered Butcher Boy's they found it was standing-room only. A frazzled-looking hostess with drawn-on eyebrows and too-black hair said, "It'll be a few minutes."

The atmosphere was friendly, a nice small-town feel. Everybody seemed to know everybody. Judging from the way the clientele was dressed, they all seemed to be going to the rodeo, like Buster and Joiner. The food smelled wonderful. Hearty. Joiner thought he might starve, but they finally got a table at six forty-five.

Buster ordered a chicken-fried steak with mashed potatoes and Joiner had a burger. Hunt told him to get onion rings so he followed the chef's advice. When the server brought their food, Buster's steak hardly fit on the plate. It was thin and crispy, and slathered in gravy. The burger, not too thick, was delicious, and the onion rings were the best Joiner had ever eaten.

"How have I lived an hour away from this place all of my life and never known about it?" Buster wiped his mouth and pushed his seat back from the table.

"It's probably a good thing for your arteries that you didn't."

"Maybe so, but now I do. So watch out." Buster grinned. "You'll have to extend my compliments to the Cowboy Chef."

Joiner laughed. "Will do. And he'll be happy to know you watched his show."

"Well." Buster cleared his throat. "Stella does. Not so much me. Wouldn't want that to get around."

"Oh, it's Stella who makes you watch it. I see."

"Yeah." Buster insisted on paying the bill as they exited, and they were off to the rodeo.

They missed the Mutton Busting, but got to their seats in plenty of time for the opening pageantry and introduction of officials. As Buster watched from the edge of his bleacher, Joiner mostly kept his eyes on Buster. The look on the older man's face during the grand entry was priceless.

Scores of men and women in costumes performed choreographed routines on horseback, with a stirring musical accompaniment and dramatic narration by the rodeo announcer. Like every rodeo Joiner had ever attended, it had a Western patriotic theme. To his world-traveling, polo player's eyes, it all seemed pretty, uniquely American, traditional and also kind of funny. But Buster was a little kid on Christmas morning. This was his happy place. Seeing the older man so excited almost made the hell he'd have to pay with Stella worth it. Almost.

The first event was bull riding, then came steer wrestling. Buster provided commentary through it all, recognizing names, both of contestants and animals. When it came time for bareback riding, however, Buster was all business.

The announcer called, "Ladies and gentlemen, allow me to introduce the aptly named Colt Millsap! This young cowboy is a three-time college champion from the home of the Aggies, College Station, Texas! He's hoping to advance to the finals with Blue Smoke. Let's show him some support tonight!"

The crowd erupted in screams as the chute burst open. Out came a stocky, grayish horse with a life-size cowboy rag doll on top of it. Joiner watched, mesmerized, as the horse twisted and danced, kicking its heels in the air and pounding the dirt. Blue Smoke seemed to hate his rider. More than that, he seemed possessed by some kind of horse-demon.

Colt Millsap leaned back on the horse so that his head almost touched its rump. His hat fell off in a puff of dust. He raised one hand in the air as if he was praying, and Joiner thought he'd better be. The cowboy's bright red chaps bounced and banged up and down, fringes swaying, till it seemed every bone in his body would break. Joiner bit his lip. Would eight seconds never end?

Joiner's heart beat fast, he broke out in a sweat and his throat went dry as a bone. "Way to go, Millsap!" he yelled as the buzzer sounded.

Buster slapped him on the leg. "Now, that was quite a ride."

On the way home Joiner quizzed Buster about everything pertaining to broncos. Buster was happy to oblige him. Before they knew it they were pulling up in the driveway at the ranch. "If you're really this interested, I finally heard from my buddy. He wants me to come help him next week."

"I'm there," said Joiner. "I'm so there. You just name the time and place." Buster's enthusiasm for bronc riding was contagious. It reminded Joiner of how much he loved and missed polo, but maybe busting broncs could be a good substitute...

CHAPTER EIGHTEEN

IT WAS ALMOST EASTER. Stella stood on the threshold of her house looking outward across the yard. In every direction, in every color and kind, there were lilies blooming. She snapped a picture with her phone and sent it to Cha Cha, who was in Little Rock for her chemo treatment. Stella hoped the picture would bring her a smile.

The fall after Stella's mother died, just before the first frost, Cha Cha had driven up in her hybrid. The rear was riding low. It was a Saturday and as was their tradition, Stella was sitting on the porch swing waiting for Cha Cha to arrive.

When Stella bounded down the steps to greet her, Cha Cha handed her a gift bag. Inside were gardener's gloves and a trowel, unusual to say the least. *What's this for*? Stella remembered asking. And then Cha Cha opened her trunk.

That weekend they planted over five thousand lily bulbs. Cheryl, Buster and Stella. Along the walkway, along the drive, in the flowerbeds, by the mailbox, in the fence rows. Cha Cha had ordered every type of lily available in the US: daylilies, calla lilies, stargazer lilies, tiger lilies. On and on went the list. But the one she brought the most of were Easter lilies. Stella's mother's favorite.

Stella stopped to smell one as she walked to the barn to begin her day.

Joiner was already there, as he often was. His herd of mares had been in the pasture a week, and he liked to ride through and check on them before beginning his day at Star Stables.

"How's it look out there this morning?" she asked as she approached the stall where he was brushing and feeding Pistol.

"Pistol and I are falling in love." He smirked in a way that melted Stella's heart.

"Is that so?"

"Yep. Only Pistol has twenty-five ladies he's wooing."

"Do they seem to be getting along?"

"I think so. They seem to have already established a pecking order, and Majesty is the boss."

"Oh wow. I could have guessed that would happen."

"I know, right? She's just got that regal air about her, an alpha. Certainly is well named."

He ran the brush through Pistol's mane. "Bella, Suzy Q and Racy are the next three in command at this point."

"Poor Pistol may have trouble keeping all of them happy."

"It will be a tough job. But you're up for it, aren't you, boy?" He patted Pistol on his star. "Yeah. You're the man."

"Aren't you glad you only have me to keep in line?" Stella entered the stall cautiously, but Pistol didn't seem to mind.

Joiner narrowed his eyes at her. "Girl, I don't believe anyone could keep you in line."

She moved in behind him and put her arms around his waist. "I think Pistol's starting to warm up to me."

"I agree. It's about time."

Pistol snorted.

"'Course you weren't always courting his favor."

Stella laughed and laid her head against Joiner's strong back. He was so warm, and such a rock for her. He tried to help her relax and enjoy life, and Cha Cha had reminded her that she needed that. "I'm so glad you're here."

She closed her eyes and felt the rhythm of him, his breathing, the motion of his arm as it moved the brush. It was something so simple, an everyday thing, really. But Stella was able to savor it. To appreciate it for the gift it was.

When he was finished, Joiner dropped the brush and turned to kiss her, enfolding her in his arms. "Me, too, babe. I'm glad I'm here, too."

They kissed again, more passionately. Soon, their cowboy hats collided and fell to the floor. If Joiner noticed, he didn't let on; instead, he pulled her closer.

Stella raised her hands to feel the lush beauty of his hair. She breathed in the scent of leather as her face touched against his smooth neck. As she lost herself in his dark waves, Joiner lifted her boots off the floor. She wrapped her legs around his waist, and he walked forward, backing her up till she was against the wall.

The cedar wallboards were rough against her shoulder blades, even with her shirt as a barrier. Everything was the scent of leather and hay. Then his mouth was on her, kissing her up and down her neck.

As Joiner's kisses intensified, Stella felt as though she was going to explode. She dug her fingers into his hair, pulling him closer to her, as though she could somehow merge their bodies and souls. She covered his lips with hers and kissed him greedily. Never before had she experienced such hunger. It was as if somehow she'd been starving her whole life and now here, in this moment, was the one thing that could satisfy her. Joiner Temple. This wild and wonderful man.

When Stella opened her eyes, he was gazing down at her. A crooked grin edged its way across his lips. "Why are you staring at me?" she asked him. He was still holding her against the wall.

"That's an easy question." He shifted her onto one hip.

"Answer it then, if you're so smart."

"Because you are beautiful. And I enjoy looking at beautiful things."

Stella shook her head at him. She didn't know what to say. What *was* there to say to something like that?

"You have beautiful skin, a beautiful face, beautiful eyelashes, a beautiful nose."

"Really? You were staring at my nose?"

"It's asymmetrical. Just the kind of nose I like best."

"You are crazy, you know that?"

"I suppose you are the pot and I am the kettle."

She giggled. "Well, put me down."

He held her tighter. "Something you need to

understand, madam, is that while you are my boss at Star Stables, you are not my boss in matters of this kind. You cannot command me at will to put you down. I will put you down when I decide."

"Joiner, put me down!" She banged her fists on his shoulders.

"There is no point in resisting. It will only make matters worse."

"How you are speaking with a straight face?"

He confessed, "I have no idea, but that is entirely beside the point."

"Okay. Don't put me down. Hold me like this forever. Even if the world walks in and sees us."

"The world is of no consequence to me."

"Even if Pistol rams us."

"Pistol is quite too much of a gentleman to ever do such a thing."

Pistol stomped his foot as if concurring...or disagreeing.

"Even if your back breaks."

"That is becoming an issue, I must admit." He shifted her onto the other hip. "I may be a cowboy Superman, as you have so fittingly described me, but even Superman has his limits."

"Well, I'm not going to tell you to put me down again. I'm perfectly happy to sit on your hip all day. It is entirely your choice whether or not your back breaks."

He dropped her gently on her feet.

They left a puzzled Pistol to rest in the stable, and went forth together to face the day.

DURING THE LATE MORNING, Stella worked with Cade and two other children, new clients who also had sensory issues. They did some group therapy to improve their social skills. When Jacob and Daune arrived, they each took one of the children and put them on horses, Cade on Daisy, and the other two on Dakota and Picasso. They led them into the arena for occupational and speech therapy using new equine techniques they'd learned at a workshop in Dallas.

Joiner was in the arena, too. While their mother watched from behind the fence, he was giving a riding lesson to seven-year-old twin girls named Adelaide and Sophia. They were out in the center with Pistol, and as a threesome, were the cutest things Stella had ever seen.

The girls were not identical, but both had enormous blue eyes. Sophia had sandy blond hair and Adelaide's was as white as cotton. The twins stood about four feet tall, long and lean, and as it was their first day they were not in riding gear.

Instead, it appeared they had both dressed for the part of a rhinestone cowgirl. They wore matching bedazzled white shirts with purple bandannas, matching jeans that were studded with stars down the sides, matching belts that were embossed with their names, matching cowgirl hats and matching purple boots.

"My goodness," Stella called as she approached with Cade on Daisy. "I didn't know we were working with rodeo queens today."

The girls grinned, showing gaps where they'd both lost teeth.

"Hey there, buddy!" Joiner waved to Cade.

"Hey." Cade lifted his hand.

Stella watched out of the corner of her eye as she and Cade circled the arena. Joiner showed the girls each piece of equipment and how it was used. Then he helped them practice getting on and off Pistol, who seemed amazingly calm.

Joiner's way with the girls reminded Stella of how Buster had been with her when she was younger, and she couldn't help but think how he'd be a good dad. As he led Adelaide and Sophia on a little ride out of the arena and over to their mother, Stella also couldn't help but notice every female in the vicinity, regardless of age, seemed smitten with the violet-eyed cowboy. Of course, when it came to being smitten, she was the worst one of all.

But Joiner wasn't sure what he wanted or where he wanted to be, and she was afraid that one day—maybe soon—he would find something more exciting than being ranch hand for Buster and her assistant at Star Stables. In her heart, he was already so much more.

CHAPTER NINETEEN

IF YOU'D ASKED Joiner Temple before he'd come home whether he'd have ever dressed up in a bunny costume, hop around hiding plastic eggs and pose for pictures all day long with sugar-crazed kids, he would have said *there's no way in Hades*. But that was before Stella Scout came into his life. And that's exactly what he did on the Saturday before Easter at Star Stables.

Clint Cavender, who'd hired a bouncy house as well as lemonade, popcorn and cotton candy vendors to provide free refreshments for everyone, got to dress in his usual mode of designer cowboy. Buster presided over the petting zoo in clean overalls and a new pastel T-shirt. Stella looked her usual Sundance catalog model self, and Jacob Hunnicutt was as professional as always. Daune Holzman was the only other one who sported an Easter-themed costume. She'd come dressed in a yellow chicken costume that made her look like a giant marshmallow Peeps.

Meant as a fun day for clients and their families as well as an advertisement for the riding school, the event was a smashing success. Cade, Adelaide and Sophia were there, as well as most of the other regulars. They were joined by a host of people from the community who came to see what hippotherapy was all about.

"After this day, I'm going to be really ready for bronc riding next week," Joiner whispered in Buster's ear as he hopped by a group of children who were in line to pet Minnie and Violet. "I've got to get my man-card back somehow."

"A bronco bustin' bunny is something I have to see," Buster growled back through his perma-smiling lips. "That should be somethin' else."

ON WEDNESDAY NIGHT he got his chance. Stella refused to speak to him about it, as it contradicted everything she was trying to accomplish at her school, but Buster was chomping at the bit. He had been ever since he first got the call.

One of his old rodeo friends had asked him a while back to give him some tips on busting broncos. Now, it seemed, his buddy's setup was finally ready. Buster didn't really know the extent of it and he didn't have to. His friend had had him at the word *bronc*.

And Joiner's interest had only fueled Buster's fire. So he went with the older man to visit Alex Hickey, and Stella stayed home to worry.

Alex met them at his newly constructed arena, equipped with chutes for bulls and broncos. He was a wiry fellow with greased-back black hair under a tall, tan Stetson. Joiner supposed the tallness of the hat was intended to make up for the shortness of the man, who he estimated to be about five feet eight inches.

Alex embraced Buster heartily.

"This is Joiner Temple," Buster told him. "He's kind of my ranch hand."

"Well, hi, Mister Kind-of-Buster's-Ranch-Hand." Alex slapped his shoulder. "You any kin to the other Temples around Kilgore?"

"Yes, sir. I am." His answer just kind of hung there in the air, so Joiner left it at that. His family name had been met with suspicion for most of his life, which was one thing he hoped to cure during his time at home by doing something good in Pap's honor.

Buster interjected, "Joiner tried to buy part of my land but I couldn't let it go. So he's working for me some and helping Stella with a business she's starting, as well as breeding his horse out of one of our pastures. He's got quite the interesting background."

Hickey nodded. "I see."

Joiner wasn't sure why he felt the need to explain himself. "I played polo at UT in Austin, and graduated with a master's degree. Then I traveled overseas with a few different teams. I've come home to be near my brothers for a bit." He looked Hickey directly in the eye. "I have a purebred Argentine stallion I'm breeding with twenty-five mares this season. And I'm also researching care for wild mustangs right now. Long-term, I plan to establish a trust in my pap's name to do just that."

"Well, it's nice to meet you, Joiner. You sound like a man with a plan," he said sincerely enough. Hickey turned to Buster. "Wanna see my setup?"

"I didn't know you were made of money," Buster said to Alex as the other man showed them around the place. "Even if you did win a bull-riding championship or two."

"Pretty, ain't it. This is all of my life's savings."

"Shoot yeah, it's pretty."

Alex spat tobacco into the dirt. "But I need it to work for me, too, and that's why I asked you to come here, Buster."

"What do you want me to do?"

"Well, believe it or not, I'm going to give rodeo lessons."

"You? Really?"

"Me. And some others."

Buster snorted. "Well, if that don't beat all. You know, my daughter's doing equine therapy with people. Has her own little school on the ranch—that's what Joiner's helping her with. Seems like everybody's into teaching people to ride horses these days."

"You're right," Alex said. "In our day, you just got on an animal and learned it. Heck, I worked on my daddy's ranch. That's how I learned to ride."

"I busted feral horses before I ever thought about riding them in the rodeo," Buster declared. "That was the hardest riding I ever did."

After he decided Hickey wasn't a Temple-hater, Joiner liked listening to the two old cowboys swap stories. They'd grown up in a different world than he had. He could learn from them, and was afraid their kind was a dying breed. Still, his ears perked up when their talk returned to the reason he and Buster were actually there.

"Buster, the fact is you were the best bare-back rider in the country for a lot of years. You're an invaluable resource for young riders who want to improve their skills. Would you consider teaching some lessons here? You can set your own schedule."

"That's tempting," Buster acknowledged. "But my daughter wouldn't like it at all."

"What do you mean?"

"Well, after her mother died falling from a horse, Stella gave up on the rodeo. She believes it's way too dangerous." Buster rubbed his beard. "That's the reason I quit all of this in the first place." He motioned around the arena.

Alex raked a pile of dirt with one of his boots. "Hmm. Well it seems to me she makes a good argument for why you ought to give lessons, then. So these young boys know what they're doing, take all the necessary precautions." He turned to Joiner. "You ever busted a bronc, polo player?"

"No, sir."

"Buster, at least let's go look at some of my animals. You might decide to give Joiner here a lesson—and a chance to become a real cowboy." Alex winked at Joiner. They followed him into the stables.

Hickey's rough stock were some of the roughest Joiner had ever seen, and he couldn't wait to get on one.

"Okay, okay. Give us that sturdy little girl.

The Appaloosa. That is, if you're up for a lesson, kid?"

Joiner remembered the stony expression on Stella's face as they'd left earlier that day. But then the skin on the back of his neck prickled and he started to feel the rush that he'd been chasing all his life. An uncontrollable grin swept over his face. "I'm game," said Joiner. "Bring that sweet girl on."

ALEX ASKED A HELPER to take the horse, whose name was Starfall, and get her ready in the bronco shoot. He let Buster pick out gear for Joiner from the supply closet: spurs, gloves and rigging, which looked kind of like a suitcase handle with girth straps.

"Fit your glove in here," Buster directed Joiner. "It has to be tight, but not so tight you can't get the glove out if you need to."

That sounded a little foreboding.

"Normally, I'd have you practice on a bale of hay," said Buster. "But you've got a lot of experience on horses so we'll skip that part."

Joiner was thankful for that decision; riding a hay bale didn't sound very exciting. He donned the chaps that were also provided, and slipped a tailbone pad down the seat of his jeans. They walked together back to the arena. On the way

Buster instructed him how to fall and how to get up. Of course, Joiner had done both a million times as he'd learned the sport of polo.

"These horses are different than polo ponies," Buster warned. "She'll be trying to stomp on your guts."

"So I fall on my side, roll out of the way and get up as fast as I can."

"That's right," said Buster. "And don't die. Now visualize the ride. I want your shoulders back, stomach tight, chin down and free hand skyward."

Joiner threw his hand in the air the way he'd seen the cowboys at the rodeo do it. Buster smiled.

"Keep your spurs high so they'll set in your horse the first time she lands out of the shoot." Buster continued, "Your first goal is to stay on for eight seconds. The second goal, which is less important at the moment, is to do it with style."

Joiner nodded. Then, before he knew it, he was dropping gingerly onto the back of the horse. She felt like a tightly wound spring about to explode. Almost immediately Joiner's right leg started shaking uncontrollably, and Buster hunkered over the chute, whispering advice to calm him.

It didn't work. Joiner's mind was honed in on the thousand-pound she-devil he was sitting on, who he could tell already wanted him dead.

"You nervous?" Hickey grinned, a little too happy.

Then the gate flew open and the animal plunged out, bucking madly as Joiner clung to the leather handle. Joiner's upper body flopped wildly across Starfall's back and sides while she practically levitated off the dirt floor in paroxysms of protest. Joiner, whose other arm jerked around as though attached to a jackhammer, felt a sense of control while at the same instant being on the verge of certain disaster. At one point, the four-legged murderess darted dangerously close to the metal fence, but Joiner's adrenaline kept him from letting go.

Finally, after eight seconds, a whistle blew and Joiner wriggled his glove out of the rigging. He slid off Starfall's side, landing on his feet, and scurried to safety.

Buster's face was beatific. He pumped both fists in the air and hollered, "Whoooeeee! Did you see that polo player ride?" He slapped a stunned Hickey on the back and ran over to Joiner on wobbly legs. The older man almost knocked him down with the force of his hug.

As Joiner's heart slowly settled down into his

chest, his whole body sagged with exhaustion. Even his teeth felt as if they'd been rattled out of his gums.

But if he had to sum up the ride—the whole experience in one word—he'd use this one: *awesome*.

CHAPTER TWENTY

AT THE RANCH, Stella sat on the couch with her laptop and a cup of decaf coffee, surfing the internet. Mugsy and Mitzi flanked her on either side. Compiling a digital folder she was considering naming "Doomsday," she saved video after video of bronco rides gone bad.

Then she started adding articles: Friends and Family Mourn Death of Bronc Rider, Indian National Finals Bronc Rider Dies, Rodeo Rider Dies after Horse Pins Him to Fence, Rider Paralyzed after Bucked by a Bronc, Bronc Rider in Wheelchair after Tragic Fall…

The scary possibilities were endless.

By the time Buster returned from the rendezvous with Alex Hickey—Joiner had wisely decided to go straight to his RV—she had amassed quite an arsenal of information.

"Well, good evening, little lady!" Buster's eyes were undeniably lit up with joy.

"Hey, Pops."

He sank into his recliner, appearing utterly satisfied.

"What have you been up to while I've been gone?"

"Oh, just a little research on the dangers of what you were doing."

"That sounds…kind of freaky."

"Pops, you know how I feel about the rodeo, and especially bronco busting."

"Yes, I know. I know." Buster leaned back and started to snore.

"Are you…asleep?"

"No, just faking. But I should go to bed. These old bones are tired."

"Aren't you going to tell me anything about your evening?" Stella demanded.

"I didn't figure you wanted to hear it."

Stella angled her head to one side, waiting.

"Alex has built a complex on some land out west of town. It's a state-of-the-art arena, with a gorgeous red barn attached. Sort of like your setup, though the barn has rooms for instruction and equipment in addition to regular barn stuff."

In spite of herself, Stella's interest was stirred. "What kind of instruction, exactly? He's not going to compete with us, is he?"

"Not hardly." Buster chuckled to himself. "He wants to teach people to rodeo."

Stella brought her hand to her mouth, gasping.

When she recovered slightly, she said, "What on earth does this have to do with you?" Then, as everything clicked together in her mind, she gasped again. "He wants you to teach bareback riding, doesn't he?"

Buster kicked down the footrest of his recliner and sat up straight. "Yes. Yes, he does."

"Are you going to do it?"

"I haven't made up my mind yet." Buster lifted his bushy eyebrows. "But I'd be lying if I said I wasn't interested."

"Pops," Stella pleaded, "how can you do this? After all we went through with Moma?"

He walked over and sat beside her on the couch. Mitzi bolted into the recliner as if she was afraid he would sit on her. Stella and Buster both had to laugh at the dog. A moment of comic relief.

Then Buster got serious again. "Pretty, I think somewhere along the way I failed you in helping you deal with your mother's death. Maybe it was because I'd been a traveler all of your life, and when everything happened I wasn't as close to you as I needed to be. I regret that, I really do."

"You didn't fail me, Pops."

"I did, though. Hear me out." Buster patted her on the leg. "Maybe it was my own grief. I'll never know, I don't guess. And quitting the rodeo—that was a good thing. The right thing for both of us."

She nodded.

"Whatever the reason, I failed to teach you the difference between being scared of dying and being scared of living."

"What do you mean, Pops?"

"We're all scared of dying. And when a person loses someone like we did—well, it's terrifying. He or she will go to great lengths to try to make sure nothing bad happens again, because she doesn't think she can stand it if it does."

"Well, I'll readily admit that. After losing Mama, I wouldn't survive if I lost you, too."

"But you're going to, one day." Buster looked her straight in the eyes. "It will happen."

Stella averted his stare.

"I hope it will be when I am very old, and in my bed."

Stella wiped a tear from the corner of her

eye. "It will be. Pops, where are you going with this?"

"Stella, I believe you are so afraid of dying that in some ways you don't let yourself live."

She started to protest, but he cut her off. "And I have catered to that, reinforced it. I think I did it to make you feel safe. But it wasn't right."

"So you're going back to the rodeo in order to really live? Is that what you're telling me?"

"No. What I'm saying is that when my time comes, I would rather die happy, doing what I love, like your mother did. With no regrets." He let that sink in a minute. "Your mother was not afraid of death. She was afraid of the unlived life. And so should we all be."

Stella stared at him for a long moment. Then she said, "That's all fine and good. But 'really living' doesn't mean you have to do stupid things and be crazy and reckless all of the time."

"I totally agree." Buster nodded.

"In fact, I think that's wrong. It's throwing away the gift of life."

Buster studied her face. His eyes were tender. "Do you believe that's what your mother did? Squandered her life away? Is that really what bothers you?"

"I don't know," exclaimed Stella. "I don't want to think so, but I just don't know!"

"Well, maybe that is a question you need to answer for yourself. It could be the answer to letting *you* live." He picked up the amulet she never took off, then let it drop back against her neck.

THE NEXT MORNING Joiner came limping into Star Stables. He was not late by any means, just later than his usual early time. Stella saw him out of her office window, and rushed to meet him as he entered the barn. "What happened to you?"

"Mornin', Boss Lady." His violet eyes looked sleepy, as though maybe he hadn't slept well through the night.

"Good morning, yourself." She tried to control the panic in her voice. "But why are you limping?"

"I went for the ride of my life yesterday evening."

"What?"

"You mean your dad didn't tell ya? I stayed the whole eight seconds on a bronc! My first time ever!"

Did he expect her to be proud? He did—she could see it in his eyes!

Her heart was in her throat. *Deep breaths. Deep breaths.*

"Boss Lady? You okay?"

Remain calm. Visualize. Happy place. Happy place. Lake Lily.

"Stella?"

"What? Oh yes. Yeah. I'm okay." She rubbed her head, her eyes and face, and then folded her hands underneath her chin. "I'm just…I thought…I was just worried because you are limping."

They walked on together toward the horses' stalls, Joiner's pace much slower than normal.

"I'm as sore as all get-out. That horse pounded me in the butt and rattled my brains. It was crazy! But it was so much fun—I can't wait to do it again!"

Stella's head was spinning. She couldn't deal with this.

"Joiner!" Stella exploded. "Do you hear yourself? You're an idiot!"

He stepped back as if she'd punched him in the gut.

But she wasn't finished. "What is your problem? Are you trying to kill yourself?"

"It's hardly killing myself to have a little fun," he spouted, none too kindly. "You should try it sometime. I bet it wouldn't kill you, either."

Unwelcome tears stung Stella's eyes and slid down her cheeks. "Do you get some kind of sick joy out of hurting me?"

Joiner reached for her but she shrugged him off.

"Stella?" His voice was low. "I'm so sorry. It's just—"

"Maybe we'll talk later," she said weakly. "I—I've got to do something in my office right now." Stella bolted away, leaving him holding a rake at the door of Pistol's stall.

AFTER CLIENTS STARTED ARRIVING, the day got extremely busy, which helped Stella put Joiner and her father and their death-wish ways out of her mind. At least for a while.

Cade came for therapy at his usual time. He was starting to show real improvement, which thrilled Clint as well as all of the staff.

They also had five new children who'd registered with the school after the Easter Eggtravaganza. It was so exciting to watch their journeys begin—and a privilege to have a little part in it.

Allie was a twelve-year-old with Down syndrome. Her mother explained that she was afraid of animals, and Allie seemed terrified of the horses at first, even crying when Stella and Daune brought her near Dakota. But as Allie brushed Dakota's coat and fed her snacks, her tears turned to laughter. And Daune and Stella then had tears streaming down *their* faces. By the end of her ninety minutes, Allie was sitting on the horse.

Another new client was Eddie. He was born three and a half months early with cerebral palsy affecting the left side of his body. Another physical therapist in town, one of Stella's friends from PT school, had recommended his parents try Stella's program to strengthen his torso and possibly help him start to walk. At two and a half years old, Eddie was the youngest child at Star Stables.

That day, his first day, his dad said it would be a miracle if they could even get him near a horse, much less ride. He was scared of everything—noises, parking lots, dogs and cars seemed to send him into a panic. And when Stella brought out Picasso and walked the horse over to him, Eddie did start to panic and pointed in the other direction. Following her gut, however, Stella said, "Hand him to me and go inside the barn."

She could tell Eddie's dad thought she was

crazy. But he did what she said anyway. She put Eddie on that horse and away they rode, and the little boy didn't cry or scream. Eddie's dad watched from behind a glass window in the viewing room of the barn. When he waved at his son, there was a knot in Stella's throat.

The new clients were essential to the bottom line, and Stella was equally thankful for the volunteers who had signed on in the past couple of weeks.

Harper, Grace and their cousin Madeline were college students who were using the time they spent at Star Stables to fulfill volunteer hours they needed for their particular fields of study.

Madeline, the youngest, was a tiny, free-spirited blonde. She was a sophomore kinesiology major who excelled at anything physical. Although she didn't have much experience with horses, Stella guessed that if she wanted to, she could have become a great barrel racer, or even a female jockey. After less than a week, she was already dancing to country music from the horses' backs as if she'd been born there, to the delight of all of the clients.

Madeline's cousin, Harper, was a premed student. He was genuinely interested in the idea of using horses to heal people, and asked Stella and the other therapists a lot of great questions. And he was really talented at translating what he learned to his activities with the clients. All of the little girls had crushes on him, and Stella understood why. With his dreamy blue eyes, wheat-colored hair and dark complexion, he looked like he could be a movie star.

Grace was Harper's sister. She was the oldest of the three. She already had her degree in teaching, and was working toward her master's in gifted education. A guitar-playing, grown-up Taylor Swift type, Grace also had a spiritual quality about her that was a welcome addition to Star Stables. She often prayed for clients and their families and with them, if they desired it. Stella had the feeling she prayed for her, as well.

With the school's financial problems mounting, Stella hoped she did. She needed all of the prayers she could get.

When the day was over, Stella decided to go for a relaxing ride on Vega. She hadn't spent much one-on-one time with her horse lately, and she wanted to be alone with her thoughts and try to sort through how she was feeling.

She grabbed her phone, thinking she'd also check in with Cha Cha. Then she saddled up Vega and headed out into the open range.

They took their time getting out to Lake Lily, just breathing the fresh spring air and watching for wildflowers. When they finally arrived, Stella stretched out on the big rock while Vega munched on some grass nearby.

"Cha Cha? Can you hear me?"

"Hey, sweet girl. You're loud and clear."

"Oh, great. I'm out on the north forty beside Lake Lily. Reception is not always great out here."

Cha Cha sighed on the other end of the line. "Oh my gosh. Such a beautiful place. I've not been out there in forever. You'll have to send me a picture when we get off the phone."

"Okay, I will. How are you doing?"

"Today's a good day. But it's the first one I've had since the chemo treatment. And before we know it, it will be time for another round."

"Argh." Stella's problems suddenly seemed very small. "Tell me what it's like."

"Well, the worst thing is that it's unpredictable. I think I'm going to be able to do something so I plan it, then I have to cancel because I'm in bed. Or throwing up. Or both."

"Poor baby."

"I know! Poor me!" Cha Cha laughed. "But today I got to go eat lunch with my parents in Springdale, and my mom and I went to T.J.

Maxx. Now I'm back home in my recliner. Oh, and it's catfish night at The Wooden Spoon, so Steve is bringing dinner after work. And we're watching *Lost* tonight. So I have no complaints."

"You never do have many."

"Right, I am such a saint."

Stella laughed at that.

"What's going on with you, sweet girl? Tell me something about that good-looking cowboy."

"Oh Lord. You don't want to know."

"Yes, I do!" Cha Cha exclaimed.

"Well, with the aid of my father he has now taken up a new hobby—bronc riding."

Silence at the other end.

"Did you hear me?" Stella asked.

"Yes…"

"Well, what do you think about that?"

"I'm trying to figure out what I think before I say anything."

"Oh," Stella said. "Well, some people say that's a good idea. Not that I've tried it lately."

Cha Cha giggled. "Yeah. Me neither. I'm horrible at it."

"Well don't do too much thinking now. Just tell me what that news sounds like to you."

"Okay," Cheryl began. "I'm glad that he and

Buster are bonding, and that they have some things in common."

"Go on," Stella urged.

"And I always did think rodeo guys were sexy."

"Cha Cha, for Pete's sake!"

"Yes, yes." Cha Cha sighed. "I know it probably stresses you totally out."

"Bingo."

"And I can't say that I blame you. It's a risky sport."

"Yeah, it is! And he's thirty-one years old. Not exactly the time to be taking up a new, physically demanding and highly dangerous hobby!"

"Why not? I mean, if you enjoy that sort of thing? It's not as if he's old and decrepit like me."

Stella measured her words carefully. "Well, because he's just given up on playing polo. He said himself that he's moved home to try to reinvent his life. Why on earth would he start busting broncos now?"

"First polo, then bronc riding? Maybe your cowboy needs an adrenaline rush."

"But why?"

"I can't say, honey. Why do any of us need what we need?"

Cha Cha's question lingered in Stella's mind long after she hung up. It was still there as she mounted Vega and galloped, racing the sunset, back to the barn. In fact, even after dinner with Buster, a long, hot bath and a little texting with Joiner, it remained on her mind. And it was still there—lodged like a burr under her saddle—when she snuggled into her quilts, turned out her bedside lamp and tried to sleep.

At one o'clock in the morning Stella stopped fighting it. She got out of bed, grabbed her laptop, and typed this email:

Dear Joiner,
I'm sorry for brushing you off today when you were so excited about riding that bronc. You are important to me, and I want to support you in your dreams.

I don't know whether I've communicated how strongly I fear danger and risky behavior. I'm not sure I even know the extent of how that fear affects my daily life. All I can say is this: ever since my mom died, I am terrified of losing people I care about. And I've ordered my entire life to do anything I can to prevent that from happening.

Just recently Buster pointed out to me that maybe I go too far in this extreme. He said something I have really never thought about, that a person can be so afraid of dying—or in my case of other people dying or getting hurt—that she never really lives. I don't want to be that way, but I think maybe I am.

I admire your zest for life. I'll admit I don't understand your desire to get on a bronco. And you might as well know that it stresses me out that you and Buster are pursuing this hobby, or whatever it is. But I need to give up being so afraid all of the time, and the OCD that results from that. Like Adrienne Rutella talked about that night, that fear is keeping me from really living. It kept me from sharing your excitement today, and I regret that.

I am sorry my issues with this have hurt you, both today, and even in the situation with Cade and Pistol. I promise to try to do better, though I can't promise to be happy about what you are doing, or the idea that it could take you away from me.

I hope you can understand. Stella

In the morning she received this reply:

Stella,
No worries. We all have our issues and I do understand you.

Will you support me in my dreams of going

on a date with you tonight? No dangerous or risky behavior planned, unless that includes kissing.

You are important to me, too.

Joiner

CHAPTER TWENTY-ONE

SUMMER HAD COME to the ranch. It was as hot as a firecracker outside, and with kids out of school, Joiner's side of Star Stables was booming. Apparently word had gotten out that he had a handsome new assistant from the college, because it seemed as if every teenage girl in Kilgore had signed up for riding lessons. Thank goodness Harper had riding experience and could pretty much handle lessons on his own. Joiner had to recruit Buster to teach on the regular schedule, as well.

Joiner was happy to be busy, however, because the business brought in revenue for the school and he just didn't know how long he would be there to keep the lessons going. Riding lessons were cheaper than therapy, of course, but at least everybody who signed up for them could pay. Stella continued to add clients who needed the therapy services but didn't have the money to pay what it cost, so the hippotherapy side of things was a little touch and go.

But of course, Clint had a solution for that: another fund-raiser, this one for July Fourth. They'd called it the Star Spangled Stables fund-raiser.

If Clint Cavender wasn't such a darn good person, Joiner would be tempted to hate his guts. But Clint *was* good. And a great friend. Still, it killed Joiner that he just couldn't compete with the Cavender fortune. And it seemed every time Stella needed something for the school, Clint was Johnny-on-the-spot with some idea for how to help her get it. His solutions were creative, but on some level they usually meant he'd be hauling out his moneybags to save the day. That was sure to happen again on the Fourth of July.

The fund-raising event was sure to draw a crowd and lots of money for the school, and Joiner felt guilty for even thinking negative thoughts about it. It really was kind, and it really was generous, and it really was a good idea. But it really was annoying, too.

And if it wasn't for comparing himself to Clint, Joiner would have been more excited about what he was accomplishing by breeding Pistol. Things were going great, with a third of the mares bred already, and if all continued as planned, Joiner stood to make about a quarter of a million dollars. But what was a quarter of a million compared to Clint's millions? And, why was he comparing himself anyway?

He knew the root of it was his relationship with Stella. Things couldn't go on as they were. For one thing, the yearning he felt for her was powerful, but he wanted to keep it pure. He was finding that more and more difficult as time went on, especially since he lived in an RV that was practically in her backyard. But that needed to change, as well. He didn't want to take advantage of Buster's generosity.

There was no way Joiner could justify using Buster's pasture for breeding again next year. He'd kept up his end of the bargain with Buster—to get the ranch in shape by mending fences, doing odd jobs and helping Buster with whatever he needed done. He'd also helped Stella establish Star Stables. They'd opened the doors together, and he'd been instrumental in building its reputation every step of the way since. The school was thriving, as long as it was funded. No one could question the quality of the services they provided.

The arrangement had worked for all of them. The ranch and Stella's school were all up and running. Breeding season was almost done. Everything outward said it was time for him to move on. Pocket the money he'd clear with Pistol, buy himself some land and move forward with his hope of clearing Pap's name.

But everything outward wasn't everything there was. The bigger picture was that Joiner was emotionally attached to Stella, an attachment that went deeper than any he'd ever had with a woman. So how could he move on?

Joiner pondered this conundrum as he measured shampoo into a bucket. His nieces had spent the afternoon with him at Star Stables, and before he took them home he was going to let them bathe Pistol to help keep him cool.

Carrie, Meg and Hope had come into Joiner's life when his younger brother Cullen had married their mother, Sarah. The girls' father had died several years ago, leaving Sarah a widow. She'd ended up meeting Cullen when she went back to school at the university where he taught. Their relationship had been transformative for Cullen, and a big part of that was the chance it had given him to be a father. Now that he was in Kilgore for a bit, Joiner was happy that he was getting the chance to be an uncle, as well.

"Meg, go get the water hose."

She unwound it from its stand beside the barn and dragged it over to him. He filled the bucket till the shampoo turned nice and sudsy. Then he carefully wet Pistol down with the hose.

"Okay, Hope, you start with his side here." He handed the youngest girl a soft brush full of the soapy water. Then he positioned Meg on the other side. For the more difficult places on the horse he would work with Carrie, the oldest.

"Uncle Joiner, when are you going to take me to the movies?" Hope asked as she dipped her brush back into the bucket. "Like you did with Carrie."

"Yeah. Me, too," said Meg. "I wish I could have gone to *The Fault in Our Stars*."

"Well, Mom said you were both too little for that movie," Carrie retorted. "I was the only one who was old enough to go."

Hope exhaled loudly. "I don't care about the dumb old fault in our stars, anyway. I want to go see *Sponge Bob*."

"Is there a new one?" Joiner asked as he cleaned Pistol's hoof.

"Yeah, and it looks awesome."

"I don't want to see that either," Meg confided. "I want to go to my own movie with Uncle Joiner."

"Yeah," said Hope. "I want to pick where we

eat and go by Cavender's Clothing Store just like Carrie got to."

"Me, too, Uncle Joiner," Meg pleaded. "Can we?"

The hope in her eyes was irresistible.

By the time they finished bathing Pistol, Joiner was hooked up for two more movie dates. It seemed the other girls needed their due, which was fair enough. He remembered what it was like to grow up with three brothers. He wanted each one of the girls to feel they were unique and special to him, because they were.

Splash! The unique and special Meg sprayed him with the hose when he returned from putting up Pistol. He looked as though he'd wet his pants!

"You're going to get it now!" Joiner took off, chasing her with the bucket of suds.

When Carrie got in on the action, hitting him in the arm with her sponge, he dumped the bucket in her direction. All he accomplished was splashing her shoes. Out of danger of the suds, Hope jumped on his back while Meg sprayed him some more.

When he collapsed in the grass by the barn, the three girls dog-piled him. He was on the bottom of the pile wrestling one on one leg,

one on the other and one on his shoulders when
Stella walked up with her camera and snapped
a picture.

Joiner groaned.

"This will be great for our new website.
Thank you, girls!" She winked at them and
sauntered away.

Joiner figured it was about time he took the
girls home. Cullen was in the backyard grilling
pork chops when Joiner and the girls drove up.
Sarah directed the girls to set the table while
she fixed the side dishes, and sent Joiner outside with two glasses of iced tea, one for him
and one for Cullen. She insisted that he stay
for dinner. For a bachelor like Joiner, it wasn't
a hard sell.

Their dinner of steaming baked potatoes,
green salad with fresh tomatoes and onions
from the garden, barbecued pork chops and
homemade rolls was delicious. The talk around
the table was sweet, first about the girls and
how much fun they'd had at the ranch that day,
and then about Cullen and Sarah, with their
genuine interest in each other and the family. Watching their easy banter, the way Sarah
touched Cullen, casually laying her hand on
his arm, and the way he served her, Joiner felt
as if he was in the midst of a miracle. It was

hard to imagine that this same Cullen used to keep himself so guarded and buried in books.

"But that's just it. I'm not the same Cullen," his brother said later when Joiner mentioned the observation to him. They were cleaning the kitchen while Sarah put the girls in bed. "Falling in love with Sarah and her girls changed my life completely."

"How did you know it was right? I mean, how did you know she was the one?"

Cullen looked up from the baking dish he was scrubbing. "There are so many things I love about Sarah, Joiner. She's strong and beautiful and good. And the girls—they make me laugh. They need me. They remind me of what really matters.

"But the way I *really* knew she was the one— the thing that changed everything—was when I had to face my cutting and tell her about it."

Joiner took in the faded network of tiny scars on Cullen's arms, visible because of his rolled-up sleeves. He nodded. "I remember that night."

"You actually helped me a great deal."

"Me?"

Cullen laughed. "Yes. Remember? You all came over here with Alma and Felix, and I was having so much trouble talking about the cutting I had done as a teenager, and you just blurted it out?"

"Oh yeah." Joiner felt a little sheepish at the memory.

"It was good, Joiner. Because in that moment I realized you all knew, and loved me anyway. And that helped me to be able to tell Sarah. Even though I thought I was risking everything with her."

Joiner took the dish from Cullen and rinsed it. Then he dried it off with a towel. "So, let me get this straight. And I promise I'm not trying to be stupid. I really need to understand."

"Okay?" Cullen urged him on, an understanding smile on his lips.

"You knew you were in love with Sarah. But the thing that made it a forever kind of love was that she helped you confront the truth about yourself and quit hiding it?"

"Yes," Cullen said. "She reached me in a very deep place, deeper than anyone else ever had, and helped me not to feel so alone."

Joiner bristled. "But you were never alone. The Brotherhood was always there."

"I know, but she even helped me appreciate that more fully."

"Well, what do you mean by alone, then?"

"Sarah completes me. I'm not sure how else to say it but that. And I knew it the moment I saw her I had to—and learned that I could—trust her with my deepest, darkest secret."

Joiner put down the towel. "That's really beautiful, man. And philosophical and poetic. If I wasn't convinced you were totally serious, and hadn't witnessed it with my own eyes, well, I might not believe it. But I do. You've given me a lot to think about."

"Are you getting pretty serious with Stella?" Cullen asked. "I didn't realize things were moving that fast."

"I don't know," Joiner answered. "I have no idea where our relationship is going. I really like her a lot."

"Do you trust her?"

"Yeah. That's what I was thinking when you were talking. I could trust her with anything. But she's already aware of my past. It's pretty obvious I'm a washed-up polo player. That's not something I could really hide."

"Well, it's a cliché, and I hate worn-out sayings, but this one has been true in my own experience. 'When it's right, you'll know it, just like when you know it's wrong'."

"Uh, I've never heard that saying in my life, Cullen."

Cullen threw the dishrag at him. "Even better, then."

CHAPTER TWENTY-TWO

"HOLD STILL!"

Joiner squirmed more than a worm in hot ashes.

"That tickles!"

"I am never going to get the stars right if you can't be still."

Joiner, who was seated on a lawn chair, straightened like a soldier from the waist up and saluted. He was still for a total of five seconds. Then he burst out laughing again as the paintbrush swooshed across his right nipple, covering it in white paint. His whole chest erupted in spasms, cracking the paint on her masterpiece as if it was painted during the Renaissance.

"I give up!" Stella stepped away from her human canvas and placed the brush in the jar of water that was on the table beside them. "You're going to have to find another artist."

He grabbed her wrist gently. "What if I don't want any other artist?" Then he pulled her toward him, careful not to smudge any paint.

"I simply cannot work under these conditions," Stella protested, but his eyes were already working their magic on her.

"I'm sorry. It's just that I'm not accustomed to a beautiful woman painting my chest."

Stella shook her head. "You are impossible, you know that?"

"But you are crazy about me."

"I guess there's no denying that." Stella kissed him on the lips.

"You guess?"

She kissed him again.

"That's a little better."

She picked the brush up again and pointed it at him. "Now, are you going to hold still or not? I just have a couple more stars and we will be done."

"Sir, yes, sir!"

When she finally finished, even Joiner had to admit it was perfect. Stella had taken a pair of jean shorts she'd bought for the occasion and painted them with white stars on one leg, and red-and-white stripes on the other. Using her shorts as a pattern, she had then painted Joiner's torso and arms to match. He had become a human flag. She even painted the lines with a bit of a curve, as if the flag was flying in a breeze.

"Selfie!" She pulled out her phone. In her shorts and white shirt, standing beside his flag torso paired with jeans and boots, they were a matching pair. The only problem was that Joiner looked so sexy she wasn't sure she wanted him going out in public. Could this really have been her idea? Well, it was too late now.

They drove up to the palatial Chateau Cavender early, as Clint had instructed. Waiting for them on the circle drive, a valet took Joiner's keys and went to park the truck elsewhere. Clint bounded down the stairs like a kid on Christmas morning. He then led them back up and onto the extensive grounds, which had been transformed into a sight to behold.

There were flags everywhere—both the national and the Texas state flag. From the giant balcony in front of Clint's home, as well as every window, patriotic banners were draped in half-moon shapes.

He'd gone all out on refreshments, too. Everywhere she looked there were silver barrels full of iced-down drinks. A station with a galvanized watering tank for horses, large enough to be a swimming pool, said Seed Spitting Contest. The tank was full of Black Diamond watermelons, also on ice.

Underneath Clint's beautiful oak trees, there were tables set up—long, white tables—with patriotic flower centerpieces and metallic confetti the shape of stars sprinkled everywhere. They all faced a stage where a live band was setting up. Servers in black-and-white uniforms stood at the ready with iced tea, lemonade and water.

And oh, the smell of the food. Stella's mouth began to water before she even saw Hunt and his catering crew. They were there from Temple Territory with loads of his special-recipe barbecue brisket, coleslaw, baked beans and sweet potato fries. There was also an ice-cream sundae station, with blueberries and strawberries as toppings to continue the patriotic theme.

"What are you charging per plate?" Joiner asked Clint, trying to make some sense of how much the event might raise.

"It's donation only—and all of the proceeds go to the school."

Stella didn't know whether to laugh or cry. This event—and Clint's overwhelming support—seemed too good to be true. But it was key if she was going to be able to operate Star Stables the way she wanted to. Stella didn't want to turn anyone away. And she couldn't expect Joiner to stay around teaching lessons forever, though she couldn't bear to think of him leaving. But even with her handsome ranch hand, she was like David up against Goliath when it came to covering the costs for people who couldn't pay.

Right beside the food, another station featured information about Star Stables. Jacob Hunnicutt was there already, sporting a cowboy hat and wearing red, white and blue. There were brochures, sign-up information and printed testimonials from parents. A sign beside a fishbowl read that they would be drawing for two one-year scholarships to the riding school, compliments of Cavender's, Inc. Stella was blown away.

"Clint, I can't believe you have done all of this!"

"You like it?" He grinned broadly.

"*Like* doesn't begin to cover it. But I feel indebted—" Stella began.

"I am the one who is in your debt." Clint stared into her eyes for a long moment. "Look over there."

Stella turned to see another station in the distance. There was a circular pen with four ponies. Inside, Daune Holzman—in an Uncle Sam outfit—led a horse around with Cade on its back. The boy noticed them watching. He raised his hand, not quite waving, and smiled.

As guests started to arrive, she and Joiner tried to mingle. It was strange to not be the official hostess of an event that benefited her school, but Clint had insisted on handling everything. Daune told her that he'd paid everyone, including her and Jacob, to man their stations, not expecting them to donate their precious time.

With that knowledge, Stella began to relax. Buster showed up after helping out over at Hickey's arena, and challenged her and Joiner to compete with him in the seed spitting contest. They walked over to the watermelon tank, where Harper was cutting slices.

"Hey, man! Where'd you get that cool shirt?" Harper asked when he saw Joiner.

Joiner flexed his muscles for Harper, popping his pecs. Harper shook his head, and Stella rolled her eyes, laughing. "Dude, this thing is custom-made," Joiner bragged.

"Did you paint that?" Harper turned to Stella.

"Yes, and as you might imagine, it was no small chore."

Harper laughed. "Well, it's really cool." He handed a slice of watermelon to each of them.

"Mr. Scout, you ready to show them how it's done?"

Buster stepped up to the line. He reared his head back, pulling downward on his beard, and spit that Black Diamond seed as hard as he could.

"That's pretty good," Harper declared. He marked the spot with a piece of tape and then handed a slice of watermelon to Joiner. "You think you can beat that, Joiner?"

"I do, but I'm going to let the lady go first." Joiner handed his slice to Stella.

She took a piece with a seed and handed it back to him. "Oh no you're not," she told him. "You're going next so I see what I have to beat."

"It's not going to matter." Joiner made a big production of rolling the seed around in his mouth. Then he bent his legs, and sprang up like a Slinky, jumping and spitting with all of his might. His seed landed a little bit past Buster's.

"Okay, Miss Stella, it's your turn." Harper backed up to show his support.

Stella looked at Joiner's seed, then she found a mark in the grass just beyond it and concentrated on that mark. With no fanfare, she took in a breath and spit her seed.

Harper dropped down on the ground to measure. "It's gonna be a close one!" he taunted.

Joiner was squinting to see, but Stella wasn't worried. Her seed had hit the mark.

"Stella Scout wins!" Harper yelled, his movie-star teeth shining in a smile as big as Texas. Then he gave her a blue ribbon, which she proudly displayed on her shirt.

The three of them walked around together to all of the other booths. It was set up like a county fair, and it seemed all of Kilgore had showed up for it. When they had the opportunity, they talked to people about the riding school and all of the services they offered there. It seemed people had been hearing good things, and many were interested in learning more.

This was why Stella would never dream of leaving Kilgore. This town and its people had always been there for her, and she would always be there for them. She couldn't understand why Joiner seemed determined to reject this kind of support and love.

When it was time for dinner, Clint gave a short speech about Star Stables and the way it was changing people's lives, including his and his son's. He recognized Stella and asked her to stand and share some of her vision. This was the one thing she had expected about the night, so when one of the servers brought her a mic, she was prepared.

"Hi. And thank you, Clint, and the community represented here tonight for your support and generosity." Stella willed her voice not to shake. "As many of you know, Kilgore is my home. The people here have celebrated my successes, such as when I won the National Barrel Racing Championship."

There was a burst of applause, mixed with a few goose calls.

Stella smiled and thanked them. Then she continued, "Even more importantly, however, you surrounded me with love and encouragement when my mother passed away." A lump she did not expect rose in her throat, and she fought it back down, pausing a few long moments. "This town is like my family. And that is why I chose to go to college here, earn my degree in physical therapy and establish Star Stables. It was my way of giving back to this community, and helping the people here who are in need. Please be reassured that if you or someone you love could benefit from any service we provide, you will not be turned away. Come and see us." She smiled and took her seat as everyone clapped again.

Next Clint invited Allie's and Eddie's parents

to the stage so that they could each give a testimonial. The things they said about what hippotherapy, and specifically Stella and her staff, had done for their children, warmed her heart. Joiner reached out and held her hand. As the band played, Clint urged people to head on over to the Star Stables station and register to win a scholarship, or of course, make a donation.

Night fell. It seemed not to come slowly, but rather, that the darkness dropped over the gathering like a cloak and suddenly it was time for fireworks. Clint had everyone move to a spot on his extensive grounds that had been prepared with quilts to sit on, and chairs for those who couldn't easily get up and down from the ground. Stella and Joiner lounged on a quilt with Harper, Grace and Madeline. Families gathered their kids onto quilts, and older people chatted in the chairs. Buster stood not far away on bowed legs talking with longtime friends. It was a moment of joy. Fireflies lent a magical quality to the air.

The fireworks began with a loud *boom* and then showers of colored sparks. Like nothing Stella had ever seen before, except maybe at Walt Disney World, they kept coming and coming and coming. They were not very noisy, which she thought was a nice touch, but they were over-the-top. Every round had a star—giant star designs that painted themselves across the sky, starbursts in all colors of flames, scatterings of stars that seemed flung across the sky by an unseen hand. The grand finale was a hundred rounds—which equaled a hundred stars—sent up into the sky as a salute. It was spectacular.

"You really outdid yourself, man." Joiner shook Clint's hand as they were leaving. "This was an awesome event."

Stella gave him a big hug. "I am overwhelmed, Clint. Thank you so much. Everybody needs a champion like you."

CHAPTER TWENTY-THREE

EVERYBODY NEEDS A champion *like you.* The words roared in Joiner's ears as he slid onto the back of the horse, a twelve-hundred pound gelding Hickey had just added to his rough stock collection. Buster had been wary of letting him try it out, but after several weeks of lessons, Joiner felt he was ready. Heck, who was he kidding? He was born ready.

Why couldn't Stella understand how important it was for him to ride? To push himself to the limit? She'd been distant all day because of his plans tonight.

Maybe she'd prefer someone safer, like Clint. She'd practically said as much. He was her *champion.*

The gelding pulsed underneath him like a volcano about to erupt. *Bring it on*, thought Joiner. Anything to get those words out of his head, even for a little while.

The horse flew out of the chute like a shot from one of Samuel Colt's revolvers. Joiner's spurs hit pay dirt just as the horse landed from his first assault, and sent him into orbit again. The gelding twisted and kicked. He bucked and jumped as if he'd been stung by a bee. Joiner held on for dear life, determined to beat him, but the horse had another trick.

He lunged to the right, and before Joiner could correct his balance, the gelding rammed him into the metal fence. Joiner heard a loud pop, saw stars and then everything went black.

HE WAS LATER told that the gelding had tried to stomp him, but Buster had jumped over the fence and chased it away, only to be kicked himself. When he came to a few minutes later, Buster was beside him on the ground.

Joiner reached out to him. The movement sent spasms of pain through his head, and he felt as if he might vomit. "Buster?"

"I'm okay." The older man turned on his side, and Joiner could see his leg through his torn pants. An angry bruise glared at Joiner from Buster's left thigh. His lip was also busted, and there was a cut on his forehead.

"You don't look okay."

"You don't look so great yourself." Buster grimaced, trying to rise to his feet. "'Course you always were ugly."

Somehow they drove themselves home. If Joiner had his wits about him, he might have been concerned that Buster was driving his truck with a bruised tailbone, having to sit sideways in the driver's position. But of course he did not have his wits about him. He was lying across the backseat trying to hold his head on, simultaneously willing himself not to throw up. He managed to make it till Buster opened the door of the truck to help him out.

"Lord have mercy," Buster cried, jumping back. He held a hand over his mouth as if he might vomit himself, then recovered. He waited patiently. "Can you make it to the porch?"

Joiner nodded. "Yeah. I'm okay now."

Buster held out his hand. As Joiner attempted to stand, he saw stars again. They flashed on and off from every direction, white-hot and too bright. His head felt as though someone was boring into his skull from the top with a giant screw. Cold sweat dripped in rivulets down his back and his hands were clammy.

Buster gripped him hard by the arm. The pressure anchored Joiner to reality. They walked together—if it could be called walking—toward Buster's front porch. Really, Buster was dragging him while badly limping himself. Joiner might as well have been a deadweight. "I'm sorry, man," he mumbled.

"You stay here," Buster instructed, depositing Joiner into a wicker chair. "I'm going to get Stella. You're going to the doctor but I'm not the one to take you."

Joiner sat in the chair, elbows on his knees with his head in his hands. *Deep breaths*, he thought. *Deep breaths*. He heard the door close softly and breathed in the smell of rain with a little twist of lemon. Hope had never smelled so good.

Stella's face came into view, and Joiner saw the only star he wanted to see, his North Star, the only star in the sky. Her eyes were full of concern and compassion.

He rose to a sitting position, squeezing his eyes closed to shut out the pain. When he was steady, he opened them and pleaded with her. "Don't make me go to the doctor."

"Spoken like the idiot you are." She touched his face gingerly, as though it might shatter in her hand. Her touch was cool and soft, so refreshing.

"I'll be fine."

"We're going to the doctor." She kissed his cheek and patted him on the chest, as though making sure he wouldn't fall over. She left him sitting there, and within a couple of minutes, her car was pulling up through the yard to within a few feet of the porch.

"Crazy woman driver." Joiner leaned on her shoulder on one side, and Buster gripped him on the other. They guided him down the steps and into the car.

"Get in, Pops. You're going, too."

"I'm not." Buster was firm. "I can take care of myself. But this cowboy needs his head examined."

By some stroke of luck, Kelli Robertson was the doctor on call in the ER. She'd been the valedictorian of Joiner's high school class, as well as the homecoming queen, and they'd always been friends.

"I don't really need to be here," he told her as she checked his pupils.

"Yeah, right. I see you haven't changed a bit."

She hadn't changed, either. She still had naturally curly chestnut hair, flawless skin and was sassy as all get-out. Not your typical science nerd. "What's that supposed to mean?"

"I remember when you got your head smashed in that football game."

"In junior high?"

Dr. Robertson nodded, studying Joiner's left eyeball with her own large brown ones.

"Luckily it was the last game of the season."

Dr. Robertson looked at Stella. "He remembers. That's a good sign."

"Ha-ha, very funny."

"Did you go to the doctor then?"

"My dad was a doctor so he treated me at home. Mostly I just lay around." Joiner thought for a minute. "They didn't let me play video games, I remember that."

"Right. You're not supposed to have much stimulation when you recover from a concussion." She switched to the other eye.

"Yeah. It kind of stunk."

"That was the last game of the season. But you came back and played several more seasons after that, as I recall."

"Sure. I was okay. And I haven't had any problems since."

"Ever fall off a horse and hit your head playing polo?"

"I fell off plenty of times, but never on my head. And we wear helmets anyway."

She was finished with his pupils. She sat down on a stool by a desk with a laptop on it. "What were you doing when you hit your head this time?"

It was the strangest sensation, but Joiner couldn't recall.

"He was riding a bucking bronco." Stella furnished the answer.

Dr. Robertson shared a look with Stella and nodded. "Okay. And presumably not wearing a helmet."

"Who wears a helmet in a rodeo?" Joiner interjected.

"And is that where you were? At a rodeo?"

Joiner's face flushed red. He had no clue where he had been.

Stella touched his shoulder with her hand. "He was out with my father at a friend's arena, practicing."

"I see." Dr. Robertson typed all of this into her computer.

"Joiner, do you know what time it is?"

Eight o'clock? No. Maybe twelve o'clock. No, that wasn't right, either. He decided to make a joke out of it. "It's five o'clock somewhere."

"Well, at least you haven't lost your sense of humor." Dr. Robertson laughed. It was a comforting sound.

She continued typing her notes and then glanced up at him. "Joiner, we're going to do a CAT scan. I want to see what your brain looks like before I decide whether to admit you tonight."

"We can find out if he actually has a brain," Stella kidded.

"Why do I have to be at the mercy of two women?" Joiner kidded back. "It's cruel and unusual punishment." But in his heart he was thankful they were both there, because for the first time in his life, he was afraid.

CHAPTER TWENTY-FOUR

STELLA WATCHED JOINER while he rested. He had not been admitted to the hospital, yet, but they were in some kind of room at the back of the ER where there was a bed. A kind of holding pen. A place where, presumably, a patient could rest while waiting for the results of a scan.

Joiner barely fit in the bed. His long legs were bent, but still his feet hung off the end. His hat was off, of course, just like his boots, and they lay on a counter beside the pile that included his jeans, shirt and belt. He'd been humiliated by having to wear a hospital gown for the CAT scan. But when he got back from the scan he was so cold he didn't even mention putting on his clothes. He just asked for more blankets. Stella and the nurses piled them on, tucking them all around him, until he was warm and comfortable. Now he was sleeping. The only skin she could see besides his face was one arm folded across his chest. It looked like sculpted marble. The other one was under the covers.

She took his free hand in hers and waited. She'd studied his face many times before, but never as he slept. The five o'clock shadow, the tiny blue veins underneath the transparent skin of his eyelids, the hint of a cleft in his chin. The hollows in his cheeks where dimples would form if he was smiling. Stella almost felt as if she was intruding on something sacred. He'd never looked so vulnerable before.

The long black lashes fluttered open. "Who are you?" he whispered. The corners of his mouth turned up in a wicked grin.

Stella laughed, and a tear spilled out of one of her eyes, rolled down her face and splashed him on the cheek not far from his lips.

He stuck his tongue out and licked it. "Yummy," he said. Then he raised his hand and stroked her face. "You're so beautiful."

"I was just thinking the same thing about you. So beautiful, and so naughty."

Before Joiner could protest, Dr. Robertson walked in. "You guys having a moment?"

"We were, till she told me I was naughty."

"Well, I'd say she knows you pretty well." Dr. Robertson smiled at Stella. Then she spoke more somberly to both of them. "I took a look at your CAT scan."

Stella's heart began to beat faster.

"The good news is that we did find a brain."

"Well, that's a relief." Stella laughed more cheerfully than she felt.

"The bad news is that you have scar tissue from a previous concussion. This one will probably leave another scar, though it takes three to six months for it to manifest. More scarring increases your risk of seizures, which can be extremely serious."

"So, what are you saying?" Joiner asked.

"I'm saying that you are lucky you haven't had seizures already. But I think you will heal and be fine if you go home and get a lot of rest." Here she turned to Stella. "And that means doing basically nothing physically or mentally taxing for at least three weeks."

"Three weeks?" Joiner exclaimed. Then he automatically grabbed his head because he'd hurt it by rising up too fast.

Dr. Robertson shot him a warning glare. "Do I make my point clear, cowboy?"

Joiner sighed. "Yes."

She bent down to his eye level. Her voice was kind but firm. "Look, Joiner. I know you love your sports and your horses. But you need to listen to me now. You cannot do anything to put your head in jeopardy again. Nothing! If you do, you could really mess yourself up for the rest of your life."

IT WAS QUIET in the car as Stella drove them home. Joiner insisted on going back to the RV instead of staying in Buster's guestroom. He said he'd imposed on them enough, that he'd be fine. But Dr. Robertson had told Stella that someone needed to stay with him overnight, just in case. So while Joiner was getting ready for bed, Stella sat down on the red couch and called Buster to let him know where she was.

Joiner came out of the bathroom in sweats and a T-shirt. He looked like a frat boy instead of a cowboy, and Stella grinned at the thought.

"Thank you for taking care of me," he said to her. "I wish I could walk you home."

"Well, you're far too much of an invalid for that."

He smiled but his eyes were sleepy. "Guess so."

"Here, let me help you get to bed." Stella rose from the couch and led him to the bedroom. She pulled back the covers on his bed and he climbed inside.

"I feel like a baby."

She tucked the covers around him, then kissed him softly on the lips. "You are a baby. A great, big baby."

"Thanks." His eyelids were getting heavy. "See you tomorrow?"

Stella sat down on the side of the bed and took off her boots. "Nope."

Joiner's eyes widened. "Surely you're not going to try to seduce me in my weakened state?"

Stella elbowed him gently as she crawled onto the bed beside him, pulling up the afghan Alma had thrown across the foot of the bed as an accent. "You're a horrible man, you real-ize that?"

"Just voicing my dying wish."

"You're not dying. But you also shouldn't be alone tonight. Doctor's orders." She laid her head on his broad chest, wrapping one arm around him, and snuggled him tightly.

Joiner sighed with contentment. "I've never loved Kelli Robertson more than I do in this moment."

Stella raised her head and looked at him in-credulously.

He continued. "Although this is not what I had in mind for our first sleepover."

"You're going to tell me how much you love another woman right now, really?"

Joiner laughed deeply—Stella's favorite sound ever. She laid her head back on his chest and pretty soon he became quiet. She could hear his heart beating; feel the rise and fall of his chest as he breathed. He ran his fingers through her hair.

"I love you, Stella Jane Scout. You, and no other."

"And I love you. You and no other."

CHAPTER TWENTY-FIVE

ALTHOUGH HE ENJOYED being babied by Stella, the next three weeks were torture for Joiner. He had never been so bored in his life. All he could manage to do was walk outside, sit at the school—but not touch the horses or a rake or saddle or anything—watch the mares and Pistol in the pasture, and walk back to the RV. For meals he walked to the house to eat with Buster and Stella, or he ate whatever his brothers and Alma brought him. It was nice having them visit. Occasionally one of them also took him on a nice, smooth car ride. But by the end of the three weeks Joiner was about to lose his mind.

And one of the things he missed most was going to the arena with Buster to ride broncs. As it was looking as if that might never happen again, Joiner was also battling a touch of depression. He didn't like being sidelined—again.

It didn't help that the heat of late summer in Texas was bearing down on Kilgore. It seemed as if the very air was oppressive.

Finally there was an evening toward the end of the three-week hell that seemed a little bit cooler. It was the night before he was scheduled to go see Dr. Robertson, in fact. He was so hoping she would release him to be normal again.

Buster was at the arena, giving lessons, and Joiner and Stella ordered pizza. They both liked their crust paper-thin and their pizza covered with pepperoni. It had been hilarious the first time they had pizza delivered to the RV. The young guy knocked on the door, obviously expecting someone different than Joiner and Stella to answer. But by now they'd done it enough times the delivery people were unfazed.

They ate it out of the box on the couch and watched *Downton Abbey*, which to Joiner was mindless activity, therefore safe for his injured brain, though to Stella it was edge-of-your-red-couch thrilling.

"I have plans for you," she said when *Downton* was over and it was dusk outside.

"Thank God," said Joiner. "Please tell me it involves danger, or at least something risky."

She rolled her eyes. "This is me we're talking about here, cowboy. Now where's a quilt?"

"A quilt? Are we building an indoor fort?" He rubbed his hands together.

"Okay, now you're just being downright rude."

He feigned innocence. "An indoor fort would be fine with me if we could get into it and kiss."

"That's too strenuous. At least for one more day. Now do you have a quilt?"

"In the closet in my room. Top shelf." He followed her in there, and found her standing on her tiptoes, unable to quite reach.

"Here, let me exert myself just a little." He extended his arm, feet flat, and grabbed the quilt.

"Thank you. Now get on your boots and come outside with me."

Joiner obeyed.

She spread out the quilt in the area away from the trees with patchy grass in front of the RV, which they laughably called his front yard. Then she went back in and retrieved a pillow for his head, turning off the outside light of the RV so it was darker. She took his hand, leading him to the quilt, and said, "Come on. Lay down here with me."

Joiner began to feel some of the restlessness ebbing out of him as he lay beside her on the quilt. The last time they'd laid on a blanket, deep in the meadow, acres away, they'd been like two pieces of flint, igniting a fire as they touched. But in the weeks since his accident, he'd come to appreciate the comfort of her presence, as well.

He nuzzled her neck. The scent of rain, the softness, the sweetness, of her was equally alluring—at least equal—as the fiery passion. She was a safe place for him to land. With her, he almost felt as though he was home.

"Look eastward."

Joiner glanced up. As the dusk deepened he noticed sparkling blue-white star clusters. Haunting nebulae spread their gossamer beauty across the sky. It was breathtaking. He reached out and found Stella's hand. "I never really saw the stars before you."

She rubbed his arm. "Summer is ebbing into fall. There's a change of positions with the change of seasons. See Vega, shining the brightest in the summer triangle?"

"I do now."

"I feel like some changes are happening between us, too, Joiner. Can I talk to you about something important?"

"As long as you're not breaking up with me."

She hit him playfully on the arm. "Be serious for once."

"I was being serious." If only she knew how seriously he meant it.

"Okay, well. I've been thinking."

Why did stuff like this always make him so nervous?

"You remember how you told me you love me? Me and no other?"

"No, I cannot remember saying that. Something must have been wrong with my head."

"What about all of the other times since then?"

"I don't remember them, either. But for the purposes of this conversation, since it is obviously an integral part, allow me to say it once again. I love you. You and no other."

"Okay. Well. I've been thinking about you, and about us, and I need to tell you two important things."

He could hear the fear in her voice, and it helped him get control of his own, and quit joking around. Her voice was shaking but she was pressing on anyway. That was brave. "Whatever it is, it's okay, Stella."

"The first thing is that I've changed my mind about the bronco busting."

"Okay…"

"Remember when I emailed you, and I said I would support you in it even though it made me nervous, because I wanted not to be controlled by fear so I could really live, and I wanted to encourage you to do the same?"

"Yeah…?"

"Well, I don't know if you've noticed, but I really did give up fear that night. I mean, as much as I could. I'm sure it will always be a struggle. But as far as you and Pops were concerned with the broncos, I let it go."

Joiner agreed. "I did notice. And I appreciated it."

"Well, I've changed my mind, Joiner."

He felt a churning start up in his stomach. "Why? Just because of my accident?"

"Yes, because of your accident."

"Listen, I've done a lot of reading on the internet, and I think Kelli went a little over-the-top about all of this seizure stuff."

"Joiner, I'm sorry, but I'm not going to listen to that."

"Why not? She's just one doctor, and she's probably being overprotective because she's a friend."

"No, I believe she's right."

"Stella, you are letting your fear cloud your judgment on this. It's like you were looking for an excuse."

"Joiner, listen to me." Stella's voice didn't waver. "You are wrong about me in this situation, and you are wrong about the bronc riding. You can live in your crazy little world if you want to, but I'm not going there with you."

He lay still and quiet for a long time, feeling sick to his stomach. Finally, he said, "I thought you said there were two things."

"I'm not sure the other one matters anymore."

"Try me." He hated that he sounded so mad.

"It was just that I love you. More than anyone or anything. I know our relationship has kind of happened fast, and maybe we need more time, maybe…" Her voice cracked. She was crying.

Joiner reached out to her in the starlight. He wiped her tears with his thumbs. "I'm sorry for being angry. I'll consider what you said. I don't want to live in a crazy little world all by myself."

Stella laughed.

He laughed, too, relieved. "And whatever else you need to say matters. I want to hear it. And I hate it when you cry. So would you please do me the honor of finishing your second thing?"

Stella took a deep breath. "I just wanted to say that I think we could make a go of it, together. The school could be ours. It's ours already, but—"

"You want me to be your business partner?"

"I'm going to knock you in the head myself."

"I love you, Stella Jane Scout. And I can say for sure that I love at least one of your ideas." He'd have to think about the rest. Was he ready to give up his own plans? Joiner wasn't sure. But he knew he loved her.

He kissed her then, and neither cared whether it was too strenuous or not.

CHAPTER TWENTY-SIX

STELLA WASN'T SURE whether Joiner had taken her seriously or not. She knew he loved her. Yes, she knew that. And she thought that he wanted to be with her in the future, though she couldn't be sure he was ready to settle down in Kilgore right now. While he was so authentic, so "real," as she'd said to Cha Cha that time, there was something about him that was an enigma, too.

For example, why was it hard for him to give up something that could kill him? He seemed such a rational, intelligent person. And yet he still wanted to ride broncs even though it could mess up his brain.

It didn't make any sense. Stella stabbed a Granny Smith apple with her paring knife, and peeled for all there was in it. She did this for six apples, and then sliced them all ever-so-thinly.

During their visit, Cha Cha had posed the question, "Why do any of us need what we need?" Stella had thought Cha Cha's question had pertained to her. She'd needed Joiner to be safe because she was afraid of something happening to him, but her fear was misplaced. Too demanding. Too controlling. That's why she had let it go. And it had given her the freedom she needed.

Sprinkling sugar and cinnamon over the apples, she tossed them around in the bowl, coating them with the mixture, and none too gently, either. Oh well, they'd all turn to mushy yumminess when they cooked anyway.

She had let her fear go in other areas of her life—with Buster, as much as she could, and with clients and she even worried less about funding for the school. But Joiner's accident had taught her there had to be a balance. The right amount of fear is not wrong. It's responsible. And bronc riding, at this point for Joiner, was irresponsible. So why did he still feel as if he *had* to do it? That was a question he would have to answer before they could move forward. And she wasn't even sure he could.

Stella measured three cups of flour, added a pinch of salt and began to cut butter into it with a pastry cutter. She obliterated more than two sticks of butter by the time her mixture was the right consistency. Then she tossed in a few tablespoons of ice water and stirred.

At least Buster was on her side. After Dr. Robertson released Joiner for all "reasonable and normal" activity, he told Joiner he refused to give him any more bronc-riding lessons because he wouldn't be able to live with himself if Joiner got hurt again. That was pretty big stuff coming from Buster. But would it be big enough to get Joiner's attention?

Stella rolled out the dough for her pie crust. Her phone rang beside her, so she put it on speaker.

"Hello?"

"Hello there!"

"Cha Cha! What's happening?"

"I'm on the way to Little Rock for another round of chemo so I thought I'd call and check in. What is that sound?"

"I'm rolling out some pie crust. My occupational therapy assistant, Daune, dared me to enter the pie baking contest at the Kilgore fall fair."

"Well, it sounds like you're beating it to death."

"Have to take out my aggression some way."

"I'm getting ready to take out some aggression myself if Steve doesn't watch the road!" Cha Cha shrieked out the last part.

"Hey, Stevie!"

"Hey, Stella!"

Uncle Steve's voice. Then laughter.

"How many more of these treatments till the surgery?"

"Two more, they think."

"I bet you're so ready."

"Well, I hate the chemo, but I'm not exactly looking forward to getting my boobs cut off, either."

"No kidding. I wouldn't be, either, especially when you put it that way."

Cha Cha laughed. "Well, it is what it is."

"I know."

"But I just take things one step at a time. Have to view it all as part of the process…steps I have to take in order to get rid of this junk and be healthy."

"You amaze me with your attitude."

"What choice do I have?"

"Plenty. You could choose to be sad, mad, bitter—"

"Well, I can be all of those things on any given day, just ask Steve."

Steve said, "I'm not saying a word."

"But you don't stay there," Stella commented.

"Nope. Not gonna stay there."

"I love you."

"I love you, too, sweet girl. Now tell me about you. What's going on at Star Stables?"

"Things are great. It's hard work, but I love it. My only worry is keeping the doors open. Seems like there is never enough funding."

"And the violet-eyed cowboy?"

"He's back at work, which is great. I never fully realized how much he does around there before we had to do it without him."

"I bet he's glad to be back."

"Yeah, he is. He was getting pretty bored having to take it so easy."

"Must've been tough." Cha Cha chuckled.

"Yeah!"

"How about the bronc-busting thing?"

"Just waiting to see what he'll do, I guess. He's noncommittal. Buster refused to teach him any more, but Joiner's still keeping his options open."

"Good for Buster!"

"I know, right?"

"Well, I was thinking about you and him and all of that and I had an idea. Why doesn't he play some polo?"

"What do you mean?"

"I mean, if he's got to have a hobby on a horse, why not play some polo just for fun? You could even try it."

"I'm not sure about that. For one thing, he's the only polo player I've ever heard of from Kilgore."

"There has to be more. Or at least there should be some in the area. Why couldn't you guys start a little polo club?"

Stella had never thought of this. "I guess I could talk to him about it."

"At least it might be worth a try."

"Cha Cha, you're either crazy or a genius."

JOINER RANG THE DOORBELL as if it was a regular date. Mugsy and Mitzi barked and ran to the front door as if they were in a race. When Stella opened it, her heart skipped a beat. She felt like a silly schoolgirl for being so thrilled to see him, but there it was.

She was so glad she'd splurged on the new Miss Me jean shorts to go with her full blossom boots from Old Gringo. They were her favorite short boots, red leather emblazoned with a free fall of embroidered flowers. Paired with a new chambray shirt with cutwork lace and her red Justin, Stella felt presentable.

Joiner tipped his black Justin and smiled, eyes crinkling in the corners. The week outside working had brought color back to his face. He smelled like leather again instead of soap, which for Stella was much preferred. His eyes, always that intense, exotic color, held so much acceptance, so much approval of her. She was instantly put at ease.

"Evenin', gorgeous."

"Good evening to you, cowboy." She invited him in for a moment so she could go retrieve her pie from the kitchen.

When she returned he admired it, breathing its intoxicating smell in deeply. "You know, we could always stay here and just eat that pie, and maybe go for a ride out to the north forty."

"No. I promised Daune. Besides, we should look at the stock to see if we want to buy something for the ranch. Buster is interested in a pig, as well as a few new chickens."

She'd said "we" but Joiner still hadn't said how he felt about settling down and making a go of things together. She hoped he would decide to stay, but with or without him, she had to keep moving on.

With that in mind, she'd decided on something else. "I'm thinking of going into the cattle business."

"Are you serious?"

"Well, at least a few cows, maybe. For beef."

"Like, to eat?"

"It's just an idea right now, but I want to be

more self-sufficient. You know, farm-to-table, all of that good stuff."

"You're always thinking, aren't you?"

"I have to, if I want to stay solvent."

"You're full of surprises." He grinned. "Well, whatever you say. Your chariot awaits." He opened the door for her, and they walked to his truck.

On the way she talked to him about Cha Cha's idea of starting a polo club as a substitute for bronc busting. Joiner was seemingly touched by the offer, but he didn't seem too excited. "It's not the same," he told her. "That would be like giving more riding lessons."

"How?" She genuinely wanted to understand.

"I mean, it's cool and all, and I get that it's a way to share my passion for the game with others. But it won't challenge me. Push my limits."

Stella groaned inwardly. Would he never get over the need to live on the edge?

The Gregg County Fairgrounds were just outside Kilgore. Joiner and Stella registered her pie before walking over to watch the livestock show. On the way he bought her a snow cone. She picked the rainbow flavor, and they shared it.

Watching the livestock brought back memories for Stella, who used to show goats when she was little. Her mother had been a sponsor for 4-H, and the county fair had always been a big deal for her.

They had just found seats in the bleachers when someone yelled, "Joiner!"

Adelaide and Sophia ran up in their sequined cowboy boots and bedazzled shirts paired with blingy jean shorts. They both had their faces painted with horses that looked like a galloping Pistol with glitter strung out behind him. Their mother followed close behind.

Joiner jumped up and held out his arms to them, enfolding both girls in hugs. Then they each sat on one of his knees, swinging their boots and licking suckers as big as polo balls. Their lips were stained red.

"Hi, Miss Stella," they said in near-unison. She was obviously an afterthought, but Stella didn't mind. She understood their devotion to Joiner.

As she watched the little girls sitting on his knees, describing the thrills of the Tilt-A-Whirl and the Octopus rides, Stella's heart melted. Joiner gave them his full attention, laughing and gasping at all of the appropriate places in their stories. Their mother, who Stella thought resembled a worn-out Barbie, stood on the other side of Stella and admired the threesome.

"He is so great with my girls."

Stella smiled at her. "They are such little sweethearts."

"Thank you. They really enjoy coming to the school."

"Well, I am glad they do."

The girls' mother leaned in conspiratorially. "I think I have as much fun watching as they do riding."

"I know what you mean. They are adorable."

"And that ranch hand of yours is sure easy on the eyes." She winked.

Stella tried to control the anger that rose up within her, even though she was sure it showed on her face. After all, the woman couldn't be expected to know that she and Joiner were a couple. It was natural for her to be with her ranch hand at the livestock show, right? Yes. Sure it was.

"He certainly is," Stella agreed. "I pay him extra for that."

"Is he single? I mean, I'm sorry to put you on the spot. It's just that it's not every day someone comes along who is so good with kids, you know?" The woman's blue eyes were wistful.

She wasn't really that bad. But she also wasn't getting a chance with Joiner.

"We're actually together," Stella said bluntly.

"Oh." And then after a few minutes, "Girls, it's time to go."

Stella looped her arm though Joiner's, holding his biceps in her hand. He flexed it, making a ball the size of a softball. She squeezed it.

"Be careful, you might break something," Joiner whispered.

"You're not that fragile."

"I wasn't talking about me."

"You better lose that naughty grin on your face."

"Or what?"

"Or this." She grabbed his face and planted a kiss on his lips right there in public.

He laughed. "Remind me to grin naughtily more often."

They watched as cute kid after cute kid presented their animals. Stella ended up buying a hog named Wilbur, and a wife for him currently named Olivia, but she was going to change it to Arkie. She snapped a picture and sent it to Cha Cha. She also bought ten chickens and three heifers. Or Buster did. He'd insisted on donating the money from his bronc-busting lessons to the school, and Stella had to admit her whole life seemed like an experiment in irony.

After making arrangements for transporting her purchases to the ranch, she and Joiner walked around the fairgrounds.

"Do you like rides?" he asked her. "The Tilt-A-Whirl and Octopus come highly recommended."

"No Tilt-A-Whirl for you."

"Huh?"

"I read it on the internet. Bad for your brain."

"Oh. My poor brain." Joiner rolled his eyes.

"But we can ride the Ferris wheel."

They stood in line with quite a few teenagers who were all on their cell phones. When they got on, Joiner immediately started rocking their car. And that's when everything made sense for Stella.

"You're an adrenaline junkie, aren't you, Joiner?" Stella blurted out.

"Huh?"

She exhaled loudly. "I just figured it out."

"You figured out what?"

"That you're addicted to danger. You are, aren't you?"

Joiner stopped rocking and looked at her. "Stella, you are a genius. And an amazing psychotherapist. You figured out my deepest, darkest secret, sitting here beside me on the world's smallest Ferris wheel."

Stella started to engage him but bit her tongue. He could make light of it all he wanted to. But it was all fitting together now. He'd said himself he had a need to push the limits.

In Stella's heart she realized she'd finally drilled deep enough to hit a geyser of truth. But would it change anything?

CHAPTER TWENTY-SEVEN

BY MID-SEPTEMBER, all of the mares had been successfully bred and had gone home to their owners. Joiner was back where he started—it was just him and Pistol—except he was two-hundred-and-fifty-thousand dollars richer. It was time to make a move, but to where?

His best laid plan had been to work for Buster and Stella, stay in the RV, breed Pistol and make some money so he could go out on his own. He still wanted his own land, and since the breeding operation had worked out so well, he planned to expand it once he had his own ranch. He figured if he had his own place he might also board horses, and he would continue to teach riding lessons, as he enjoyed it. But maybe for more serious riders than what his clientele was at Star Stables.

That made him think of Adelaide and Sophia and he grinned. The truth was he loved the school and all of the kids. And he loved Stella. Star Stables had everything he needed, and there was plenty of work to be done there to last Joiner a lifetime. But the land belonged to Buster. And even if he and Stella settled down together, pooled their resources and made a go at a quiet life together, would Joiner ever truly be at home?

It was times like this he sorely missed playing polo. When he'd discovered the game in college, it had offered him the exhilaration and frantic pace he'd needed to keep his mind off things. He'd been able to keep his life going, even earn a master's degree, without asking these kinds of hard questions. As long as at the end of the day he could get on a horse and play polo, he was all right. It was something he'd excelled at from the beginning.

His first polo pony, the first stick and ball—it had just felt natural. When he was playing polo he never wondered where his place was or what his life was supposed to look like. There was always another chukker, and one thing to focus on: the goal. Life made sense in that context. But now his polo career was over, and Joiner was back in the real world of Kilgore, afraid of getting too emotionally invested with a woman, a ranch and a town that hadn't felt like home since he'd lost his parents. It would take a lot more than a polo club to make him settle down.

"Hey, man." Clint Cavender walked over to where he was giving Picasso a bath.

"Hey, Clint. How's it going?"

"I just dropped off Cade at the barn. Jacob wanted to do some speech therapy with him in a group setting before he gets to ride."

"Well, I don't live with Cade, but from what I see here he seems to be really developing his communication skills. What's your feeling after six months of equestrian therapy?"

Clint shook his head. "I just can't say enough good things about this place. I realize it sounds cheesy, but it has really brought a lot of hope back into my life."

Joiner smiled at him. "I'm glad to hear that, buddy. You deserve good things to happen to you. You do a lot of good for other people."

"Ah, I just do what I can."

Joiner sponged Picasso's big brown splotches. He'd always thought paints were such fascinating horses, even when you understood the genetics behind what gave them their strange coats.

"What about you, Joiner? What are your plans? I know you've been breeding Pistol, and I heard that went well. You plan to continue here?"

"I'll admit I've been thinking about the future, even this morning. This was just supposed to be a temporary gig." He wiped the sweat from his brow. "I originally approached Buster about buying some of his land, and then we made this arrangement instead, for me to live and work here while I got started breeding Pistol, and Stella was getting her school off the ground."

"I see. Well, those two things seem to be up and running." Clint squinted into the sun, taking in the sizable operation Star Stables had become. "You know, if you're ever interested in a job…"

Joiner smiled. "That is kind of you. But whatever I do, I've got to be outside. I wouldn't look good in all of those fancy suits you wear, even though you do spice them up with some great hats and boots."

Clint laughed. "Thanks. I think."

"My brother Cullen asked if I'd be interested in teaching literature at Kilgore Community College."

"Really?"

"I guess my family's worried what I'm going to do, too. But I told him I'd stay a ranch hand forever if the alternative was standing in front of a classroom and grading essays." Joiner laughed. "I admire people who can do that, but I do not have it in me."

Clint straightened his hat. "Joiner, what do you know about the school's finances?"

"Kilgore Community College?"

"No, dude." Clint shrugged. "Star Stables."

"Well, it seems to always be iffy. Stella runs a tight ship but health-care staff are expensive, and so are horses."

"It's a mess," Clint admitted.

Joiner added, "I am sure she appreciates all of your help."

Clint sighed. "I've thought about trying to buy the school from her, as an investment, and bringing it under the Cavender Holdings umbrella. She'd never have to worry about money again, but I'm not sure how she'd feel about selling."

His statement seemed more of a question directed at Joiner. Hiding his initial shock, Joiner decided to dig for a little more information. "Well, it is her baby. But what would that offer look like, exactly?"

Clint hooked his thumbs through two belt loops at the front of his starched jeans. "However she wanted it to. She'd retain total control, of course. From my perspective it would just be a way to protect her, protect the school so it could go on as long as she wants to keep doing it, but without all of the constant worry."

Joiner felt his soul shrinking when it should be expanding. "That is very kind."

"It's not completely unselfish, Temple. Like I said, Stella and this school are the best thing to happen to Cade and me in a long time. And it's possible the school might someday become profitable."

Joiner should be glad that Stella and her school would be fine when he moved on. So why did the idea leave him unsettled?

JOINER COULDN'T BELIEVE he'd let Stella talk him into this. They were driving to a little town called Fouke, Arkansas, where Kandan and Georgiaberry Mobley lived, friends of Stella's since childhood. The three of them had been part of a homeschool co-op that included every counterculture kid in the tristate area.

Kandan came from Louisiana, and Georgia-berry was raised in Texarkana. They'd settled in Fouke after graduating from Homeschool High and were now raising little countercul-ture kids of their own. Besides the fact that they were some of Stella's "oldest and dearest friends," she wanted to go to Fouke to talk to them about organic farming. Stella said they were experts.

Joiner figured they were also hippies, and by the time he turned down the dirt driveway toward the Mobley house two hours later, he was already way out of his comfort zone. He could only imagine what awaited him.

What Joiner found at the end of the driveway was a complete shock to his preconceived notions. A neat, sturdy cabin was the centerpiece of lavishly landscaped gardens with every kind of blooming flower. Purple clematis climbed French-style columns that framed the front porch steps, which were sandstone. They climbed these steps to knock on the cedar-trimmed door.

A luminous woman answered. Her eyes were an otherworldly color of greenish blue. She wore no makeup and her skin seemed translucent. Strawberry blond hair drifted past her shoulders in waves. She had a beauty mark above her lips, which were the color of ripe apricots. She was dressed in jeans and a white linen shirt, and her feet were completely bare.

Stella elbowed Joiner and stepped forward to enfold Georgiaberry in a hug. Then she introduced them. Georgiaberry's eyes danced as she shook his hand. "A real cowboy!" she exclaimed, obviously amused.

They stepped into the cabin and were immediately in the living room. One whole wall was books—there must have been a thousand of them—on floor-to-ceiling shelves, and another whole wall was windows. Rounding out the room were a mismatched couch and chairs that looked comfy, and an old beat-up chest that served as a table.

"Kandan, they're here!" Georgiaberry called, and then invited them to sit.

Joiner and Stella took the couch, while Georgiaberry sat in one of the chairs. It was green, with an orange-and-brown granny-square afghan folded across the back.

Kandan Mobley appeared with a tray in his hands, which he set on the table. On it was the strangest cake Joiner had ever seen—at least, he presumed it was a cake—and a china teapot with four nonmatching teacups. There was also dark red jelly, honey and what looked like milk. Joiner found out later it was cream from one of their grass-fed cows.

Kandan sat on the edge of the other chair after he set down the tray, crossing his birdlike legs under him and studying his guests. Then he bounded up again and kissed Stella on both cheeks, shaking Joiner's hand heartily.

"I've made you this king cake. It's a Mardi Gras tradition. And of course it's not Mardi Gras but it's such a fantastic cake GB said I should make it. And I always do what my lovely young wife says. Well, almost always. And this is fresh currant jelly."

His eyes were the kindest Joiner had ever seen. They were dark amber and seemed to contain a fire that was kindled from the inside. At the same time there was sadness in his eyes, and Joiner wondered what they had seen to make them be that way. But only for a moment. Because then Kandan's eyes were crinkled around the edges by a smile that said *I am so happy you have come.*

With tiny hands that were rough and worn, he served the cake while Georgiaberry poured tea. She towered above him. He wore cargo shorts, an old T-shirt and a leather strap around his neck with an amulet like Stella's. His dirty-blond hair was tied back in a ponytail.

"He has the same necklace as you, Stella," Joiner observed, as they sipped tea and devoured the delicious king cake.

"Yes. She got it for me. I lost my brother a year after she lost Lily. It's for healing. We made a vow to take them off when we were healed from our losses, didn't we, Stella? I always planned to give mine away to someone who needed it more. But you see I cannot part with mine. I still need its comfort somehow."

Stella pulled hers out of her shirt. "I've not taken mine off, either."

As the conversation continued, Joiner began to understand Stella's attachment to these people. There was no small talk. They fully engaged with him from the beginning as if he was as well-read as they were. Whether it was politics, literature, science, culture, they had ideas. And they wanted to know his.

It was kind of like being inside another world, in their house. They behaved as if this way of communicating was the norm. And so it was, in their world. It reminded him of an honor society he'd been a member of in college.

They showed Joiner and Stella their greenhouses, which they'd built with their own hands, and where they grew every imaginable vegetable. They explained how it had to be done to be sustainable for the earth. Kandan spoke with such passion about organics and health that he sounded like an evangelist. After a while, Joiner's head started to hurt from all of the knowledge he'd been exposed to, but he was close to being converted.

Georgiaberry led them to a small warehouse where she gathered her Sunshine for Dinner. This was the name of her business, and it was also what she shipped all over the tristate area to individuals who paid her monthly. Into lined boxes she placed whatever was ripe—radishes, carrots, lettuce, squash, cucumbers, basil, onions, peppers, okra. Then she added a carton of brown eggs from her "hardworking hens."

As Joiner and Stella left, Kandan invited them back in the winter for "hog killing time," when he and Georgiaberry would slaughter a hog and dress it themselves. Kandan's description of the bacon was enough to make Joiner want to try it. Kandan also sent them home with a plastic bag full of frozen beef from his last butchered cow, and Georgiaberry included a box of vegetables.

"Your friends are great," Joiner said as they drove out of Fouke.

"Thanks. I think they are. It's a joy for me to spend time with them."

Surprisingly, Joiner thought he would like to visit them more often himself.

"They seem so settled—so invested in each other and where they are."

"I love that about them."

"But do you think they ever get bored?"

"With what?"

"With being so settled."

"I doubt it. At least not for long. It's something we have in common, actually."

"You mean your commitment to Kilgore?"

"Yes. I may have other issues, but I know what I want to do and where I want to be."

Joiner wished he could be so certain, but he wasn't. The subject made him feel uncomfortable, so he decided to change it. "Will you tell me about your necklace?"

"What do you want to know?"

"Why haven't you taken it off? I mean, it's okay if you never do. I'd just like to understand your feelings about it."

Stella fingered her amulet. "I guess it's like Kandan said. I've never felt completely healed."

"Do you think you ever will be?"

"Are you? I mean, since you lost your parents?"

"Maybe not. Maybe we never are."

CHAPTER TWENTY-EIGHT

STELLA HAD DONE well with releasing her fears and relaxing more. For the most part, she no longer stressed out over Buster, and since Joiner hadn't gotten back on a bronc it was easier to keep her fears in check about his safety. Cha Cha was another matter, but she had to trust that the chemo was helping. And unlike Joiner, at least Cha Cha was not hell-bent on tempting fate. Instead she was fighting for her life, and though Stella worried about her constantly, she believed Cha Cha would come out the winner.

Aside from Cha Cha's battle, what was keeping Stella up at night lately was the school and its endless financial troubles. It just seemed she never could get ahead of them. Soon Stella might have to start turning people away who couldn't pay, which went against the very core of what Star Stables was to her. If she had to do that, she would have to change her whole vision for the school, and that was devastating.

The facilities themselves, the horses and the

equipment needed for therapy had taken almost every penny initially donated, in addition to what she and Buster put in. Now, along with maintenance on those things, there was the problem of paying her workers—she and Joiner rarely saw a dime—and the seemingly endless costs involved with being compliant with all of the different health regulations. Trying to stay cutting-edge by sending staff to training or adding anything interesting like a new piece of equipment just wasn't even on the table. So when it came to Star Stables, Stella was in survival mode.

She was pouring over her budget for the fiftieth time when she heard a knock on her office door. It was Clint Cavender.

"Could I come in for just a moment?"

"Sure, Clint." It was always good to see him; since that first meeting at Common Grounds he had been the school's biggest supporter. And after how closely they'd worked together to help Cade, she also considered him a friend. "What can I do for you?"

He sat down. "Stella, we need to talk."

"Okay. What's on your mind?"

"To be honest, *you've* been on my mind. You and this school that has come to mean so much to Cade and me."

"Well, I appreciate that. Cade's involvement and your support mean a great deal to the school, as well."

"I have a proposition for you."

"Clint, I know we talked about a hayride and some kind of fall festival to raise money but I think it's too soon after the event in July. It doesn't feel right. There has to be another way." Stella set down her books and ran a hand through her hair.

"I'm glad you said that."

"Really? I thought you might be disappointed. I know how you love hosting these swanky gatherings."

"Fireworks, pony rides and a watermelon-seed spitting contest can hardly be called elements of a swanky gathering."

"Okay, you have a point there."

"But I agree with you that there's another way."

"What is it? Have the financial gods you run with come up with a new solution for small, not-for-profit operations like this one?"

"Well, I think I may have."

Stella's interest was piqued. She was well aware of Clint's reputation as a financial genius.

"Stella, sell Star Stables to me."

She couldn't believe what she'd just heard. This man was supposed to be her friend. Stella took a deep breath.

"Listen, I don't want to take anything from you. I'm only trying to help you here. To give you something you need."

"By buying me out?"

"Yes, actually." Clint leaned forward and placed his hands on the desk. "If you sell the school to me I can place it under the protection and backing of Cavender Holdings. We can make you CEO and you can run the school the same as you do today, except with no financial worries. I'll put it in a contract. No strings attached."

"You'd do that? Why?"

Clint's voice was tender. "Because I trust you. Because of what you and this school have done for my son. I just want to make sure it's always here, and we can help all of the people who need it."

A tear slid down Stella's cheek. She wasn't sure this was a solution she could live with, but just the fact that Clint shared her vision was comforting. He got it. It had become a passion for him as it was for her. And he was willing to buy it to preserve it. "Clint, I don't know. Even if I could sell the school, it's so tied to the ranch. And Buster doesn't want to sell the ranch—not any part of it."

"Oh, I didn't tell you!" Clint's face lit up in a smile. "That's one of the beauties of the arrangement I've come up with. I could buy Star Stables as your intellectual property. A business, per se, a service. An idea but not a place. We can keep it where it is but rent the facilities and land from Buster. And of course I will pay you a good salary as CEO. That way everybody wins!"

Was he out of his mind? Stella couldn't believe her ears. This was certainly not the kind of thing that had earned him his reputation in the business world. "Clint, this sounds too good to be true. And I was raised that when something sounds like that, it probably is." She cocked her head to one side. "How would *you* be winning?"

"Well, it's complicated from a business standpoint, I'll admit. But I think I can make it work as a tax write-off, if nothing else. Also, this is a way Cavender Holdings can invest in the community. That's something else about your vision that has always appealed to me."

There was nothing in Stella that felt Clint was being insincere. He'd proven himself to be her friend in the past several months, and

Joiner had been friends with him for years. It seemed a crazy move for Clint Cavender financially, but then again, his biggest motive was the health of his son. She reached across the desk and squeezed his hand. "Clint, you are a good man. I will think about all you have said, I promise."

CHAPTER TWENTY-NINE

"Joiner, this is an intervention."

His brothers were his favorite people in the whole wide world, but sometimes they could be really annoying. They'd just shared a magnificent meal around Mac's dining room table. Hunt had brought his fancy sweet-and-sour slaw to go with the pork ribs Mac had smoked all day over mesquite in his smoker. Joiner had contributed sweet corn on the cob he'd ordered from Sunshine for Dinner and an apple pie Stella had made when she found out the Brotherhood was meeting. And Cullen had baked homemade rolls from their grandmother's recipe. So why were they all suddenly determined to ruin such a wonderful evening?

It was cool but not too cool, the perfect Texas autumn weather. Moonlight shone on the lake outside Mac's great room, inviting them onto the deck. Joiner had thought they might play a few hands of cards after they cleared the table.

Instead his brothers had gathered around him like buzzards on roadkill.

"Stella called us and she is concerned."

Stella was in on this, too? Traitor.

"She told us you were considering going to ride broncos again."

"And we've talked it over with Alma."

"And she agrees."

Enough was enough. "Look, guys, I appreciate your concern. All of you—the women, too." Joiner exhaled slowly. "You've never understood everything I do. But I am a grown man. And if I want to ride broncos I'm going to do it."

Hunt said, "That's just the thing, dude. We do understand."

"What?"

"Everything you do."

"What in the heck do you mean?"

"We understand. The riding fast, the riding hard, the polo, the broncs, everything."

"We are the Brotherhood," Cullen said, rolling up his sleeves. "Remember? We know." He traced the outline of one of his scars.

"You guys are weird. That's all I have to say."

Mac took over. "What the twins are trying to say, in their fairly strange and even creepy way, is that we understand more than you think we do. And, quite possibly, more than you understand yourself in this situation."

"What situation?" Joiner demanded. "The situation in which a grown man decides to pursue a hobby without seeking the permission of his brothers?"

"Joiner, you know the story *The Rocking-Horse Winner* by D. H. Lawrence?"

"Um, yes. Because that has so much to do with what we're talking about, Cullen."

"It does, actually. Remember how the little boy rides his rocking horse till he dies because he's trying to win his mother's love?"

"Yeah, sort of. As I remember it has a couple of different themes."

"Oh, for heaven's sake!" exclaimed Mac. "We think you want to ride broncos because you need an adrenaline rush to help you deal with stress and grief."

"What…?" Joiner was dumbfounded. "Wait a minute, what did Stella tell you?"

"She only confirmed our theory," Cullen said.

Hunt chimed in, "Yeah, and Alma said she's always known."

"Known what?"

Mac set his glasses down on the table.

"Joiner, we all had certain ways we coped when Mom and Dad crashed."

"Yeah…"

"Well, we all figured spending time with horses was your thing."

"It was. That has been established."

"But it never seemed destructive before so we all thought it was a good thing."

"Unlike my cutting, for instance." Cullen was matter-of-fact.

"Okay."

"Except now it has become destructive."

"How?"

"Because a doctor we trust has advised you that riding broncs can kill you."

"Now wait just a cotton-picking minute—"

"And yet you're determined to do it anyway."

"And that's crazy!" Hunt interjected, making a circular motion with his finger by his head.

"So," Mac began again, shooting Hunt a look, "Joiner, I want you to think about why you're doing this. Just tell us why it is so important to you."

"Mac, I really—"

"All kidding aside, now, Joiner. We love you and we really need you to do this."

Joiner thought as hard as he could. But he didn't have an answer. "I don't know. It just is."

"Can you see that it doesn't make sense?"

"Rationally, I guess, yes."

"Do you trust us?"

"Yes."

"Do you trust Stella?"

"Yes."

"Joiner, we're all begging you not to get back on a bronco, even if it means we all have to go to therapy with you."

"Why on earth would I go to therapy? I mean, Cullen only had to go because of his cutting."

Cullen nodded, unfazed. "Something I learned in therapy is that cutting relieved stress for me, and became a sort of addiction. Does riding broncs relieve stress for you?"

"Yeah. I guess so."

"Well, we do irrational things when we have an addiction. And it is irrational—you acknowledge that yourself—for you to get back on a bronc."

As JOINER DROVE home from Mac's, he tried to consider the things his brothers had said. It was easier to be defensive and not give them a second thought, but he had to be honest here. All of his brothers had gotten together to talk to him. Stella agreed with them. So did Alma.

Buster had cautioned him in the same way, refusing to give him lessons anymore. His doctor, a friend and a person he respected, had advised him against bronc riding. Essentially everyone who mattered to him, everyone he loved, had reached out and said no. He was causing them stress over it, enough that they'd staged an intervention. He'd be a fool if that didn't get his attention.

His phone buzzed in the console and he hit Bluetooth to answer it. It was a number he didn't recognize. "Hello?"

"Hello? Is this Joiner Temple?"

"It is. Who is this?"

"My name is Piet Quade."

"With the German national polo team?"

Piet laughed. "Oh, this is a good thing. You know who I am."

"Yes, of course." Joiner's heart began to race as if he was being carried away by wild horses.

"I hope it is a convenient time to call."

"It's fine. It's ten o'clock here."

"Oh, it is later than I thought for you in Texas."

"It's no problem, really."

"Well, um, Joiner. I've seen footage of some of your matches when you were with the Dutch team a few years ago."

"Yes, sir. I remember we played you guys a pretty hard match."

"You obliterated us." Piet enunciated every consonant.

Joiner laughed. "It was a good match for the Dutch, and their one American."

"Well, as you apparently know, I have recently acquired the German team. I would like to make you an offer you can't refuse."

"Like in *The Godfather*."

Piet laughed. "Yes. Just like that."

"Well, what's your offer?"

"Come to Europe to play polo for Germany. I will offer you a salary of six figures a year plus we'll cover all of your horses and gear. Help me build a winning team. And when you retire, you will have your own place training horses and riders at my facilities outside Berlin. Money will not be an issue. That is my commitment to you."

"Are you serious?"

"Yes, Joiner. I am in need of a player with your particular skills. I hope you will consider the offer."

Joiner didn't know what to say. If this call had come a few months ago, it would have been the solution to everything—his restlessness, his finances, losing his identity as a polo player.

His heart began to race like a fast horse. But now he had a nagging feeling—a part of him that wondered if this was still his dream. He'd been happier than he ever imagined he would be, carving out a new life on Buster's ranch. With Stella. Was there a way to say yes to one future without giving up the other?

CHAPTER THIRTY

WITH THE COMING of fall, Stella had to adjust the schedule at Star Stables once again. Kids were back in school, so that left the hours between eight and three much more open than they had been in the summer.

Cade and the other clients who'd starting coming shortly after she'd opened pretty much went back to the same schedule they'd had in the spring. But during the summer she'd added so many school-age clients, it was a little tricky figuring out how to schedule them all in either the early mornings or afternoons. Some of them had modified school schedules, of course, which made them easier to schedule during the day, but still, she was going to have to start working earlier every morning and later than normal on at least three evenings per week.

She'd also been able to start a new partnership with the nursing home in Kilgore. The leadership there had heard of the great things happening at her school, and had requested a meeting with her. They'd worked out a deal and now geriatric patients were coming to Star Stables for physical and occupational therapy on Stella's horses. And residents who weren't quite as ill could come and interact with the horses on Joiner's side of things. The whole arrangement was really a win-win, and had been a boost for Stella as well as the nursing home and the community. Still, it wasn't enough to make up for her financial shortfall, and Clint's offer weighed heavily on her mind.

But this weekend she was going to leave all those stresses behind. Usually the third weekend in October meant a trip to Cha Cha's for the War Eagle Mill Arts and Crafts Festival, not far from Cha Cha's home. It had been a tradition since Stella was tiny, when she and Lily and Cha Cha had made the first pilgrimage. They'd kept it a priority every year since. It had been especially important for her and Cha Cha to continue in Lily's absence, a way to stay connected, a way to remember.

But this year Cha Cha couldn't go. She'd had a double mastectomy a month before, and the doctor said there was no way she should go out among a crowd. So, Stella and Joiner had decided to go together, and they were going to spend two nights with Cha Cha so Joiner could meet her, and she could check him out.

Stella hoped Cha Cha would be able to give her some insight into the man after she met him. She still wasn't sure. Was he the staying kind?

When they arrived on Friday night Cha Cha was on the porch as usual, wrapped in a fuzzy afghan and sitting in a chair. She didn't get up, but waited for them to climb the steps, and invited them to sit down in her porch swing.

"You don't know how hard it is for me not to hug you," she told Stella. "I'm getting tired of all of these doctor's orders."

"It's hard for me, too," Stella replied. "But we'll do whatever we have to do to reduce your risk of germs."

"Stella's pretty germy," Joiner said. "I risk my life every time I hug her." He gave Stella a side squeeze.

"She told me you were funny."

"Cha Cha, meet Joiner. Joiner, this is my Cha Cha."

"The famous Cha Cha." Joiner took off his hat and bowed.

Cha Cha laughed. "I hate it that you are meeting me in this state. I am usually so much more glamorous, aren't I, Stella?" She touched a hand to the pink turban that covered her bald head. "Wait, don't answer that."

They chatted for a few minutes on the porch and then Joiner excused himself to go to the bathroom. While he was gone, Cha Cha showed Stella her prosthesis.

"It looks really nice," Stella said.

"Well, it's as heavy as a sack of lead. I'm only wearing it in your honor."

"I am very flattered—thank you so much!"

"Well, I could hardly go around with a scooped-out chest with that cowboy in the house."

"I thought you looked fine without it the last time I was here."

"It is certainly more comfortable without this thing. But I just hate the way my clothes hang if I don't wear it."

When Joiner returned to the porch, Cha Cha rose carefully. "Do you mind if we go in? I love it outside, but it's a little chilly without the sun."

He held the door open for both of them to go through, and then said, "I'll just bring in our bags."

While Cha Cha and Stella were settling into the living room, Cha Cha whispered, "He is gorgeous."

"I know," Stella said. "I know!" Joiner was

dressed in his usual casual cowboy style, exuding effortless sexiness. She was so glad Cha Cha could finally see for herself all of the things she'd been telling her about Joiner.

"Why don't you just put those here for now?" Cha Cha said to Joiner when he brought in their bags. "We can take them up later. I'm going to put you in the two guest bedrooms upstairs."

He set them out of the way beside the foyer and came into the living area to join them. He sat beside Stella on Cha Cha's couch.

"So I know you must be tired from work and driving. Are you hungry?"

"We stopped on the way in and got something to eat."

"Tell me your plans for the morning."

"Well," began Stella, "We're not in a big hurry. I thought we'd have a slow morning, maybe leave about nine, and then drive out and spend the day at War Eagle. We'll be back here at suppertime and I thought we could pick up whatever you'd like for us all to eat on the way."

"I am so mad I can't go with you! It's the first War Eagle I've missed in twenty years."

"I hate it, too. But you will be there next year. And maybe Joiner will like it so much he'll want to come with us again."

Joiner grinned. "I have the feeling this will

be a one-time gig for me, but I am happy to stand in for you on this one occasion, Cheryl."

"You can call me Cha Cha. Are you not the arts-and-crafts type, Joiner?"

"I made a bracelet once for my adopted mom. That's about it."

Cha Cha laughed. "Steve wouldn't step foot at War Eagle."

"Where is Uncle Steve?"

"He's gone to a meeting, and then I had a grocery list a mile long for him."

"He sounds like a pretty good minion," Joiner observed.

"He is. He has been amazing to me during this time of illness. You just never know when you might be called on to live out those vows, in sickness and in health."

"Well, you'd do the same for him."

"Yep. I would."

Cha Cha asked Joiner questions about his growing-up years, college, polo and his brothers, which led to the inevitable discussion of Hunt's TV personality as the cowboy chef.

"I bet it's nice to have his cooking in the family."

"It is. I'll freely admit it, especially since I can't cook a lick."

"All of his brothers are cool. I've met them,"

Stella said. She would tell Cha Cha later about how they'd worked together to stage Joiner's intervention.

"Why don't you let me get up in the morning and make omelets? Joiner can help me." Omelets were their War Eagle morning tradition. "Is Uncle Steve getting the stuff?"

"He is. And I'll help make them if I feel like it. I'm not a total invalid." Cha Cha grinned.

"Okay. It's a deal."

That night Stella took what had always been her bedroom at Cha Cha's, the one at the front of the house. Joiner's was the one next to it, and there was a bathroom down the hall. All of the rooms, including the bathroom, were full of old-house charm—odd angles, fun little nooks. And as Cha Cha was, well, Cha Cha, they were all decorated to the hilt.

It felt a little strange to be so close to Joiner in this way. They brushed their teeth together, and she noticed they both dressed in sweats and T-shirts for bed. Then he walked her to her door, but didn't step through, even though there was a sitting area and everything.

"You can come in if you want. I'm not afraid of you."

Joiner stroked her face. "I'm afraid of myself."

She kissed him and his response was sweet, tender, careful—as though she could feel his restraint.

"It's like there's a wild horse rearing up in me, Stella, and I have to put on the bridle. Force him to be tamed."

"It is the same for me."

"If I knew where things were going between us…"

Where are *things going between us*? she wanted to scream, but she didn't. She'd already told him what she wanted that night under the stars. To say more would feel too forward, too degrading. He was going to have to figure it out.

"I'm sure you're tired and we have a big day ahead of us, but I need to talk to you about something."

This was classic Joiner. They had driven several hours in the car together, talking about the day, Cha Cha, War Eagle, where they would eat. For part of the time they'd listened to music, then she'd slept as he drove. They'd even commented on how nice it was to be able just to be quiet together. But now, when it was time for bed, he was ready to spill some beans.

She sat down on her side of the doorway, and he sat down on his. He took her hands in his.

"I have two things to talk to you about."

"Okay." She rubbed one of his hands with her thumb.

"The first thing is that I am done with bronco riding."

Stella couldn't contain her joy at this news. A huge smile spread across her face and she closed her eyes, breathing a silent prayer of thanksgiving.

"My brothers finally talked some sense into me, and I heard you had something to do with that. I don't know why it has taken me so long to figure it out, and I am sorry. But I realize now that I do seek ways to escape to avoid dealing with my life. It's not healthy, and I want to change it."

Stella was impressed by his ability to articulate everything. "Gosh. Those words can't be easy to say. I'm so proud of you, Joiner."

"Looking back over our relationship, I want you to know that you've helped me to grow. From addressing your own fear and overcoming it to being patient with me, I appreciate your strength." His eyes were deep purple, and they seemed to see into her soul.

"You asked me when we went to the Mobleys' about whether I'd healed after my parents' deaths. I think there's a part of me that never has healed." Joiner's eyes looked as if they might spill out a river of tears. "I've done a lot of honest searching, and I realized that I've been running as hard as I could—and as far as a horse could take me—in order to outrun the pain of losing my parents."

"I understand that pain."

"I know you do. But while you ran to safety, I ran to danger, and specifically, to adrenaline. It's been the drug I used to medicate all of the hurt I felt when my parents died. Running wild and free on my horse was the only way I could get away from it after it happened, and I just never stopped. I guess I never wanted to stop, because I never wanted to experience that sense of loss again."

"Well, you can stop running now." Stella reached across the invisible line of the doorway to hold him. He shuddered and lay his head on her shoulder, crying silently in her arms.

CHAPTER THIRTY-ONE

THE DRIVE FROM Cha Cha's to War Eagle Mill was breathtaking because the fall leaves in northwest Arkansas were at their peak. As they crept along the tiny winding road in bumper-to-bumper traffic, Joiner imbibed every hue on the spectrum from pale yellow to fiery orange to scarlet red. Hillbillies in cabins built from rough-hewn logs hung homemade quilts out for sale. Fat cows with shiny coats dotted the landscape. A quaint church sign offered Beans and Cornbread, and Homemade Pies.

This was the Arkansas of folklore. Like the Romantic Road fulfilled a traveler's vision of storybook Germany, the descent into War Eagle inspired people to say that Arkansas was the United States's best-kept secret. For the first time, Joiner was inclined to believe them.

They parked in a pasture with hundreds of other cars. Then they walked a quarter mile to the fair, which on one side of the river consisted of five circus tents full of booths, and on the other, more acres of booths that were not in tents. It was a festive atmosphere. Stella liked to look at everything, she said, so Joiner walked with her through every tent.

Joiner divided the vendors into three rough categories. There were what he would call crafters, the ones with stuff Joiner wasn't sure what to do with. Then there were food booths with items that generally looked good. Stella picked up a few different dip mixes and a jar of salsa at two different ones. "For Cha Cha," she said. "We always get these."

The third group was the true artisans. And even though Joiner couldn't relate to having an art like this, he could appreciate it. There was some exquisite pottery. The prettiest was created by a lady who pressed real leaves into her pieces. She made the customer pay for it, too. But Joiner splurged on a platter for Alma that featured an oak leaf.

Stella bought a new rolling pin from a wood-carver; it was made out of walnut and was therefore a deep, dark brown. The carver obviously took great pride in his work. When she paid him for it, he handed it to her as if he was handing her the moon.

The favorite booth for both of them was owned by a Native American who made turquoise-and-silver jewelry. He was able to show them the different grades of turquoise, and why some pieces were more expensive than others. When Joiner saw that Stella was crazy about a pair of earrings in the shape of stars, he plunked down his money and bought them for her. She squealed with delight.

They bought lemonade from a stand and munched on kettle corn as they filed across the wooden bridge. Once on the other side, it was more of the same. There was gorgeous stained glass, ironwork and an interesting soap-making operation. In the end they came away from that side of the fair with a leopard-print turban for Cha Cha and a coffee mug for Buster, bought from another amazing potter.

When they made it back across the bridge, they walked down by the water and found a place to sit and rest. It was nice to enjoy the late afternoon sunshine before they left, hear the water turning the water wheel of the Mill and watch children feeding ducks. Joiner spread out his legs, leaning back on his hands, and Stella fitted herself into him, leaning against his chest. He kissed her cheek and smelled her sunbeam-colored hair, which smelled like rain and lemon. It was these moments that he wanted to last forever.

"Joiner?" she said softly, touching her cheek to his.

"Uh-huh." He stole a quick nibble on her neck.

She giggled, but turned to look him in the eye. "You remember last night you said you wanted to talk to me about two things?"

"I did?"

"Yes. You did. But we only talked about one."

"Well, the other one can wait for now. Let's just sit here together and be happy."

"When are we going to talk about it?"

"How about on the way home?"

"Home to Cha Cha's or home to Kilgore?"

"Better make it Kilgore—that way there's plenty of time."

Maybe by then he would have figured out how to tell her about Germany—and how to convince her to come with him. But Joiner knew in his heart that would never happen. It was asking too much. If she left her home she'd become someone she wasn't. Just like he would, if he stayed.

WHEN THEY CALLED to see what Cha Cha wanted them to pick up for dinner, she still wasn't feeling well. Stella's face fell at the news. That morning, Cha Cha had stayed in bed as they'd made their own omelets and visited a few moments with Steve, who told them Cha Cha had had a bad night. Everyone was hopeful she'd get good rest during the day and be able to visit that night, but it seemed as if that wasn't going to happen now.

In fact, Steve said he was getting ready to take her to the emergency room.

Stella and Joiner drove to the house quickly. They silently gathered their things and headed to the hospital in Siloam Springs. Cha Cha was already in a room waiting on the results of blood work. She looked very pale and small.

"What are they saying? What's going to happen?" Stella suddenly seemed to Joiner much younger than she was.

Cha Cha shrugged. "I don't know."

Steve spoke up. "They'll send her to Little Rock if there's a sign of infection."

Stella had flown from Dallas to Little Rock the month before for Cha Cha's surgery. It was a four-hour drive from where they were now. Joiner was weighing scenarios in his head when Cha Cha seemed to come alive.

"You kids need to get on the road. If you're not going to stay at my house tonight, you should get going. It's a long way to Kilgore."

"I'm not leaving you."

"Oh, I'm sure it's nothing. And anyway, if it is, what can you do? You have to go to work on Monday to keep your school going." Cha Cha cringed in pain. "Steve and I can handle this. You can't be gallivanting around the country trying to take care of me."

"I'm not leaving you," she repeated.

"And I'm not leaving Stella," Joiner added.

Cha Cha grabbed Joiner's arm. "I'm glad to hear you say that, Joiner. But I want you to make her leave with you and go back to Kilgore now."

They stayed another hour till it was clear, even to Stella, that it was doing Cha Cha more harm than good for them to stay. She was in pain, and their presence seemed to agitate her.

"Why do you think she wanted us to leave?" Stella asked as they drove away from the hospital.

"Probably because she loves you so much. It's her way of protecting you."

"Then, I shouldn't let her do that. Not if she needs me. I should stay anyway."

"No, she needs your respect more than she needs you to stay with her right now." He let that sink in. "Besides, I think she really will be okay. She and Steve have got this."

"I sure hope you are right."

As it was late and things had taken this turn, Joiner hoped she would rest and not ask him to talk about his other thing. He had to tell her about Piet Quade's phone call. But he still had no idea what he was going to do about it. And this was not the time to add another problem to Stella's already long list.

CHAPTER THIRTY-TWO

STELLA FELT SICK about leaving Cha Cha. After she and Joiner got on the road back to Kilgore, she continued to text both Steve and Cha Cha. They reported that there was an infection, and as there was no ambulance available, they were sending Cha Cha by helicopter to Little Rock. Steve was going to follow in their car.

At midnight, Steve texted to say that the helicopter had arrived, and they were getting Cha Cha boarded. It was all so heavy, Stella felt as if her heart might break. First Cha Cha couldn't go to War Eagle, an outing she truly loved. And then she'd been so sick, she'd stayed in bed that morning, which Stella knew Cha Cha hated to do. She'd been so excited to spend time with her and Joiner. Now, after a night and day of pain and restlessness, she'd found out she had an infection and it was serious enough that they were transporting her by helicopter to Little Rock.

"How much can a person take?" Stella cried out to Joiner. "My poor, poor friend!"

Just then the phone buzzed again. The text was a picture of Cha Cha hooked up to all kinds of equipment, an oxygen mask over her face and her body strapped into the helicopter. The message she'd typed in? Luke, I am your father.

Stella burst out laughing and crying at the same time.

After they'd stopped at Starbucks and continued down the road a bit, Joiner commented, "Your Cha Cha is a pretty amazing person."

"I know. There's nobody else like her in the world."

"Thank you for taking me to meet her. I'm sorry it had to end this way."

"Me, too," Stella agreed. "But I'm glad you met each other. Thank you for going."

"You can lean your head over here and go to sleep if you want. That Starbucks stop will do me for the rest of the way home." He took a sip of his venti caramel macchiato.

"Really, I'm not sleepy. I'm waiting for her to text me to say she arrived safely, and there's still that other thing you wanted to talk about."

"Nah, that can wait," Joiner said. "Let's just focus on what's happening with Cha Cha and get you home."

"Joiner." Stella pressed his knee. "I want you to talk to me."

"Okay," he said, setting his drink in the cup holder and taking a deep breath. "I got an interesting phone call the other night."

Stella's mind immediately went to the idea of an old girlfriend. Or possibly Adelaide and Sophia's mother?

"It was Piet Quade from Germany."

"Who's that?"

"He's a multimillionaire, for one thing. Made all of his money in computer technology. He owns a company in Germany that we might compare to something similar to an online dating service, except that it matches people all over Europe with potential employers."

"What did he want with you?"

"He recently bought the oldest and best polo team in Germany." Joiner's hands twisted on the steering wheel. "Stella, he wants me to come play for them."

"Oh my gosh, Joiner, that's amazing!"

He turned to her and smiled. "Really? You think so?"

"Well, sure! I mean, when would you go? And when would you get back?"

Joiner exhaled slowly. "It's not like that. He wants me to move there. Sign a contract for a number of years." He rubbed his chin. "The guy's basically offering me a job back in professional polo. But a more secure one than I ever had before."

Stella felt her heart drop to her feet. "Oh. I see."

As panic threatened to sweep over her, she willed herself to stop it. She would not live a life of fear. Even if it killed her, she would let her fear go. As she told herself these things, she realized another—she would have to let Joiner go, too, if that's what loving him required.

"Now you talk to me, Stella."

"I don't know what to say."

"Say something."

"Well, Joiner, I'm very happy for you. This is your dream, isn't it? Hasn't it always been?"

"It has. It is. It was. But I'm not sure anymore, Stella."

"What do you mean you're not sure?"

"I never thought it would be an option again. I assumed polo was over for me, that I'd had my run." Joiner sighed. "When I met you I was re-creating a life, reinventing myself as a cowboy, in Kilgore, where I could hopefully make a home. You know all of my plans."

"Have you done that, Joiner? Is Kilgore home?"

"Kilgore's always going to be where I'm

from. It's where my brothers are. It's an important place in my life. But—"

"But it's not necessarily home."

"Stella, I don't know if I have a home. Ever since my parents died, I've never really felt like I had a home…except when I'm with you."

A tear slid down Stella's cheek, and then another. She was glad it was dark in the car, glad Joiner couldn't see. She didn't want her weakness to play any part in his decision.

"This is so selfish. Buster will kill me but I have to ask." Joiner looked at her. "Would you ever consider going with me?"

This idea had never occurred to Stella. She had no idea what to say. What would it be like to leave everything she knew and loved— besides Joiner, of course—behind? "Hmm. Wow. I'm not sure what to say to that. Leave home? My school? The ranch? Buster? Cha Cha?"

"It's wrong of me to ask you that. Forget I ever said it."

"I'm glad to know you thought of it, Joiner. That you would want me to come along. I just…"

The phone buzzed with a text. Arrived safely at UAMS. Getting checked into a room.

Stella typed in Okay, thanks for letting me know. I love you!

Love you more! Cha Cha replied.

Joiner leaving. Cha Cha seriously ill. How would she cope if she lost one—or both—of them? Stella's fear was like a monster inside her that she fought hard to keep at bay. She squeezed Joiner's hand, taking deep breaths and praying it would not overcome her.

CHAPTER THIRTY-THREE

JOINER SLEPT IN for the first time in as long as he could remember. When he'd finally made it to the RV after driving home from Cha Cha's, he'd been completely spent. Emotionally, physically, mentally—at the point of total exhaustion. His first thoughts upon waking were of Stella. He hoped she had slept in, too. He knew she needed the rest.

It was Sunday. He slowly slipped into jeans, boots and a flannel shirt, and put on his hat. Looking in the mirror, he could hardly make out his former self. *Am I still a polo player?* he wondered. *Do I even want to be?*

Pistol was in his stall stomping, as if he'd been waiting for Joiner. He noticed Vega was not in her place. That was strange. But maybe Buster had turned her out for some exercise. He saddled up Pistol and went for a ride.

Joiner hadn't necessarily planned to ride out to the north forty, but that's what he did. Pistol remembered where the lake was, and headed that way, presumably for a drink. When they were still several yards away, he could see the silhouette of a girl and a horse beside the water. He slowed Pistol down and they walked to within feet of them.

"I guess we had the same idea."

"I guess so."

Pistol pulled up by the water's edge and Joiner slid off the horse. Stella turned to look at him and her brown eyes were sad. She pulled her Fair Isle sweater tight around her. It didn't look as if she'd slept in, or gotten much sleep at all. She faced the water again.

"What are you thinking about?"

"Lots of things, I guess."

"Want to talk?"

She sighed and shrugged. "Clint offered to buy Star Stables."

"What? When?" Joiner asked her.

"Not long ago. I was going to tell you."

"Why didn't you?"

"I didn't want to worry you, I guess. It happened right around the same time as the intervention. Anyway, it's just a business decision I have to make."

"What were his terms?"

Stella looked up and the sun shone on her face, turning her skin golden. "Kind of too good to be true, really. He wants to buy the school, pay me a fair salary to run it however I want to, rent the facilities and land from Buster, and there would be no strings attached."

Joiner pondered that last part. Were Clint's motives really that pure? Or did he see this as a way to get closer to Stella—a way to buy his way into her affections? Did Clint somehow guess Joiner might be leaving? He knew it was wrong to think that way, but he couldn't help it.

"What do you want, Stella?"

She stared down at the water. "Well, I have to admit it would be nice not to worry about the school's finances. Then I could focus my energies more on helping people instead of stressing all of the time about funding."

"Are Clint's terms something you can live with?"

"I'd have to see it all in writing, but I think so. I trust Clint. He wouldn't do me wrong."

"I trust him, too," Joiner admitted after a while. "Clint's good people."

"And he has an interest in keeping the school around," Stella said. "Namely, Cade. He said the school had given him hope again for his son. He also shares my vision of helping as many people as we can, and serving this community."

The words *he shares my vision* were a punch in the gut to Joiner. But he knew it was true—Clint had been all in from the beginning.

"He feels the same deep connection to Kilgore that I feel. It's his home, too."

Another punch in the gut, though she wasn't saying the words to hurt him. "Want to sit down?"

They shared a seat on the rock they'd sat on the first time they'd rode out to Lake Lily together. It seemed to Joiner that had been a lifetime ago. "I don't want to leave you, Stella." He caressed a vein on the back of her hand, following it with his thumb as though it was a little river.

"But you can't stay here, can you? Not when you have the chance to live your dream?"

Joiner didn't know what to say. He saw a tear slip down her cheek.

"And I can't go. I can't leave everything I've worked for, my home and my dad. He needs me. I'm all he has."

"What will you do? I mean, about Clint's offer and the school?"

"I'm not sure yet. I don't want to sell it, because it's mine. You may have figured out that I like control." She grinned up at him, blinking away tears.

Joiner smiled back at her. He wiped a tear from her cheekbone.

"But this year so far seems to be full of lessons on giving that up. Maybe I'm supposed to give up control of the school, too."

Joiner shook his head. "I wish there was a way I could help you with that. It's too bad I didn't have a richer daddy."

Stella laughed. "Yeah, me, too."

"I like the dad you've got, though."

"Buster's a keeper."

"Have you talked to him about all of this? The school and Clint, I mean? What's his take?"

"I haven't talked to him yet. I really don't want to. In fact, I haven't talked to him much about the school's finances since the initial setup. We both thought it would pay for itself better than it does." Stella picked up a flat rock and skipped it across the lake. "It will only stress him to see me in this difficult position, and he'll want to try to fix it. But of course he can't." She hurled another rock.

"Have you considered turning people away who don't pay?"

"If I do that, I lose the heart and soul of what I'm trying to do, Joiner. It becomes like any other place at that moment, where those without money lose. I wouldn't want to go on."

This was one of the many things he loved her for. But he had no answers. "Well, I think I'm going to talk to Buster today about Germany. Sort of make an exit plan. You want to be there?"

"When will you exit—I mean, if you go to Germany?"

"Piet wants me there as soon as possible. But I'm not going to leave the school in a lurch."

"I can get Buster to cover your riding lessons, at least until I can hire someone else. And maybe Harper would want to pick up a few hours even though he's back in school."

"I'll talk to Buster about that and also find out if there's anything else he needs done on the ranch before I go."

She nodded and straightened her back. "Maybe it's all for the best."

JOINER'S TALK WITH Buster went really well. The older man was gracious, as he pretty much always had been. He seemed to understand Joiner's need to chase his dream of playing polo on a more personal level than anyone else did. Even though Stella and his brothers were supportive, it was Buster who seemed to really get it. And he loved Stella enough to do whatever he had to at the school. After Joiner's talk with him, things really started moving fast.

Joiner called Piet Quade, and they agreed on a starting date. Joiner booked his airline tickets, got his travel documents in order and made all the necessary arrangements for Pistol. That was hard. But, just like things with Stella, Joiner told himself it was for the best. He couldn't overthink things right now or he'd lose his chance with Piet and polo. He had to keep moving.

CHAPTER THIRTY-FOUR

"ARE YOU OUT of your ever-loving mind?" Cha Cha's voice was raspy from the tubes she'd had down her throat when she was in the hospital. Her throat was healing now that she was back at home. Voice or no voice, she was just as spunky as ever.

"What do you mean?"

"You're going to let that cowboy ride off into the sunset without you? To Europe no less?"

Stella felt more miserable with every word of the conversation. "I told you. It's his choice. He's the one choosing to leave."

"Yeah. To pursue his lifelong dream. And he invited you to come with him!"

"How is that different than me pursuing my lifelong dream here? I'd be happy to have him stay and be a part of it, too, and I made that perfectly clear."

Cha Cha snorted. "I don't know. But this can't be right. It just can't be right for you to be apart."

"That's exactly how I feel," said Stella. "But as I said, he made this choice."

He could make money breeding Pistol, share her school, be close to his family and live a great life in Kilgore. She loved him and would even marry him if he asked. But instead he was choosing a game over her.

Stella knew that wasn't completely true, but that's how it felt. Her stakes were much higher. "I can't leave my school, and Buster, and you."

"Oh yes, you can leave me! Don't you even say you can't! Your mother would roll over in her grave!"

"Let me rephrase that. I don't want to leave my school, or Buster, or you. My life is here. What am I going to do in Europe?"

"Oh, let's see. Tour amazing museums, eat great food, visit some of the world's wonders, learn a different language, experience new cultures…yes, you are right. There is nothing to do in Europe. You should definitely stay in Kilgore, Texas."

Stella sighed. "Okay. It's not that. It does sound glamorous to live the lifestyle of a professional polo player in an exotic location."

"Now you're talking."

"But really, Cha Cha, I just can't see myself leaving home—everything I've worked for and everyone I love—to follow a man. No matter where he's going."

Cha Cha sighed. "I think I've misunderstood how you feel about him, then. If that's the truth, then you're right. You can't follow him. And he is not the man for you."

STELLA HAD A going-away party for Joiner at the school on the Friday evening before he was scheduled to leave on Monday. She and Daune decorated the conference room with black, gold and red—the colors of the German polo team. She pulled Hunt in on the act and he catered an assortment of yummy German breads with appropriate wine and cheese selections, as well as fruits, pastries and chocolate marshmallow treats for the kids.

The Brotherhood were all there along with Joiner's two sisters-in-law and three nieces, and Jacob and Buster, as well as Cade and Clint, Adelaide and Sophia, Grace, Madeline, Harper, all of the volunteers and several other clients, including the nursing home women, who all loved Joiner. They shared stories, and laughed and visited for a couple of hours, wishing Joiner well. It was bittersweet but a fun time, and Stella felt as if Joiner was honored. That was her main goal anyway.

Clint handed her a sealed manila envelope before he left, and after she and Daune finished cleaning up, she sat down in her office to read over the document inside. It was several pages long, and there was lots of legalese, but the parts she highlighted were these:

Purchase Price of Star Stables Equestrian Therapy and Riding School: $2,000,000.00

Rental of Facilities and Equipment to be paid to Buster Scout: $2,500.00 monthly

Salary for CEO Stella Scout: $250,000.00 yearly.

She set the papers down on her desk and rubbed her eyes. This was too big for her to digest. And reading the figures, she realized it was not her decision to make alone. She would have to talk to Buster.

You around? She texted, and for once he answered.

Maybe.

Can we talk in my office?

Snds srius. Buster's abbreviations.

Where are you?

In conf rm lkng 4 lftovrs. B there shrtly.

He brought a tray she and Daune had covered and put in the fridge earlier. It contained grapes and cheese, and he had put half a baguette he found on it, as well. "You hungry?"

"I am, actually." She grabbed a hunk of the baguette and paired it with some Gruyère.

Buster sat down in one of the chairs across from her desk. "I noticed you didn't eat much at the shindig. I didn't feel like it, either." He reached over and picked at the grapes. "Too bad Joiner couldn't be going somewhere with a steak theme, but I guess that would be here, huh."

Stella laughed. "Eat a piece of this cheese with some bread. It's good." She handed him a wedge of Gouda. "But, for the record, I think they have plenty of meat and potatoes in Germany. Just wasn't the kind of party I was going for."

"How are you, Pretty? I mean, with Joiner leaving."

"It stinks."

"Yeah, it does." Buster scratched his beard. "I guess I was pretty off in my thinkin'."

"What do you mean?"

"I just figured, well, you guys seemed pretty serious about each other. This all took me by complete surprise."

Stella sighed. "I thought we were serious, too. But it's complicated."

"How did he tell you? And when?"

"On our way home from Cha Cha's. He asked me to go with him."

Buster's eyes widened. "Oh. He did."

"I said no, obviously."

"Why?" asked Buster. "If you don't mind my asking." He smiled.

"Because I don't want to leave…the school, my home, you."

"Are you sure, Pretty? I mean, you've considered it long and hard?"

"Well, it's all been so sudden I can't say I've considered it long. But I do feel like I considered it pretty hard." She drummed her hands on the desk.

"And you're sure this is right? I mean, for you to stay?"

"Are you trying to get rid of me or something?"

"No, no, of course not. You know better than

that. It's just…I don't want you to regret it."
Buster looked into her eyes. "I'd have gone to
the moon with your mother."

"What are you saying, Pops?"

"I guess I'm just giving you a little lesson on
love to file away somewhere. If you can live
without him, he is definitely not the one. But
if you ever meet somebody you can't live without, well, then don't. Don't live without him,
no matter what you have to give up."

"I'll keep that in mind. Meanwhile, you've
got to read this." She handed him the papers
Clint had given her.

He squinted to examine them closely. "Lord
have mercy! Where did this come from?"

"Clint Cavender left it with me today."

"Well, the surprises just never end, do they?
Has the world gone crazy?"

"I definitely feel like ours has been turned
upside down."

"Two million dollars? Rent the place from
me for twenty-five hundred a month? Pay you
a quarter of a million a year to run it?" Buster's shaggy eyebrows bobbed up and down.
"What's the catch?"

Stella leaned forward. "I think the only catch
is we wouldn't be our own bosses anymore.
And we'd be beholden to the Cavenders."

"The Cavenders are good people. I just don't like to be beholden to anybody."

Stella exhaled loudly. "I don't, either. And I don't want to change my vision for the school. I'm afraid that will happen if somebody else is controlling the purse strings, even if Clint promises it won't. We'd be putting the future in someone else's hands, which makes me very uncomfortable. But right now, with all of our costs, and the uncertainty of the riding school income with Joiner leaving…I'm just not seeing another way."

STELLA TRIED TO keep herself busy on Saturday, which wasn't that difficult to do. She still hadn't found Joiner's replacement, so she and Buster interviewed several potential ranch hand/RV dwellers that day. No one seemed promising. That night she went to dinner with Joiner, his brothers and their two wives in Corsicana. They stopped at the Russell Stover factory there to get some "Texas chocolate" for Joiner to take over to Germany. He thought he could use it to make friends, he said. Stella usually loved their French mints and pecan caramel clusters, but all food was kind of nauseating at the moment. She and Joiner agreed not to prolong their goodbye when they got home, so he walked her to the door, kissed her good-night and she ran in before he could see her start to cry.

Sunday evening was a different matter, however. He'd asked her for what he called a real date—a ride at sunset on their horses and one last look at the stars. It sounded wonderful to Stella, and terrible.

Choosing her outfit carefully, she wore Legacy Destructed jeans tucked into her riding boots that were the color of blood. On top she wore a soft, slub-knit pullover with a raw-edge trimmed V-neck. Its colors were blended—crimson, red, orange, salmon pink. The color of a sunset. She wore a leather belt with it, and carried a luxurious fire dancer scarf for later if the air was cold. In her ears were the star earrings he'd bought her at War Eagle, and around her neck was her necklace.

Joiner showed up at her door in a new pair of jeans, polished boots, and a Western cord shirt the color of a ripe eggplant. When he pulled her into a hug and held her there, his shirt was as soft as butter. She wanted to sink into it and never move, but somehow they managed to wrench apart. They both trudged to the barn as if they were on a death march.

"We've got to stop being so sad," Joiner said.

"Nobody's dying. I'm just going to Germany. We can Skype every day."

"I know. It's just so far. And we have to be honest, Joiner. Our lives are taking different directions."

They saddled up Vega and Pistol. Joiner tied a quilt onto his saddle, and offered one to Stella. Then they led them out of the stables and through the gate. The horses didn't try to run. Even Pistol, it seemed, understood the somberness of the occasion.

"How are we going to get back in the dark?" Stella asked. She hadn't thought of that till now.

"I brought a light." Joiner showed her the flashlight tied on his saddle. "It's not ideal, but it will do."

They rode together toward Lake Lily, where the sun was setting on the water. Then they headed to the meadow deep in the woods. The moon was rising as they spread out their quilts and lay down to look up at the sky together.

Joiner pointed out the constellations he'd learned and said something about looking up at the same sky while he was in Germany. But Stella, who was usually so interested in stars, just lay there, memorizing the sound of his voice, the curve of his neck and the scent of leather.

"I'm going to accept Clint's offer, Joiner," she finally told him. "It will make everything so much easier, for everybody."

"You don't have to do that, Stella."

Somehow this made her angry. "Yes I do, Joiner. You don't understand! And it's none of your concern now anyway."

He reached out to hold her in the dark. "You're wrong about that," he said softly. "I'll always care about what concerns you."

She wanted to yell at him, to beat her fists against his chest. To somehow will him to care as much as she did, as much as Clint did. But that wasn't fair. Joiner had his own dreams to chase. Neither one of them were willing to leave their dreams behind to be together. As much as she'd like to blame him, it was a two-way street.

"Stella, I want you to do something for me while I'm gone." His voice was husky.

"What is it?"

"I want you to take care of Pistol."

She rose up to try to see him better, even though it was dark. "Pistol? What do you mean? Aren't you taking him with you?"

Joiner choked out the words, "No, I'm not."

"Why? He's a polo pony."

"I know, Stella. But I negotiated it out with

Piet. He's providing all of my ponies so I can leave Pistol here with you. He's yours."

"Mine? What are you talking about?"

"I gave Buster the papers. He's your horse, and you and Buster can go right on breeding him out of this ranch and make all of the money you need to supplement the school."

Stella's heart began to race. He couldn't be giving her Pistol. He couldn't. That was insane.

"I can't let you do that."

"It's already done." Joiner cleared his throat. "And if you choose to move forward with Clint, that's okay, too. Just think of this as my way of giving you choices. Options. So you don't have to do anything you don't want to do to keep your dream alive."

Stella fell on his neck, kissing him. The tears falling down her face melted into the ones he was crying, as well. They kissed, and clung to one another till they fell asleep, totally spent, underneath the stars. And they didn't awaken till sunrise.

CHAPTER THIRTY-FIVE

IN A WAY, it was good, how it all happened. When Joiner awoke in Stella's arms at sunrise he had no time to think, he just had to move or he wouldn't make it to the airport. Thankfully, their horses were grazing nearby, and they hopped on both of them and galloped home.

Stella was not taking him to the airport. On this they had previously both agreed. It would be too hard. As Mac was keeping his truck for him, Joiner was supposed to be at Mac's at eight so Mac could drive him to Tyler, where he was catching a puddle jumper to Dallas. From there it was a direct flight to Frankfurt, and then another regional flight into Berlin, where Piet Quade's people would be picking Joiner up.

"Text me when you get there." She made an effort to be perky.

"I will."

She stroked Pistol's star as they stood together in the stable. "Pistol and I will be waiting to hear."

"Pistol will be asleep and you should be, too." Joiner grinned. He wrapped a piece of her hair around his index finger and twirled it, hoping he looked more at ease than he felt. Then he cupped her face in both of his hands and kissed her, closing his eyes and breathing her in, one last time.

When the kiss was over, she told him to wait just a moment. Raising her hands to her neck, she unhooked her necklace and then slid it around his neck. "You helped me heal, Joiner. And I hope you find what you need to heal, as well."

HE SHOWERED QUICKLY, thanking God he already had everything packed. He threw on the pair of jeans and black T-shirt he'd left out, stuffing his dirty clothes into his bag. He wore the same boots as the night before, and took the dark purple cord shirt to wear over his T-shirt as a jacket. It smelled like rain mixed with lemon. He wasn't ready to part with it yet. Then he put on his hat.

When he pulled into the driveway, Mac was standing at the ready, of course, with a mug full of coffee for Joiner. He jumped in the driver's seat and headed to Tyler.

"Thanks for the coffee, man."

"You're welcome."

"That's one thing I'm going to enjoy about Germany—the good coffee."

"I know. You'll have to invest in your own espresso machine."

"I plan on it." Joiner took a big sip. "Thanks for driving me, too."

"It's so dumb that you're flying from Tyler to Dallas. I could have driven you to DFW."

"I didn't want to put you out, man. DFW is a full two hours from Kilgore, where Tyler is thirty minutes." Joiner took another sip of his coffee. "You have to work today. This just made more sense."

"Well, whatever. Can't do anything about it now." Mac straightened his glasses. "So, I keep this truck until you're sure you're not going to need it and then you want me to sell it?"

"Yeah. That's the plan. And we may have to use the money for my taxes. We'll just have to see how that plays out."

Mac nodded. "After all of that money you made breeding Pistol and now running off to a six-figure salary, I'd say your tax stuff will change quite a bit next year."

"Yeah. Might have to give yourself a raise." Joiner snickered.

But Mac was serious. "You sure you're not going to get over there and come straight back home to Stella?"

Joiner frowned. "I've already made that break, Mac. Hardest thing I'll ever have to do."

"When do you think we'll see you again?"

"I'll definitely come visit in the off-seasons, and some holidays. And you guys can always come over there."

"I plan on it," Mac said.

Joiner looked at him, surprised. "Really? 'Cause a European vacation doesn't really sound like you, Mac, even though I'd enjoy nothing more than to see your ugly mug in Germany."

"Really, Joiner. I'll do it."

"Cool."

Before Joiner knew it they were driving up to the little airport in Tyler where Mac dropped him off at the curb.

"I love you, man. Be safe."

"I love you, too, bro."

ONCE JOINER ARRIVED at Dallas-Fort Worth International Airport he had a short layover. It was ten o'clock and his plane left at twelve noon. He decided to look for something decent to eat and then sit down and read. Carrie had given him another John Green book as a going-away present and he figured he'd like it. He hoped it would get his mind off leaving Stella, because nothing else was.

He purchased a bowl of fruit and yogurt and a caramel macchiato from Starbucks. He'd be wired after drinking Mac's coffee, too, but what did it matter? He had miles to go.

He found his gate and sat down in one of the empty seats. A mother and daughter sat across from him, sharing a crepe and studying a guidebook for Europe. The two of them looked so carefree. They were both blonde and blue-eyed, the daughter an early teen, and the mother in her forties. He imagined this to be how Stella and Lily had been when they'd been together. Adventurous, content and happy together. The world full of pearls and the two of them sharing an oyster knife.

He was glad he had been able to help Stella heal from her loss, as she said, though he didn't know how he'd helped exactly. Perhaps dealing with his issues of recklessness had forced her to confront her fear. But that could hardly be considered helpful on his part. Whatever had happened, she had overcome it and decided to live her life to the fullest. She was the strongest person he knew.

He pulled out his iPhone and checked the time. One o'clock. What would she be doing right now? He guessed she'd be taking care of a client, though he couldn't remember who. On his side of things, Buster would be giving a riding lesson to the first of the nursing home ladies. They'd continue in a straight string till school got out, then Adelaide and Sophia would come on the bus. He sighed at the thought of them, of Stella and Buster, of Pistol. Of his life. He'd had a good time there on the ranch.

He felt a pang of guilt when he thought about Pistol. Buster had told him once that a man who couldn't love a horse could never love a woman. But Joiner did love his horse. The only thing that could have ever made him leave that horse behind was the reason he had left him—his love for a woman. He hoped his gift would empower her to make the choices she wanted for her life. Even if the choice she made some-day was Clint. At least his gift would take her need for money off the table for both of them.

The teenage girl across from Joiner nudged him just as he registered the flight attendant's message. "Final boarding call. Flight 1293 non-stop to Frankfurt, Germany."

CHAPTER THIRTY-SIX

STELLA WIPED THE tears from her eyes for what she hoped was the last time, but who was she kidding? The dust Joiner's truck had stirred up as he left the driveway had just settled. He was officially gone from the ranch, gone from Star Stables Equestrian Therapy, and as good as gone from her life.

She shook her head as though to clear it. It was time for her to go to work. Her first client would be there at eight. She and Daune needed to meet for a few minutes and discuss their therapy strategy.

She was glad she had Daune to rely on today. Stella could not imagine a calmer, steadier presence, or a time when she had needed such a presence, at least in recent history.

For the first three clients Daune basically took the lead and Stella acted as her assistant. At eleven o'clock she asked if Daune could handle the next one by herself. Janie was there as a volunteer; she could help. Stella needed some time alone in her office. She walked through the stable to check on Pistol. He seemed fine, as did Vega, though they were both a little worn. Then she stepped through her office door and closed it behind her. The ghost of Joiner was everywhere. She'd never be able to separate thoughts of him from Pistol, and his presence was even here in her office. She remembered him in the chair across the desk from her, then kissing her, then sitting in her chair, with her on his lap and kissing her some more.

She had not changed clothes since the night before. There'd been no time this morning before work, although she had shed her scarf in the office. Grabbing it now from her chair, she wrapped it around her, and there he was, too. The scent of leather. Tears began to flow.

Stella sat at her desk, not knowing whether it was best to try to pull herself together or allow herself to mourn. Looking at her mother's picture, it was her father's words that came back to her. *If you find the one you can't live without, don't live without him, no matter what you have to give up.* She suddenly knew what she had to do.

All of this time she'd been focused on losing her home, losing control of her school, losing her dream…but now she realized that without Joiner, none of that really mattered to her. Because even if all she had was Joiner, she'd be happy. She'd have everything she needed. It was time to throw her carefully calculated caution to the wind.

"Buster," she called as she ran past the arena where he was giving a riding lesson. "I'm leaving! You and Daune are in charge!"

The clock in her car said twelve fifteen as she barreled out of the driveway. Normally it took her over two hours to get to DFW but that was not going to happen today. Not if driving as if she was on the autobahn would make a difference.

"Call Cha Cha Smith!" Stella ordered Siri.

"Calling Cha Cha Smith," the automated voice answered.

After a few rings, Cha Cha picked up. "Hello?"

"I need you to look up a flight for me."

"What?" Cha Cha sounded addled. "Stella? What are you doing?"

"I'm racing to the airport to go find Joiner!"

"You are? Great!"

"Can you search for flight 1293 to Frankfurt out of DFW? I've got to know his gate!"

"Sho 'nuf. I'll call you back in a few."

In just a few minutes Cha Cha's call came in through Stella's Bluetooth.

"Hey!"

"Okay, it's Gate D35."

"Thank you!"

"Good luck, sweet girl! I am rooting for you!"

STELLA KEPT THE pedal to the metal the whole time. She was a person who never went over the speed limit but today was a different kind of day. She just dreaded seeing any blue lights because then she'd have to stop. She hoped since she had never even gotten a warning, the odds would be in her favor this one time.

The closer to DFW she got, the worse traffic became. She'd been to the big airport on several occasions but always with someone else. Usually, like when she flew to see Cha Cha, someone dropped her off. It was different trying to negotiate it alone. There were arrows here and arrows there. It seemed very convoluted. Finally she saw an arrow for international gates. She took it, racing the clock, which said one forty-five. Joiner's flight left at two o'clock.

When Stella found Gate D, she pulled her car up to the curb and parked it. She jumped out and ran as fast as she could.

"Ma'am," the attendant called after her. "Parking here is just for unloading."

"I'm sorry! It will have to be towed!"

The man looked completely puzzled, but Stella didn't care. She would worry about her car later. She had to stop Joiner from getting on that plane!

Once inside the terminal, she took an escalator up to D1. The wide hallway was full of meandering people, some in a hurry, some dragging luggage and walking as slow as molasses. Stella took off running with all of her might. Her boots clacked on the tile floor. She could see gate thirty-five in the distance—a long ways away. Would she ever make it in time?

She arrived, breathless, to find the seating area empty. It was five past two. Her heart pounded in her chest. There was an empty Pepsi can in one of the seats, and a candy wrapper in another. But no sign of Joiner. The gate was closed, and the desk area was desolate except for a blank flat-screen. There was no one to ask about anything. Stella put her hands on the window, looking out to the tarmac, and pressed her face to the cold glass. She watched as the huge plane taxied away. It carried part of her with it—a part she knew she would never get back.

She sank to her knees and then sat cross-legged on the floor. Still facing the window, head in her hands, she began to sob uncontrollably.

CHAPTER THIRTY-SEVEN

Joiner boarded the plane and found his seat. As he'd purchased his tickets so close to the date of departure, he'd had to take what he could get. And what he got was the seat at the very back of the plane in the aisle, right by the toilet.

"Great seats, huh?" The mother of the teenage girl was seated beside him, giving her daughter the window seat.

"Yeah," Joiner said. "How'd we get so lucky?"

"I think we're here because we bought the cheapest tickets we could find."

"Budget travelers," the girl added. It didn't seem to bother her any. She gazed out the window as if there could be some great wonder to behold at any minute.

Joiner fastened his seat belt. He stretched out his legs as much as he could, which wasn't much. This was going to be a long flight. But at least he had pleasant company.

As the flight attendant instructed them in the

rules of safety, Joiner's thoughts turned once again to Stella. She would probably have listened attentively to the flight attendant's instructions, he thought. Doing everything the flight attendant said. She'd be a great person to have by your side if there was ever an accident.

He sighed to himself. She was a great person to have by your side even if there *wasn't* an accident.

"Does all your laundry smell this good?" The lady beside him asked, pointing to his purple shirt.

What am I doing? Joiner unbuckled his seat belt and stood up, grabbing his backpack out of the overhead bin.

"Excuse me, sir, the captain has turned on the fasten-seat-belt sign. We are about to start taxiing to the runway." A flight attendant appeared from behind him.

"I've got to get off this plane!"

"But, sir. You can't. You've been checked in and everything."

"Ma'am, you've got to help me. I cannot stay on this plane!"

Joiner strode down the aisle, causing quite a fuss. The flight attendant from the back called the flight attendant up ahead and warned him of the situation. When Joiner got to the next station, a small, bald man in uniform was waiting.

"Sir, may I help you?"

"Look, dude, I know this is a problem. But we're not moving yet and you've got to help me. I've made a terrible mistake."

He could see in the flight attendant's eyes a hint of compassion. A desire to help.

"Okay. But you have to do exactly as I say."

Joiner nodded.

They moved forward to the cockpit, the flight attendant very speedily leading the way. The other man spoke to the first mate. Then he whispered to Joiner. "Grab your stomach. Act like you are about to be sick."

The first mate glanced at Joiner, then hastily opened the door to the ramp. The other flight attendant pushed Joiner through it.

"Thank you," whispered Joiner.

"Yes, sir," the man said loudly. "Go to one of our desks as soon as you can to change your ticket. And I certainly hope you do not have the swine flu."

The airline workers who were in the tunnel wrapping things up gave Joiner a wide berth. He held his hand over his mouth, keeping up the charade, till he came to the entrance, which had been reopened for him. That was when he saw her.

"Stella?"

She turned from the direction of the window, wiping her face on her sleeve. Her face was splotched red and her beautiful eyes were puffy. He lunged forward as she stood to her feet, and they fell into one another's arms.

Not wanting to let her go, he picked her up and carried her to a seat, where he held her in his lap like a baby. Stella, for her part, kept her arms around his neck. He had the feeling she was finished letting go of him, but he wanted to hear it from her own lips.

"What are you doing here, my love?"

"Did you see me? Is that why you got off the plane?"

"No," he admitted. "I had no idea you were here. I was just sitting there in my seat and I realized I could not leave you. I don't know what in the world I was thinking even getting on the plane." Joiner smoothed her hair back from where it was matted to her face. "Polo is fun, and it used to be my dream. But you are my dream now, Stella. You and nothing else. Do you hear me? I am yours—body and soul. I don't even care where we are or what we're doing. But I know that none of it means anything to me unless I have you."

He stroked her face as she digested all of his words.

"Well, you don't have to give anything up, Joiner." Stella touched the amulet on his chest. "I came here because I'm going with you. I do love my school, and of course I love my family. Kilgore is my home—or so I thought—until you left." She wiped her face again with the back of one hand. "I tried to work this morning—to go on without you at the school—and that's when I realized I don't want that dream anymore if you're not a part of it. Let's go buy my ticket. If you're going to Germany, I'm going, too!"

Joiner hugged her to his body, enfolding her tight in his arms. He kissed her on the mouth, softly at first, and then with powerful intensity, as if releasing all of the pain and confusion he'd ever felt.

"Stella, I don't want to go to Germany."

"What? But I thought—"

"I thought so, too. But my home is with you in Kilgore. I want us to run the school. I want my brothers, and Pistol, and the ranch, and even the RV till we can afford something better." His eyes twinkled. "And I want Buster to be a grandpa someday and he can teach our little kids to ride broncs."

Stella jerked her head up sharply.

"Just kidding about the bronc part. But I'm serious about everything else." He set her gently in the chair and got down on one knee. "Stella Jane Scout, will you please marry me?"

CHAPTER THIRTY-EIGHT

IT WAS AMAZING how much of a wedding could be planned online. After they set the date for New Year's Eve, Stella picked out her dress at Stardust Celebrations in Plano, where Joiner, his brothers and Buster were also fitted for their suits, and then she headed to Cha Cha's in northwest Arkansas for Thanksgiving. With a short time-out for turkey and dressing with Cha Cha's parents on Thursday, they spent the entire long weekend piled in Cha Cha's bed picking out wedding things on her laptop.

For these moments, however, Stella could not have been more grateful. Even though they might have preferred shopping in Dallas for the big occasion, Cha Cha's health just wouldn't allow it. This bothered Cha Cha more than Stella, who had never been a big shopper any-way. The important thing was that they were together.

And really, everything they needed was at their fingertips. Stella didn't even have to do much. This was Cha Cha's passion and area of expertise. By the time Stella had to leave for home on Sunday, they had a photographer booked, flowers picked out, decorations chosen, music lined up and everything else you could imagine on order and scheduled for rush delivery.

The Christmas season flew by in a whirlwind, although Joiner and Stella managed to take in the Festival of Lights in Kilgore, and Daune and company threw a shower for the couple. She and the other employees, along with Clint Cavender, pitched in and hosted it at Common Grounds.

With the money Joiner hoped to make breeding Pistol, they'd decided not to take Clint's offer. Star Stables was their shared dream now, and they hoped to always be able to run it the way they wanted to run it. Clint, as ever, had accepted their decision graciously.

They got lots of neat housekeeping gifts, and some that were hilariously funny. Most surprising was a gift from Garry Clubb—or the sea captain, as Joiner called him—he gave them a telescope. It was used, he said, but very valuable, a gift to him from his late wife. Stella had had no idea that Garry's hobby was studying constellations. The gesture was touching. And it was something they'd definitely enjoy.

The most interesting gift was Buster's. He wrapped up a miniature RV that closely resembled the one on the ranch. When they opened it, he explained that he was giving them the RV to live in, and then he handed them another gift. Inside that box was a birdhouse he'd made, and it contained a paper that was rolled up, sticking out of the hole. The paper was a deed transfer for the north forty acres, made out to Joiner and Stella Scout Temple. He explained that the birdhouse represented the new house they could build and live in, if they wanted, on the north forty.

When everyone clapped at this, Buster blushed. "Well, you're lovebirds, ain't ya?"

The three of them drove to Gentry for a quick visit on Christmas Eve. They took lunch, as Cha Cha had started chemo again and had very little energy, but she was hoping "the stars would align" and she'd recover enough to feel good at the wedding. Steve had the Charlie Brown lights on for them even though it was daylight when they arrived.

Joiner chose the moment after lunch, before Cha Cha had to lie down, to do two things that were very special. "I have some jewelry for these two ladies," he said. "The first is for you, Cha Cha."

He took Stella's necklace from around his neck. "I know you gave this to Stella when she lost her mother. She gave it to me, with a wish for my own healing, and I believe I have found it. Now I want to pass this necklace back to you." He walked over and placed the amulet around Cha Cha's neck. "You are so very important to all of us. And we pray every day for your healing."

"Thank you, Joiner." Cha Cha wiped a tear away.

They all did. But Joiner wasn't finished. Lightening the mood, he said, "And I think I owe this little lady a piece of jewelry, if I'm not mistaken."

Stella sat on the edge of her seat. Out of his pocket, he pulled a small black velvet box. Taking a knee as he had that day in DFW airport, he said, "I wish I had this when I asked you to marry me, but like with a lot of things with us, I've been a little late." Joiner opened the box and held it out to her. "Stella, I hope I'm never late again in showing you how much I love you. And I'm so proud you're going to be my wife."

Stella gasped. He took the ring out of the box and slipped it on her finger. The round, three-carat diamond was bezel-set in a milgrain-detailed frame. A double halo of forty single cut diamonds encircled it, in the most intricately detailed of patterns. It was an antique, from the art deco period, cast in platinum. It fit as if it had been made for her. And it was absolutely perfect.

WHEN THE BIG day came, the barn was transformed into a wonderland of soft white lights. Champagne-colored organza and tulle draped every surface, and a bower of fragrant vintage roses, provided by Kandan and Georgiaberry's garden, formed the centerpiece of the gathering place at the front. Grace sat on a stool to the side and played her acoustic guitar, with selections ranging from country to classical to spiritual. It was wintry cold outside, but the atmosphere in the barn was warm and golden.

Before a standing-room-only crowd of Stella's Kilgore family—all of the Star Stables employees and clientele, old teachers, rodeo people and friends—Jacob Hunnicutt, who also happened to be a minister, stood at the ready to perform the ceremony. An unspeakably handsome and nervous Joiner waited beside him, with his brothers all lined up at his back. On the opposite side of the aisle were Hunt's and Cullen's wives, Gillian and Sarah, and Cullen's two oldest daughters, Carrie and Meg, who were junior bridesmaids.

STELLA AND BUSTER waited in her office for the traditional wedding march to begin. He was nervous, fidgety, constantly bothering with his black four-in-hand tie. Stella straightened it for him for the seventh time. "You look very handsome, Pops," she whispered.

A tear slid down his cheek and landed in his beard. "I wish your mother could be here with us on this day," he choked out. "She would be so very proud of you."

"I believe she is with us, in spirit. And Pops?" Now it was Stella's turn for tears. "Thank you for loving me, and loving Joiner."

The music began and they walked, arm in arm, to the back of the barn. Cha Cha was waiting there in a chair to usher them in and help with the timing. Wearing the necklace Joiner passed along to her for Christmas, she smiled radiantly under her pearl-colored turban and fluffed the train of Stella's dress as she and Buster prepared to walk down the aisle. She gave final instructions to Hope, who was the flower girl, and released her to throw out her rose petals like nobody's business. Uncle

Steve, in the back row, gave Stella and Buster a thumbs-up.

Stella wore a ring of champagne roses on her head that almost matched the color of her skin. Her hair fell in soft, gamine wisps around her face, softening the line of her high cheekbones, and accentuating the beauty of her long neck. A touch of lip gloss, just a brush of bronze blusher and mascara were her only makeup. In her hands she carried a bouquet of the same colored roses and her mother's lace handkerchief, a gift from Buster.

Her gown was two shades lighter than the roses in a pale candlelight ivory. The style was Baroque inspired, with vintage lace net, a strapless sweetheart neckline and a sheer alençon lace bodice with beaded and embroidered overlay. With it, up top, she wore a matching beaded and embroidered bolero net jacket accented with pleated tulle trim. A soft, A-line lace net skirt with pleated ruffle godets on the sides and back hugged her curves. She felt as if she was gliding on a cloud that trailed out behind her in a chapel-length train. She heard the crowd catch its breath as she took her first step.

But her eyes were fixed on Joiner. Standing tall and proud at the end of the aisle, he was the picture-perfect groom. His black three-piece suit slim-fit him in all of the right places. He wore designer boots without a scuff and a new black cowboy hat, hair peeking out from under the edges of it in raven-colored waves. But what Stella focused on most were his eyes. Their deep violet color held so much love for her in that moment she thought her heart might burst from the sheer joy of living.

There was no fear in their love. She kicked off her satin boots and ran down the aisle to meet him.

* * * * *

LARGER-PRINT BOOKS!

GET 2 FREE
LARGER-PRINT NOVELS
PLUS 2 FREE
MYSTERY GIFTS

Love Inspired

Larger-print novels are now available...

LILPDIR13R

LARGER-PRINT BOOKS!

GET 2 FREE LARGER-PRINT NOVELS PLUS 2 FREE MYSTERY GIFTS

Love Inspired®
SUSPENSE
RIVETING INSPIRATIONAL ROMANCE

Larger-print novels are now available...

YES! Please send me 2 FREE LARGER-PRINT Love Inspired® Suspense novels and my 2 FREE mystery gifts (gifts are worth about $10). After receiving them, if I don't wish to receive any more books, I can return the shipping statement marked "cancel." If I don't cancel, I will receive 4 brand-new novels every month and be billed just $5.24 per book in the U.S. or $5.74 per book in Canada. That's a savings of at least 23% off the cover price. It's quite a bargain! Shipping and handling is just 50¢ per book in the U.S. and 75¢ per book in Canada.* I understand that accepting the 2 free books and gifts places me under no obligation to buy anything. I can always return a shipment and cancel at any time. Even if I never buy another book, the two free books and gifts are mine to keep forever.

110/310 IDN F5CC

Name _____ (PLEASE PRINT)

Address _____ Apt. #

City _____ State/Prov. _____ Zip/Postal Code

Signature (if under 18, a parent or guardian must sign)

Mail to the **Harlequin® Reader Service:**
IN U.S.A.: P.O. Box 1867, Buffalo, NY 14240-1867
IN CANADA: P.O. Box 609, Fort Erie, Ontario L2A 5X3

**Are you a current subscriber to Love Inspired Suspense books
and want to receive the larger-print edition?
Call 1-800-873-8635 or visit www.ReaderService.com.**

* Terms and prices subject to change without notice. Prices do not include applicable taxes. Sales tax applicable in N.Y. Canadian residents will be charged applicable taxes. Offer not valid in Quebec. This offer is limited to one order per household. Not valid for current subscribers to Love Inspired Suspense larger-print books. All orders subject to credit approval. Credit or debit balances in a customer's account(s) may be offset by any other outstanding balance owed by or to the customer. Please allow 4 to 6 weeks for delivery. Offer available while quantities last.

Your Privacy—The Harlequin® Reader Service is committed to protecting your privacy. Our Privacy Policy is available online at www.ReaderService.com or upon request from the Harlequin Reader Service.

We make a portion of our mailing list available to reputable third parties that offer products we believe may interest you. If you prefer that we not exchange your name with third parties, or if you wish to clarify or modify your communication preferences, please visit us at www.ReaderService.com/consumerschoice or write to us at Harlequin Reader Service Preference Service, P.O. Box 9062, Buffalo, NY 14269. Include your complete name and address.

LISLPDIR13R

ReaderService.com

Manage your account online!

- Review your order history
- Manage your payments
- Update your address

---

*We've designed
the Harlequin® Reader Service
website just for you.*

Enjoy all the features!

- Reader excerpts from any series
- Respond to mailings and
  special monthly offers
- Discover new series available to you
- Browse the Bonus Bucks catalog
- Share your feedback

Visit us at:

ReaderService.com

RS13